Totally Bound Publishing books by Ellen Mint

Happily Ever Austen
Pride and Pancakes

Happily Ever Austen

PRIDE AND PANCAKES

ELLEN MINT

Pride and Pancakes
ISBN # 978-1-83943-819-6

Interior text design by Claire Siemaszkiewicz
Totally Bound Publishing

Published in 2019 by Totally Bound Publishing, United Kingdom.

Totally Bound Publishing is an imprint of Totally Entwined Group Limited.

PRIDE AND PANCAKES

Dedication

For my husband, who's as weird as I am.
Special thanks to Kristi for being the best Alpha-Reader I could ask for, my editor for helping to whip this book into shape and Jane Austen for inspiring generations of women to not take societal confinement lying down.
Also to my dog, whose constant need for walks lets me create characters and stories from the ether.

Chapter One

Why isn't the car spinning out in the snow? Nothing dramatic that'd require an ambulance or the jaws of life, just a minor hiccup in her travel plans. Anything to delay her from this coming storm. But, no, Beth couldn't be that lucky.

Wringing her hands over the rented Civic's steering wheel, she glared out at the stark white landscape. It'd started muddy and drab, dawn hours away when she'd left New York City. Six hours later, deep in Vermont's snow-capped mountains, the azure skies did nothing to evaporate the dread in her heart.

The road was little more than dirt and snow packed down by wide wheels, increasing the throbbing headache Beth knew wouldn't vanish once she reached her destination. At the sign for the Honeymoon Cabin—*charming*—she turned right to follow an even thinner trail. The tiny car barely made it into the ruts dug out by a monstrous SUV, Beth listening to every *chunk-chunk* of snow splatting out of the wheel wells.

As a twist of smoke pierced the snow-peaked horizon, her editor's parting words rang through her skull. *'Land this damn interview, Cho. If you don't...'*

He didn't need to finish his threat—everyone in journalism was well aware of the always-looming cutbacks. It didn't matter how much money their website pulled in, it was never enough for investors. And the easiest way to line their pockets was by sending yet another reporter to the breadlines.

While the six-hour-plus drive in inclement leaning to suicidal weather didn't endear her, it was the subject of the interview that had Beth chewing glass. If it had been a fickle actor known for being handsy, she'd have brought her friend Bruno as an assistant. If it had been a mealy-mouthed politician—not that her employer cared about politics beyond if one was caught without pants—she'd have kept a slew of previous soundbites at the ready.

But this? This was...

Her thought snapped away when the ever-rising ground finally leveled out and she emerged before a picturesque cabin. It looked like a Victorian Christmas card had come to life. The cabin of massive red logs boasted a single chimney puffing perfect clouds of smoke into the air over snow-capped shingles. Quaint green shutters hung off the three windows she could make out. There was clearly a picture window for the living room, but it was frosted over from the encroaching cold. Pine trees lined the driveway, each one dusted in white snow as if a designer had painted them.

It'd be a lovely place to vacation or hide away in for a week while trying to hammer a book out. But that wasn't what awaited her inside.

Pulling a cleansing breath into her lungs, Beth snatched up her purse and laptop and struck out into the cold. Her leg sunk a foot into the snow, the freezing air punching into her chest and a gasp escaping her mouth. Cruel, frozen water tumbled into her shoes.

Damn it! Damn it! Damn it!

With each step she took to the cabin, more plummeting snow filled her ankle-high boots. They were cute for the city in winter but pointless this deep into the wilderness. It was doubtful anything short of a whole bearskin would keep someone warm up here. Thanks to her having turned up the heat in the car, the snow quickly melted to slush, seeping up her socks and leaving her crankier.

Despite dreading what awaited her inside, Beth dashed for the cabin. At least it'd be warm and snow-free. She grabbed onto the wooden railings with their woodland animal carvings and leaped up the three front steps. The door was a firehouse red with a wreath of cedar and holly hanging from it. Breathing in the smell of hamster bedding, she pushed on the handle and let herself in.

A flash of lightbulbs from by the fireplace interrupted Beth's entrances. Orange flames danced inside the stones there, three stockings without names dangling off plastic greenery above the fire. And standing beside it, an arm lazily draped over the mantel, was what had had her grinding her teeth for six hours.

"Tristan?" the photographer called the stone man glaring through space. "Can you turn and raise your chin?"

If he raised it any higher, all her shots would be directly up his nose.

Tristan Harty. Once a teenage heartthrob sporting floppy hair that dusted over those striking blue eyes, he'd climbed the charts with a handful of songs plucked out on his guitar. The trajectory of his career followed the majority of those who began in the same way. He'd grown older, teenage girls had moved on, his star had faded. Now, he was trying a comeback thanks to the rise in '90s nostalgia and his PR team had finagled an exclusive interview with her magazine.

Instead of the leather jacket overtop an expertly distressed T-shirt, they'd dressed him like Father Christmas. A black suit coat, tailored tight to his thin frame, lay unbuttoned over a crimson vest. A pocket watch, of all things, dangled off the vest. *Does he intend to recite some Dickens to the photographer as well?* Time had thinned the soulful mane of his younger years. Locks shorn to an inch revealed more of his forehead than any had seen in a decade.

While most men his age would have wrinkles piling up across that vast brow, the cold demeanor of Tristan Harty kept his face nearly as preserved as if he were a botoxed socialite. Somehow, his record company had convinced an entire generation of fifteen-year-olds that he was the deepest, most soulful man in existence. Beth wanted to laugh at the thought when the man in question focused away from his photographer to where she stood dripping at the front door.

Eyes bluer than a sapphire burned into her soul. She tried to swallow, but her throat constricted. Even turning her head was proving impossible as ten thousand watts bore down upon her.

"You!" a voice shouted, evaporating the confounding spell. Beth blinked, glancing back at the once bewitching man. With the glare broken, he transformed back into a snooty aristocrat hoisting up a guitar.

From the mess of photography equipment that claimed the cabin's entire living room bustled a wide man. He wasn't fat, at least not in that lovable oaf way, but his rectangular build easily fit into a doorway. He was the comedic opposite of the thin man pretending to play a song for the camera.

"Who are you?" he shouted at Beth.

She flexed her lips in a not smile. "The interviewer."

What had to be the manager scoffed. "You're late. What took you so damn long?"

"I'm afraid transporters haven't been invented yet, so I had to rely upon the old-fashioned horseless carriage," Beth snapped, in no mood to be shouted down by the reason she was in this mess. There were a dozen more interesting concerts and art house movies she could be reviewing at home instead of wasting an entire weekend in Vermont.

The manager pinged his beady eyes skyward. "What? You never heard of airplanes?"

She chewed on her tongue, keeping the caustic comment at bay. There was no chance of her company splurging on an airline ticket, seeing as how they couldn't ship their reporters as freight.

"Barry…?" A voice of reason stepped into the fray as the very subject of the interview spoke up. "Let it be," Tristan whispered. His speaking voice was soft and drifted in the tenor range, a surprise for anyone who knew his songs.

Barry the manager was in no mood to do such a thing. He was clearly incensed there was no underpaid intern to boss around and had to take all that anger out on someone. "Listen here…" Whatever derogatory term floated in his brain remained there, though he stared twice as hard at her eyes. "We ain't got time to waste here. So get this little Q&A session done fast. Got it?"

"Mr. Barry." Beth unlatched her purse, picking up her phone. "This little 'Q&A session' is part of the deal. I have full access to your…talent, and we host a release for his album." She should have been surprised at having to remind him of the back-scratching contract, but it was a wonder sometimes that most managers had the wherewithal to work a bed.

His annoyance at her tripled in strength. Beth internally smiled at her barbs when Barry pointed toward an open room. "Fine! Set up in there. I'll send Tristan in once he's finished."

"Thank you ever so much." She hefted her bag closer to her side. Just before she turned her back on the primping and posturing, another cobalt glare burned across her sights. For a foolish breath, her cheeks burned.

So I'm to work in the bedroom? While grateful she wasn't being forced to conduct her interview in the bathroom, she'd done worse. Once, she'd had to question a football player while crammed inside a food truck while an untended open fire singed an inch off her hair. Though, as she gazed around the room, a new unease settled in her gut.

While the living room and small adjacent kitchen were rustic and woodland themed, this was where the honeymoon adjective came from. The bed was gigantic, with four posters painted like birch trees, and a damn canopy, of all things. Red and pink silks hung off the posts and a shimmery duvet covered the bed itself. Perched between the ordinary pillows was one in the shape of a heart. There were no bottles of wine in a bucket on the nightstand, but a remote sat there instead. Beth was both curious and terrified to see what it was for.

She glanced at the oval-shaped mirror set in the vanity, finding in the glass an exhausted woman who'd been awake since three a.m., driven up a mountain and still had to crack this damn introvert. At least she'd thought to check in at the hotel first, knowing she'd be exhausted by the time this was over. A warm bath and a night of typing in her terrycloth pajamas was as good a reward as she could count on.

Unbuttoning her blazer, Beth set to work. There wasn't much in the way of seating in the bedroom, so she picked up the vanity's chair and placed it in the center. Hopefully, Tristan would feel just comfortable enough to be uncomfortable. Laying out her tools of the trade the way a warrior would before battle, Beth inspected the batteries' lives. Her phone was holding strong—she'd learned to keep her apps to a minimum lest she miss a vital picture or be unable to record a pivotal quote. The laptop was at seventy percent. Not great, but she'd only crack into it once she was back at the hotel.

The room felt too bright and cheerful. For some subjects, that'd be perfect. The candy-coated-sprinkle types loved nothing more than to bake cupcakes and divulge all their secrets while frosting. But not Tristan Harty. He'd been in the spotlight for over fifteen years, then out for eight. In all that time, the most people'd gotten out of him was his name, date of birth and current hit song. He was a black hole of personal information, and in order to keep her job, Beth had to get this vacuum to sing.

Cracking her knuckles, she took one last look at her reflection. Instead of the fretting thirty-year-old reporter, she saw a little girl. With her neon-pink unicorn notebook in hand, that girl in pigtails had been prepared to ask dictators and humanitarians alike the hard questions, and wouldn't stop until she got them. This Beth could handle some has-been musician.

Chapter Two

Hands tugged on his vest, and Tristan flinched before he realized the photographer was yanking off the borrowed watch. Raising his arms higher above the woman's head, he held his breath as she fished off the on-loan aspects of his attire. If she intended to pluck the suit from his body, she'd have to buy him dinner first.

"Are you finished?" Barry blustered, as he had been all morning.

"This was your idea," Tristan answered instead, growing weary at the dark cloud that was his manager.

"Yeah, a few pics to go along with the article, not this unending…" He flapped his hand at the mountain vista.

As the photographer finished folding away the white screens, Tristan risked a step closer. "All these years on, and I had no idea your leading phobia was snow."

"It ain't," Barry insisted even as a shudder ran up his spine. Pinching into his nose, the fifty-five-year-old man swiped away his proof of fear. "But we've got a schedule to keep to."

"Yes, yes," Tristan interrupted, gliding his hand along the satiny flush of the vest to cup his hip. "Despite my long absence from the stage, I do remember how it is to be crammed into a crate and only pulled out when they need the monkey to perform." He should have breathed it to himself. He would have in his younger days. Every corporate suit he'd met had praised him in one breath, then brow-beaten him with the fanged threat of being dropped in the other. It had kept him coddled and quiet.

Age has a terrible way of wearing off the patina of manners.

Before Barry pitched another fit, or did something so foolish as to cancel all of it—tour included—Tristan gripped his arm. "The pictures are finished." He glanced over at Angie Leon loading up the last of her padded boxes. "And while you inspect them, I will knock off the Q&A. Should be done in ten minutes."

The manager snorted. "Or we skip the damn interview altogether and get out while we can. There's talk of snow."

"We're in the mountains."

But Barry fished out his phone to try and dig up the latest local weather scares. *How has he become even more of a wet hen with technology's assistance?* There'd been weeks on tour when a seventeen-year-old boy had had to suffer a grown man pulling his hair out over the mention of drizzle on the road. "I'll get it done before you've even finished signing off on the photos," Tristan insisted.

The glare turned from the weather-report-of-doom to the bedroom the woman had slunk off to. "You sure about that? I know how you and reporters get on."

Tristan's patient smile cracked apart. "As if some cut-rate blogger for a gossip rag can rattle me. Ten minutes, that's all I need."

"A'right." Barry shrugged, already looming over the photographer and throwing in useless suggestions about the hue and saturation. For her part, Ms. Leon nodded along while probably not listening to a damn word from the man who couldn't work an instant camera.

Pausing before the bedroom door, Tristan pulled in a calming breath. He'd run the gauntlet of reporters before his first chin hair had sprouted, learning quickly to guard his words and freeze his emotions. But it had been years since anyone had wanted to know what passed between his ears. Any haphazard word from his lips could doom him to scandalous headlines and threats of losing sponsors and contracts.

A cough startled him and he turned to see Barry glaring at the top of his head. With a start, Tristan found his hand running roughshod over his scalp. The carefully styled locks crunched between his nervous fingers, dry gel raining down. *Shake it off, Harty. It's just another reporter.*

Not even a reporter, he assured himself while opening the door. *She's…*

A solitary chair sat in the middle of the room encircled by darkness. The blinds were drawn, letting only a hint of the snow-speckled haze puncture past. Light beamed onto the seat as if aliens were about to abduct it. Tristan's mind instantly scrolled through the interrogation scenes in every spy movie.

Movement drew him away from the hot seat to the would-be reporter. Even in the muted light of the closed shades, her eyes sparked like flint. Nearly filling her face, their size gave her an innocent and pure look. He'd dismissed the snow-bedraggled woman out of hand as she stood shivering in her mid-calf coat. But when those obsidian eyes had caught his, he'd nearly stumbled backward into the fireplace.

"Mr. Harty," she said, her hand extending from the darkness, "Beth Cho with *Thorn*."

As he accepted her fingers in his, it surprised him how warm they were. He gave a quick shake. "Pleasure."

That caused her lips to purse tight, her cheeks rising as if he'd insulted her with a single word. She reached over him to the dresser. Tristan froze, tearing his gaze from the soft pink blouse just translucent enough to reveal a hint of a freckle on her collarbone.

An unwanted flush tried to climb up his cheeks, but he tamped it down—along with the question of how many more freckles hid under her shirt. Ms. Cho's focus broke from whatever she reached for on the dresser and her gaze burned into him. "I assume you are fine with my recording this?"

She was kind enough to phrase it as a question, but Tristan knew better than to argue. In truth, he preferred being recorded. It made it harder for reporters to invent their own stories later if both parties knew there was a live record. "Please," he said, racing to find his steps in this old dance. "I presume I belong in this chair."

Perhaps it was his catching on to her plan, or his pointing directly at the interrogation seat, but Ms. Cho's deep-brown eyes darkened. Nodding, she tried to force a smile onto her tight lips. With no recourse, Tristan sat.

It surprised him to find that the light off the table lamp did not pierce into his sight. Instead, it backlit him. He stared down at his shadow leeching across the hardwood floor and she positioned herself on the bed.

With the box spring propped up on high risers, Ms. Cho's five-foot-nothing height had to jump to elegantly slide her backside onto it. And when she did, she sank into no doubt the best feather down that vacationing packages could buy. He knew better, but a snort broke from Tristan at the reporter flapping her arms to keep from tumbling back onto the bed.

She arranged herself fast though, that smoky glare narrowing upon his exposed throat. A knot plunging deep into his neck, Tristan raised his hand to tug off the kitschy bowtie. One more look from the reporter with her legs locked together in a death-cross and he froze. Digging his fingers digging into his knees, he tried to turn to face her, but the awkward arms on the chair prevented him.

"Mr. Harty," she began. "You've been removed from the music scene for a long time."

"I suppose." Tristan tipped his head, shaking more of the crunched-up gel onto his suit coat's black shoulder.

The woman spoke as if she was reading, but her gaze burned through the side of his cheek. "Once declared the next Bob Dylan when only sixteen…"

Tristan flinched at the memory and the flurry of magazine covers bearing his face. "It'd have been less damaging if they'd called me bigger than Jesus," he admitted.

She didn't even pause. "Yet, you wasted that promise with a string of weak albums in your twenties before vanishing completely."

"A promise I do not remember declaring," he insisted.

"So, when you reappear, with the world questioning why it should give you a second glance, you choose a Christmas album of all things. Why?"

A flush beat through Tristan's veins, his sight narrowing at the edges as he tried to track the woman. Despite the phone recording his every breath, she kept scribbling away at a notepad in her hands. The cheap pen swerved like a vengeful bee, making it impossible to follow. *What is she writing?*

"What's wrong with Christmas?" He struggled to keep his voice light and airy. Every other stop on his 'redemption tour' the people would smile, ask him about his songs and request a happiest Christmas memory to pad out their article or runtime. Tristan had a store of invented ones to dole out.

She flickered her hard-as-diamond gaze up from her scratch pad. "You cannot get triter than a Christmas album. Add a few helium-pitched rodents and you're on your way to starring in a rotoscoped cartoon."

He flexed his fingers deep into his knees, wrinkling the silk-lined pants in an instant. A warning bell clanged in the back of his head, telling Tristan to keep his tone light. There was an app recording his every word. Through gritted teeth, he said, "If you think so little of my latest work, why are you here?"

The question seemed to surprise her, that cursed pen pausing. To hell with the damn chair. Tristan stretched out a leg and leaned to his right side to stare directly at her. She flicked a glance at her phone, or perhaps her purse to aid in her escape, before shooting him a marrow-boiling glare.

"I'd ask the same of you," she volleyed back.

"Excuse me?"

"Why now? Why return to the spotlight after you so thoroughly shunned it eight years ago?"

Do not say the name. He glared the order at her but banged it around his heart as well. *Do not let the name grace my lips, or I will never recover.*

"One of my songs recently returned to the charts. Perhaps you hadn't heard…"

"Yes, your magnum opus, *My Half.*"

Tristan scoffed. "I'd hardly call it my magnum opus."

That struck a nerve, her eyes opening wide, and he'd swear he caught a spark rising upon the flint. "It was the song of the summer for two years in a row. Damn near every high school had it playing on repeat during homecoming and prom."

He perked up at her knowing that. It seemed hyperbole, Tristan remembering well the other teenage musical savants he'd toured with. All of them had been sold as the Next Big Thing. Some had made it, most faded.

"Well, that's interesting," he mused, his fingers finally leaving the safety of his lap to push together. Tapping the false prayer against his lips, he dissected the woman. She looked young, her skin flawless save for a tiny mole on the top of her cheek. But the right makeup and genetics could hide her age, turning a thirty-something into a lovely twenty-five or so.

A smile cracked his lips and Tristan snickered. "You're a Harty-throb, aren't you?"

"What?"

"Card-carrying member of the club? Attended all the concerts with your babysitting money? Had a poster of me on your bedroom wall?"

Fire crackled in her eyes, Ms. Cho raising her shoulders to strangle her head. "You know nothing of who I am," she snarled, leaping to her feet.

Tristan remained seated. Despite her towering above him, he had the upper hand. Gripping the chair's arms, he leaned nearer, turning his smile devious. "Was it the one with the blue guitar and the open shirt?"

For a brief second, he feared she might slap him. One hand remained locked to her notebook and the other, clutching the pen, raised back. She had enough presence to rein herself in, and snapped her calculating gaze to the phone. *Shit.* He'd forgotten about that and now she had proof of how vain the ex-child prodigy was.

Barry was right. Reporters were his Achilles' heel.

"Your song is only back in the public consciousness due to its inclusion in a movie." Ms. Cho spoke coldly, her false disinterest cranked to eleven.

Tristan returned it, focusing on the fireplace ash under his fingernails to distract himself. "That treacly cancer story. I know, though I haven't bothered to see it."

"What?" His indifference to the movie seemed to be an even greater shock than the way he didn't carry much love for his old song. "How can you not? It's broken box office records. There's talk of it snagging a Golden Globe nom for best picture."

"Because I already know how the tale goes. Boy meets quirky girl. Girl is dying of cancer. Girl teaches boy the true meaning of life. Girl dies in a pretty fashion with aphorisms for last words. Boy gets to move on with his hard-won lesson of being occasionally quirky to honor her memory," Tristan snapped back, his legs shifting in the chair. "It's opiate for the masses."

To his shock, she began to laugh at that. Not a polite chuckle either. Snorts broke from her lips, Ms. Cho trying to cover them using her notebook. With a deliberate toss of her hand, she closed the front cover and placed it to her hip.

"Here I thought you were inscrutable. This stone figure no one could pierce. But I get it now. You're nothing more than some snotty brat who lucked out and believes the world owes him everything for existing. You use thesaurus-derived words to demean your perceived lessers and inflate your ego. It must be the size of a Thanksgiving parade balloon."

A cold laugh rumbled in Tristan's chest. He cracked his neck to give himself a moment to cool. For the most part, Ms. Cho didn't even flinch at the sound, but her lush eyelashes fluttered in surprise. "You know so little of me, it'd almost be embarrassing. But I wouldn't expect much from someone who only got her job by posting a torrent of bikini pictures to social media."

It was a cruel cut, but she'd thrown the first blow. Tristan considered it his job to end the confrontation as quickly as possible. For a beat, she did stumble back on her power heels. It surprised him that a blogger would come to one of these in a suit. He'd grown used to seeing so many sheath dresses. But she was just like all the rest, hungry for nothing more than a scandal, never bothering to scratch below the real surface because it might chip a nail.

Ms. Cho glared at her phone as if it might come to her rescue. God, he was never going to hear the end of it from his manager for this hatchet job. Maybe they could email *Thorn* a quick *50 Things You Didn't Know About Tristan Harty* list to dodge this misstep.

"You still haven't answered my question," her voice rumbled while she sized him up. "Why return with a Christmas album?"

Tristan was so taken aback he leaned away from her. There were no tears, not even a hint of her struggling to hide them. No quavering. No stomping away and declaring this interview over. No, she wasn't backing down, and she was glaring as if she could ignite him with her mind.

"In fact, I did. I said people like—"

"No," she interrupted. "You phrased it as a question. You did not declare why you chose a Christmas album."

Damn. Tristan's breath caught in his throat, his lips parting. For the first time in decades, the naked truth clung to his tongue. He realized she wasn't going to give in or give up without it, without taking something from him. Something he had no intention of ever giving.

"It's—"

A knock from the angels broke upon the door. "Tris? Finish up already. We gotta split."

Tristan shrugged, staring up at the towering woman. "Managers," he said with his caustic wit in place, and moved to rise. Her hand slammed on top of his. It didn't hurt, but it pinned him to the chair as her face loomed closer.

"You promised us an interview."

"Which I sat for."

"You didn't answer a single damn question," she thundered with her face so near to him he could feel the heat of her lips glancing off his cheek. "If you blow this off, and with no other exclusive to add, then I suspect *Thorn* will find some other artist's album to fill its pages."

"*Pages?* Do you think yourself a real magazine now?" Tristan tried to buy himself time to think. It was already shaky ground to form this alliance, both the label and Barry constantly pointing out how many bridges he'd burned prior.

"Come on, Harty. The photog's off in her van. We gotta hit the road." Barry's fear of the weather was growing, his voice striking higher as he banged upon the door once more.

Ms. Cho raised her eyebrow into a near-perfect peak as she stretched just enough rope for Tristan to hang himself. "You heard him," she said, "shame you wasted all this time." She seemed to want him to break the contract.

"Go on without me," Tristan called. He heard Barry's cry of confusion, but saw a cloud drift over the reporter's brow. She really did want him gone. As if he'd give in to her wants.

"What are you on about?"

"We're not finished. Head on to the hotel and deal with all the check-in procedures. I'll call you for a pickup when we're done."

"Look, kid," Barry said to the grown man with a mortgage, "there's a storm brewing and if we don't get ahead—"

"I said to leave without me!" Tristan shouted at the door, no doubt startling the already spooked manager. It was surprising Barry didn't break it down in a huff. He'd done more than that when he was younger, often yanking Tristan out of chairs by the back of his collar when things got too dicey.

A flush rose up Tristan's chest as he turned to the female reporter who'd trapped them in the bedroom. He couldn't possibly think they were…

"So help me God," Barry grumbled, "if you get us killed in some avalanche, grizzly-bear situation just to get your rocks off…"

"I'll be finished before the storm even arrives." Tristan tried to drown out his manager's salacious assumptions.

"That ain't something worth bragging over, kid. Fine, fine!"

He knew Barry's hatred of snow and inclement weather would win out over managerial stubbornness.

"Call me the second you're done so I can send a helicopter to pluck you off this mountain."

"The SUV will be fine." Tristan sighed, not needing to fuel the 'spoiled rich kid' angle the reporter was chasing.

"Whatever." Barry rolled his parting words as if they were in the '90s again. The sound of the front door being booted open and slammed shut followed, Barry quick to abandon his post once given leave.

Ms. Cho remained stationary, glaring over at her phone. "Well…" She seemed resigned to her fate, her brow heavy. It'd almost make Tristan feel bad if she wasn't trying to upend his life for her own bottom line. Snapping open the notebook, she plummeted back to the bed and began to write. "Answer the question, Mr. Harty…"

It was going to be a long afternoon.

Chapter Three

Arrogant prick.

Beth shifted her leg, trying to uncross the double knot she'd put in her thigh while waiting an eternity for him to speak. At first, he'd tossed out noncommittal grunting or one-word responses, but as the minutes ticked by, he became so quiet she thought he'd fallen asleep. Glancing down at her notes, she flinched at the nothing in her lap.

There was a who.

Presumptuous Teenage Washout who assumed he was God's gift to women.

A when and where.

Early December at some frozen peak of Vermont, the trees creaking outside the curtained window as if a giant stormed through them.

The rest was a vast blank, leaving her with nothing to her article but 'well, here's what we knew previously about Tristan Harty before he tucked tail and ran.' *Aren't musicians supposed to be humbled by having the*

Billboard charts kicked out from under them? Clearly, he'd never got that message.

In the harsh light of the positioned lamps, she could finally spot the signs of age no makeup would hide. Wrinkles not only at his eyes but circling his cheeks. The lips were flat and looked hard as iron from his unending purse. No doubt the tufts of hair he'd find in the drain each morning were wearing on him, judging by the pseudo-bangs his stylist had given him to hide the waning hairline.

Tristan directed a blue-eyed gleam at Beth and her dismissive tone melted in spite of herself. They'd used those preternaturally blue eyes to sell his first album. Nothing more than a close-up of them staring intently at the buyer, dark hair with bleached tips sweeping in from the sides. Those were the only thing that hadn't dimmed with age, somehow growing more piercing instead.

"Hmph." Tristan gave his first hint of life in an hour. "That's a rather good-sized bed for a cabin."

What do you know about cabins?

Did you stay in many?

Were you homeless as a child and forced to survive in the woods?

Are you living in one now because you spent all the money from your music on golden jaguars and silk pants?

Beth swallowed down the preposterous thoughts. Some might have been accurate, but there was no chance she could get him to cough up an answer. He wouldn't even tell her why a Christmas album, the very damn thing he was out promoting. *Why does anyone put up with his acidic tongue?*

"It's their honeymoon suite," she said instead, digging a hand into her hunched shoulders to try and fish out a decade-old knot. He didn't even know where he was holding her hostage.

"Had to be difficult to transport something that size through the trees," was his response.

"Better to suffer the broken branches and taillights than the harsh reviews of unhappy couples," Beth said, letting her stark pessimism free.

Tristan snorted – whether in laughter or derision, she couldn't tell. Tipping his head back with his eyes closed made his pronounced Adam's apple dip. "Vows never include mention of having to stack together in a twin."

A laugh tried to rise in response to his joke, but Beth shook it off. She was growing weary of the games. She needed to get this damn article started or suffer the wrath of her editor. And the subject was proving to be a brick wall.

"Why do you have that?" he asked, a long finger jabbing to her lap.

She tapped her pen thrice upon the notebook, watching him nod that that was what he meant. When she wasn't forthcoming with an answer, he explained, "Shouldn't your recording be more than enough?"

"It cannot capture your emotions" – *not that you seem to have any* – "your body posture" – *like a man facing the electric chair* – "or your habit of flexing your fingernails into your knees to hold your tongue."

At that, Tristan yanked his hands clean off his thighs. Beth smirked from the first real wound she'd gotten under his armor. He whipped his fingers through the air as if the blood had fled from them, trying to pretend that was why.

"And, if you must pry," she continued for no good reason, "I find comfort in it."

"In the act of writing, or the feel of paper in your hand?"

That sounded rather romantic. *Interesting.* Not surprising given his oeuvre, but she'd never seen mention of him preferring the tactile sensation of writing. Beth scribbled down her thoughts on the subject. *Perhaps a dive into older millennial musicians and their approach to songwriting? It could be…*

Her skin prickled with the prey-sensation of a jaguar staring at its next meal through the thick grass. A jaguar with sapphire eyes. "I feel reassured that my notebook will never lose power or catch a virus," she said, slamming shut any thoughts he might have on them sharing a single trait in common.

"Sensible." Tristan tipped his head as if he'd sacrificed a rook to move his knight. It was foolish, but a warm beam of pride hatched in her. So she'd impressed one man? So what? An obstinate, pain-in-the-ass man with sparkling eyes. "Did you learn that trick at some social media influencer symposium?"

Beth gripped so tight to her pen that her knuckles popped bone-white. The thin plastic cracked, but it was better to take her anger out on an easily replaceable pen. For a beat, the image of her cramming the nub into his eye flashed through her mind. *Instagram model? Ha!* She did most of her work in her pajamas at two in the morning with stress playing her nerves like a xylophone.

But no. All he could think, assume, was that any woman struggling to work in this cut-throat, shriveling industry had to have shown off her tits and ass.

The urge to impale him grew stronger. Beth moved to place down her pen when she read over the nuclear option she'd laid out in her research, the reporter inside her trying to not lick her chops in anticipation.

"Mr. Harty," she began, circling the cracked pen over the name as she spoke. "While you are clearly less than willing to discuss why you returned to music..."

"Hmph," he snorted.

"Perhaps we should begin with why you left in the first place."

His lackadaisical posture snapped tight in an instant. The face that'd been scanning the room for the hundredth time scorched through her. She watched his lips mouth something. It looked like *no,* but she couldn't hear it. Taking a moment to write out a few choice curse words across her pad, Beth let him marinate in what was coming.

"Sash—"

She couldn't even finish the name before Tristan leaped to his feet. A grumble rolled from his not-so-stoic lips. "This interview is over!"

Beth's body moved of its own accord, trying to block the frustrated man from leaving. It wasn't until she stood between him and the door that she noticed that his form, while lean, was taut with strength. And how he had nearly a foot on her height, on top of the biceps straining as if he wanted to yank his hair out.

"Sit down, please." Her voice didn't tremble, her hands digging into her notepad and her shoulders down as if she was unimpressed by his sudden outburst. But her fingers remained wrapped around her pen, ready to defend herself.

"For what purpose?" Tristan asked. "To allow you to...to peck and prod at matters left in the past? To defame me for..." The flames in his eyes faded to an indescribable pain. *Was it from the loss written in red in his history or because questions related to it wouldn't cease?*

"You're a vulture," he grumbled, covering his face with a hand. "All of you are. A flock of them flitting about the successful, chewing upon the bones and viscera of whoever crosses your path."

Beth's eyes rolled as she muttered, "Melodramatic."

"Excuse me?"

God, how did this go so off the rails so quickly? She'd known he'd be cold to the point of hostility, but her hard tactics weren't winning her anything but a pink slip. Damn it, why hadn't she tried sweetening him up first?

"You are melodramatic, as are all artists who hide away under the umbrella of 'it's for my art.' One slight hiccup and you gnash and wail as if the world's coming down around you. As if you're better than everyone else in the world." *Yep, so much for that article. So much for that job.* Beth could feel it all slipping away. Her shit desk in that open warehouse, her boss demanding more and more sensational clicks with each article, the unending pressure to go viral with each post.

Tristan reared back as if she had jabbed him with the pen. His face flared so alive he stopped being that snooty bookstore owner who vanished with the wallpaper. His thin lips cranked into a snarl, a white canine tooth prodding out as if he was about to turn into a vampire. "And what are you supposed journalists?"

"Vultures, apparently," she spat back, not caring what he thought of her.

A snort answered her, as if he was mad she'd stolen his chance to play his greatest hits. "Scum, pathetic posers with a phone camera sitting outside children's soccer games in order to upend their lives. Worms who root through a person's words and twist them about until you have your hot take to burn them alive. All you care about, all you live for, is appeasing your ad revenue overlords. And the bodies you crush in the process, they're not even given a second thought."

Beth growled deep in her throat. "I have never—"

"None of them have ever. Somehow it's always the other reporters that do despite the proliferation of such pain." He rose above her, steam snorting from his nose. She too took a step closer, her head craned back to glare directly into that callous face. *Heartless* didn't even begin to describe Mr. Harty. Contempt leeched from his pores and castigation dripped off his lips.

"You know..." Beth began, taking another step closer. In doing so, her trusty notebook smacked into his gut. There wasn't much give below the crimson vest, but neither combatant glanced down.

A smirk knotted up his mouth and he stole her words, "'Nothing'? Where have I heard that one before?"

"This interview is over," she ordered, snapping her notebook closed and yanking up her phone. Jamming on the button to stop the recording, she noticed its poor battery life was nearly spent. How long had they been at this?

Tristan tugged on his hair as if confused to find it gelled. "Finally," he sighed, shaking his head and sending more dandruff cascading to the carpet. She hadn't intended to mention it before, but her hand itched to include it along with every malady on his aging body. Stop the presses! *Once-Teen Star In His Thirties Doesn't Look Like A Teen Anymore.*

Cursing at herself for the stupid headline, she watched Tristan tug out his own phone from his pants pocket. After finding the number he wanted and cupping his cell to his ear, he stared hard at Beth. She deliberately turned her back on him, not caring what he was thinking or had to say. Let him stew in his own juices. Let his manager chew him out for bungling this simple press junket.

She'd get enough of that when she called her editor.

"Barry?" Tristan's venomous voice drained as he spoke to someone it was clear he *could* stand. "We're done. Come and get me."

Her skin tingled at the leopard once again staring her down. Beth risked potential mauling by glancing at him. When he caught her look, Tristan mouthed, *"Thank God I will never see you again."*

"Ditto," she whispered back.

"Yeah, Tris, about that..." the phone answered, causing the man to press it tighter to his ear as if to make the conversation private.

"It's just a little snow, Barry. Please, please get up here to..." Tristan swallowed what might have been a plea for rescue and instead said, "Screw your courage to the sticking place."

"You are aware that's what Lady Macbeth told her husband and therefore doomed them all in the process?" Beth muttered to herself while packing up her things, but it was loud enough to ensnare the beleaguered artiste.

"Yes, yes, and you're my Birnam wood come to Dunsinane," he deadpanned before returning to his phone. "Not you, Barry."

She hated to admit it, but she was surprised he knew the reference. Sure, he wore his haughty pretentiousness like a bespoke tux, but in her experience, most with their noses in a snoot survived by knowing only a handful of things. They'd then bombard a person with them endlessly for praise. *People who tour the country with boybands in high school don't tend to correlate to those possessing vast pools of knowledge. Has dandruff, knows* Macbeth. She thought about writing it down when she caught Tristan's stricken look.

"Do not play games, Barry. I mean it. I need you here, now."

"Is your manager abandoning you?" Beth snorted, her overloaded purse tucked under her arm. She gave a quick once-over of the room, having no intentions of returning to this cabin or coming near it again. She opened the bedroom door and glanced back at the fretting man. "Your team will be contacted when the article goes up."

She expected that to be the final shot across the bow, but Tristan snickered. "Do you think you're leaving?"

"Yes, and with my tattered dignity intact, no less."

"Well, good luck then."

She tried to shake it off, to ignore him, but Beth's hackles wouldn't cease rising. Her opinion cemented that he was pricklier than a porcupine, she headed for the exit. For a brief second, she was about to point out the fireplace and how someone needed to put it out. But that was his problem.

Perhaps he was hoping she'd offer him a ride, as if being trapped in a small vehicle with the man for the twenty-minute drive to civilization was in any way appealing. With a smug smile on her lips, Beth glanced back at him. *You're on your own, artist.*

She cracked open the front door and walked into a sea of white. *No.*

No!

Freezing cold air blew the white flakes fat as erasers into her face.

"Seems the storm blew in already," Tristan mused while they gazed out at the snow blanketing away every tire track, hint of the road, means of escape. And it was climbing higher.

No!

Chapter Four

He shouldn't laugh, but watching her trudge, coat open to the elements, through the rising drifts of snow to glare at the uncrossable roads was rather hilarious. Heavy flakes built up in her jet-black hair until it looked star-speckled, but despite the white swarming across her shoulders and head, she wasn't about to give up for anything. Which seemed even more farcical when he caught what she'd driven in with.

"What are you doing?" Tristan asked, looming in the doorway. He should close the door before the last of the heat vanished from the cozy cabin, but he didn't want to be pulled into her madness either.

"Leaving," Ms. Cho snorted, naked fingers grabbing onto the freezing metal of the door handle. To his surprise, she didn't even flinch while cranking it open. Perhaps rage was heating her body.

He waited until she fell into her driver's seat before risking a step into the blizzard. That was a bit of a misnomer. He'd seen far worse storms in his younger days, but the snow was heavy from the humidity and clumping the second it struck. That led to dangerous driving conditions he wouldn't wish on his worst enemy.

Also, the last thing he needed was people asking about the reporter run off the road after interviewing him.

Clomping down into the snow, he tried to match her footprints through the cold blanket, but she'd marched with such a long stride Tristan lost it. Gripping the car's roof, he leaned closer to the woman trying unsuccessfully to dig out the snow that had followed her in.

"It won't work," he said.

"Then the heater will melt it," she sneered, swinging her legs inside. Tristan waited for the door to come slamming into his fingers, but all she did was wring out the no-doubt frozen steering wheel.

"What do you think the chances are of you making it down this mountain alive in little more than a sheet of plastic attached to a metal frame? Who even drives something so flimsy in the winter?"

"Sorry we can't all afford military-grade Hummers for day trips," she said, but still the door didn't slam.

Tristan chuckled to himself at the idea of owning such a thing. A standard truck would do much better in this. *Though…* He gazed down the fog-coated path, the back of his neck prickling when he realized he couldn't even find the road. Perhaps nothing short of a tank would make it through this storm.

"Come inside," he sighed, feeling the sub-freezing temperature whistling through the linen shirt. The cruel northern wind found its way past the suit coat and drew chills up and down his chest.

Ms. Cho harrumphed and dug her obstinate heels in. Metaphorically. Even she knew better than to try to push on the accelerator without starting the engine.

"At least to wait out the storm. No one can see in this, never mind drive." Tristan couldn't believe he was arguing to keep her around, but it was preferable to causing her death, albeit indirectly. God, he wasn't certain if he had the strength to pluck her recalcitrant body out of the car and back inside.

"I've got a better idea." She crammed her key into the ignition and turned the engine over. Tristan slid out of the way, fearing she might suddenly ram on the reverse to take him out. But the door still remained open as she spoke. "I'll wait it out here. Without you."

He glanced at the mound of snow swept up over the tailpipe and only growing higher. "As you wish, but it sounds like a good way to die of carbon monoxide poisoning."

A sneer knotted up her cherry lips, her little nose crinkling in disgust. For a foolish second, his heart wondered if there was someone in her life who'd kiss that pile of wrinkles away. What did he care? The storm would pass in an hour, a few at the most, then he'd be free of Ms. Cho.

Her fingers continued to flex and claw at the steering wheel as if she really thought she could plow her way through the snow. His best guess was that she'd make it maybe twenty feet before either losing traction and sticking or spinning off the road into a tree. Either way, he'd be forced to walk to her car and rescue her.

"Fine," she spat, honestly surprising him. After the display from before, Tristan had been counting on her smashing into a tree and him plucking her unresponsive body from the wreckage into his arms and carrying her to safety. With that much fire in her belly, her body had to be particularly warm.

The cold was getting to him. He sneered at his foolish thoughts trying to impede common sense, but it was clear she read it differently. "I'm not happy about this either," Ms. Cho said, silencing her car and rising to her feet. She wobbled once her heels struck the snow and, on instinct, Tristan reached out to grab her.

Ms. Cho gripped her car's roof as she steadied herself without his help. They stood dangerously close, his hands hanging on to the open car door and the roof. Hers nearly bumped into his to keep herself upright. Steam buffeted between them, Tristan enthralled as snowflakes built up on her eyelashes. They fluttered above her deep brown eyes and cheeks paling from the cold. She looked both as fragile as a snowflake and impenetrable as ice in the same breath.

"Will you move?"

"Sorry, sorry, I..." He scampered away, his face burning at the treachery of his body. Once away from the corona of her being, he was able to take in the cooling air of common sense. "I take it you do not intend to risk the elements like some female Jack London."

"Ha." She gathered her things and tucked them tightly to her body as if they were both a protector and a balm. Stomping to the house, she muttered, "I hope you don't expect me to pull you out of a river."

Rubbing a hand through his hair, he sighed at how he'd already worked through the best procedure for saving and nursing her back to health. *Forget the reporter, just make it through the next few hours without killing her. Or doing anything else.* Taking one last glance over the unforgiving mountains, he returned inside.

Ms. Cho was already yanking open her laptop and searching for the Wi-Fi. "What's the damn password?" she muttered to herself.

"Intransigence," Tristan said, wiping the snow off his padded shoulders.

She glared at him, the reporter recognizing the word and his cut. With a shrug, he said, "It's actually Mount Mansfield. Capital Ms and an underscore for the space."

Clearly not believing him, she entered the password quickly while keeping an eye on the man shaking off the last of the unwanted snow. When it no doubt went through, she blushed and in a quiet voice said, "Thank you."

His tongue burned with a quip of shock that she was capable of such gratitude, but he swallowed it down. Antagonizing her wouldn't help as they faced who knew how much of the waning afternoon together. He tugged out his phone and noticed a dozen texts from his manager. No doubt Barry was in fits trying to reschedule over a week's worth of gigs.

This would be over soon—snows this heavy never lasted long. In theory, a few hours in a rustic cabin by the fire would be a soothing break from the constant ruckus of the road. He caught the edge of the reporter no doubt turning in all the venomous notes she'd taken on him. *In theory, indeed.*

Staring around the cabin, Tristan tried to take stock of what was available. A small kitchen sat nestled in the back, a stove with two burners and an oven so tiny it looked like it used a light bulb. The fridge was at least five feet tall, but the chances of it being stocked seemed low. Not that it mattered—he'd be out soon anyway.

Ms. Cho was quickly spreading out across the lone sofa in the cabin. Well, less sofa more love seat, given the theme. There was a single armchair perched beside but it looked rickety and uncomfortable, with a set of antlers swooping off the back. Rubbing into the nape of his neck, he dipped his fingers into the back of his collar and accidentally tugged. At the reminder of the suit still strapped to his body, he began to unbutton the vest.

"What... What are you doing?" Ms. Cho snapped from her oasis of extenuating facts.

Tristan paused in tugging the linen shirt out of his waistband, his gaze catching hers. "Freeing myself from looking like the child forced to perform at prom."

"You—" She pointed a jagged finger at him as he shrugged the coat off onto the hanger beside the door, then the vest. "You can't be planning on...on stripping."

He expected to hear horror rolling in those words. And while, yes, her face looked as stricken as if someone had slapped it with a fish, her voice sounded discordant. *Impossible to pin down.* With a laugh, Tristan plucked up the bag Barry had left for him. "Don't worry, I'll finish away from your prying eyes. Or...?" He extended a hand out as if he wanted to invite her to watch him, as if she'd want to accept, as if he cared if she would.

Ms. Cho's body shuddered and she forced her glare back to the screen. "Do whatever you want. I'll be out of here soon enough."

With the bag strung over his back, Tristan made for the unoccupied bedroom. Closing the door, he pulled in a deep breath. She was infuriating, more obstinate than a cat, judgmental and would exit his life in a matter of hours. Still, he couldn't shake off the picture of her with gentle snowflakes trapped in her eyelashes.

* * * *

This wasn't good.

Ha. Understatement, Beth. This is a disaster.

She pinged from the open chat window to her email, watching in stomach-knotting anxiety as the little dots bounced. So she was trapped in a cabin with Tristan Harty for who knew how long. Until a damn storm blew over.

Beth used dry words and a calm tone to explain the circumstances to her boss, then turned around and panicked with her friend, Madeline. Refreshing her email only revealed a new chance for her to refinance a mortgage she didn't have.

Okay, she could survive this, assuming Mr. Teenage Soul-Stealer didn't literally suck out life force with his icy eyes. Though, given their ethereal radiance, she wouldn't be surprised. *Cold eyes to match a cold heart.*

Why had he made a fuss about keeping her around? *Aside from the imaginary soul stealing.* Beth was running on little sleep and wound up, but she didn't believe in the supernatural. Not without proof of him draining a deer in a snowy glen, anyway. He could have stood back, let her try to drive her car down the mountain, crash, and wait for emergency vehicles to rescue her. It'd have gotten her out of his hair. His crispy, twisted-up, early 2010s hair.

That hand was certainly warm. She hadn't anticipated him guarding her driver's-side door, and certainly not him failing to slide back when she got out. Even in the frostbite temperatures and with snow piling up in her hair, a surge of heat had zapped off his hand to hers. It had startled her so much she'd begged for him to get out of the way before she said or did something stupid.

It's the hate. No, hate implied familiarity. She knew nothing about Tristan Harty, which was why she couldn't stand the man. That raw anger at a near stranger could confuse the senses, convince it that…that… *He did look good in that thin white shirt tailored much tighter to his body than most men wear.*

What was going to come out of that bedroom? Tristan with tousled hair and his business suit look stripped down to the bare minimum? Dressed like a successful tycoon at leisure? Or would he be naked to try and scare her away?

How much of that wiry body was supported by taut muscle?

A *bing* out of her laptop's buggy speakers nearly sent Beth leaping off the couch.

How are you stuck in Vermont? Madeline taunted from the chat screen, then followed it up with a gif of a penguin dancing on an iceberg.

Don't want to talk about it, Beth responded, meaning it. She wanted to get as far from her current headache as possible, hammer out some tripe to appease the article requirement then start the job hunt.

Uh huh. Just you, all alone in some remote cabin in the mountains. An escape for your book?

Not alone, Beth typed. To her surprise, the ellipsis began to bounce the second her words appeared on screen. She watched it, almost hypnotized by the rapid undulation that showed her friend was typing up a storm. As it passed from thirty seconds to a minute of typing, Beth gritted her teeth. This wasn't going to go over well.

When the chat refreshed all Madeline's tag said was, *Not alone?*

No doubt she'd already worked through a dozen theories before deleting them all and asking for more info.

It's complicated, Beth responded. *Explain later.* Or not at all. She suspected she'd fall into the embrace of mother tequila to forget this entire day once safe at home. That emoji with steam coming out of its nose filled the chatbox, then Madeline's rejoinder.

Later never comes, explain now!

Beth flexed her fingers over the keys, ready to type her reply and get all the venom off her chest in one go. Just before she could begin, the bedroom door opened. He wasn't naked. While relief swarmed over her at the fact, she frowned at the niggling wonder of his potential nudity.

Every trace of the suit was gone. Instead, he wore a gray-green Henley cut tight to that thin body. The waffle-weave pattern stretched at the chest but folded when reaching his waist. The garment wasn't tucked into his dark-wash jeans, shaking off some of that patrician aura he'd begun with, though the high chin and rock-solid posture kept a good chunk of it in place.

Tristan rustled a hand through his hair, tugging down the shellacked locks. Some fell into a side part, but just enough remained glued in place to give him a cowlick. Beth pinched her lips tight at the image and focused on her laptop instead.

Forget the man in the cabin. It's only a few hours. It shouldn't be hard to do.

As she didn't make any fuss like falling at his feet and declaring her unending allegiance, Tristan wandered over toward the kitchen area. Beth ignored him, all her focus upon the chat box asking why she wasn't explaining.

It's nothing, quit prying, she wrote back and pressed Send.

Of course, Madeline wouldn't hear of it. An array of guesses flew across the screen.

A photographer? A fellow writer? An editor? A manager? A sexy park ranger?

She was gonna take a crack at every possible profession before Beth responded.

The rattle of glass bowls from the cupboards caused Beth to suck her teeth. Clinging to her high horse, she turned her back on the shadow thrusting his head into the fridge and prodded out a *No.*

What do you mean no? No to sexy acrobat or no to all of them?

Maybe she should tell Madeline, just in case things took a bad turn. Sure, her boss knew she was here. There was a paper trail a mile long, but didn't rich and powerful men buy off their 'transgressions' all the time? Why would Mr. Harty be any different? Not to mention all those dark rumors about his previous live-in girlfriend. Who was to say he didn't have a basement hole for lowering a bucket with lotion into? *And you're sounding a little paranoid there, Beth.*

Mads, I'm with a client.

Accurate enough to be true, and it might get her to shut up.

OMG!

Or not.

Is it a celebrity? Are you in a snowy mountaintop cabin with a celebrity? A-list? B?

Beth risked glancing over her shoulder to the celeb in question to see Tristan scooting his denim-covered ass onto the counter while digging a spoon into a bowl.

No, was all she typed.

Try a washed-up singer-songwriter who's eating a bowl of Cheerios with complimentary cartons of half and half for milk. When he tried to hoover up the cereal with his lips, a splash of the cream-milk splattered his cheek. Unable to help herself, Beth snickered at the childish sight of the haughty man with milk on his face.

Blue depths pierced into her and she gulped at the focus burning in them. *You're trapped alone in a cabin with some unknown hostile man for who knows how long. Do not laugh at him!* Slowly, Tristan released the plastic spoon to the watery bowl and with the back of his hand wiped the spot off. His glare never left Beth's. Years of experience wandering through untamed wilderness with her father kicked in, and despite wanting to turn away fast, she maintained eye contact. *Never break that with the prowling tiger or bear. Make them feel just as small as they try to make you feel.*

With a shrug as if they hadn't waged a pointless battle over a milk stain, Tristan resumed chomping on his cereal. He stared out of the kitchen window, watching the fall of snow blotting away the last of the green pines. A shiver curled up Beth's spine, her fingers digging into her shoulder as if she needed to warm her whole body. She wanted to say it was fear, but that wasn't accurate. Her heart slammed and her breath quickened, but…

Fear. No. It had to be fear.

A reality star?

Madeline was laying it on thick. Beth sighed at the imagined horror of being trapped in a cabin with someone whose claim to fame was the depth of their spray tan. The unending 'bros' would cause her to suffer a brain aneurysm. Somehow, Tristan didn't seem quite so bad compared to that.

Will you stop? Don't you have something more important to do? What about the furballs?

Beth typed quickly, trying to silence both her friend and a disquieting feeling in her gut. *When did I last eat?*

"Do you mind?" He glared down at her things spread mindlessly across the couch. Blushing at her slovenly ways, Beth gathered up her stacks of spilled research before wondering why he cared.

Just as the notebooks landed in her lap, Tristan plummeted onto the couch beside her. He clung to the armrest, his half-finished bowl of bachelor dinner resting upon it. But the couch was so small his knee nearly brushed against hers, his shoulder swiping against the edge of her blazer. Gulping, she struggled to maneuver her mess while the man kept on consuming without a care in the world.

A *ding* out of her laptop speakers snagged her attention. She woke it up to find Madeline quickly responding.

Got one right here in my lap. See.

What followed was a picture of a tiny kitten the size of a palm resting safely between Madeline's thighs. It was at most a few weeks old, the eyes barely open and bright blue. Mads was one of the official foster moms for most of the borough's kittens, Beth often helping since she couldn't adopt a cat of her own.

"Adorable," the form beside her cooed.

Beth swiveled her head fast, an uncomfortable warmth blossoming in her as she fell directly into the full wattage of his gaze. "Wh…" Beth gulped, her brain buzzing like a downed wire. All it could make out through the hiss was that word repeating endlessly. Adorable. "What?"

"The kitten." Tristan pointed to her laptop and her private screen, which he carelessly invaded without a second thought.

"Excuse me? Did you—" Beth slapped a hand over the chat box, her blush transforming into a fire of rage. "Did you stare at my private conversation?"

"Private?" Tristan snickered as if making her angry was hilarious to him. "You're having it out here in the open. Right beside me."

"You sat down second!" Beth sneered, snapping her laptop shut.

"Oh, for the love of..." Tristan's eyes rolled so far back it was a wonder they didn't get stuck. "I saw movement, my eyes went to it, I thought the cat was cute. This is hardly KGB espionage."

"The KGB was disbanded in '91," fell out of her mouth before she shook off the stupid thought. *Who cares?*

"Then that's..." His cheap spoon flitted through the air as he sank back into the couch. "That's my point."

Without a thought, Beth launched to her feet. She leaped so far she nearly smacked into the out-of-place Christmas tree. Spinning back to the lackadaisical man stretching out on the small couch, she ordered, "Keep your...your everything to yourself!"

"Shall I stab my eyes out first chance I get?" the smart tongue replied with.

Don't tempt me.

With her laptop, notebooks and purse crammed tight to her chest, Beth stomped away from the man left alone beside the fireplace. She needed to do work away from the subject of said work before she wrote nothing but a trash article. On instinct, she headed to the bedroom. She struggled to flip on the light, all her work nearly crashing to the floor.

At first, it seemed a good idea. There was a desk of sorts, a chair to sit in while typing. But her gaze zoomed straight to the suit laid out across the welcoming bed. The shades were drawn, turning a cozy image intimate and secretive, almost as if she'd dashed away to a man's bedroom right before or after a gala. The suit was waiting for him to fill it, for a woman to adjust the bowtie and button up the vest. Then, when they stumbled home inebriated and happy, unwrap the whole thing.

The uncomfortable burn in her gut returned at her cursed imagination leaping to such heights. With a sigh, Beth snapped off the light as she made plans to strangle her libido later. This was hardly the setting or person to trip off to such romantic heights with. And she was faced with a dilemma.

Said person of tooth-grinding interest was resting upon the only comfortable seating. Not to mention how easily he could slip off to the kitchen to read her screen over her shoulder. The bedroom was…not happening.

She could feel him attempting to unravel her thoughts, to understand why she'd walked into and out of the only other room in the cabin. Not today.

With her head held high, Beth stomped to the last door left to her, the bathroom. The second the door shut behind her, her back shuddered against it. She was hiding in the bathroom like some terrified child who hated holidays with the relatives.

Great going, Beth. Way to really show him your teeth.

Cursing at herself for being so soft, she trudged to the toilet and sat on the closed seat. Opening up the laptop, she was inundated by the piles of adorable kitten pictures Madeline had taken in three minutes. The abject cuteness soothed her most rattled nerves, but a dark one lingered deep inside. Why had she run from his suit on the bed?

Chapter Five

What is she doing in there?

At first, he ignored the woman rushing off to the bathroom to hide. Tristan busied himself with the mountain of emails that Barry kept forwarding to him. *Isn't the point of a manager to manage my correspondence?* Check this date, match with this appearance, circle in on yet another interview that'd lead to nowhere.

He pursed his lips tight at the one set for a moderate-sized local news crew on the East Coast. After that it was back to the West, Barry slotting him in as entertainment during a bowl-game parade. Walking in the chilly air, pretending to slap around his guitar while his pre-recorded voice sang out of the speakers before the bandstand? Tristan had no qualms with that pretense. But the thought of yet another reporter digging into his private life and his past set his teeth on edge.

At that thought, he risked a glance to the slammed bathroom door. No sounds came out, bodily or otherwise. If she was watching anything on her laptop, she must have headphones on. *Could be a movie. Or some funny cat videos.* Dread sloshed in his cereal-crammed guts as old press footage raced through his memory. One of a young man, red-eyed and distraught, yanking the camera out of the hands of one of a dozen paps around him. How it flew through the air to the inhuman shrieks of the crowd before splattering on the ground.

The reason Barry was so tetchy about leaving him alone with reporters. The reason reporters were cautious but also salivating about sinking their fangs into him. How many more small cuts would it take for another disaster like that to happen?

Not helping. Forget it. That wasn't me anyway. It was…it was his Hyde. When the smell of bleach and copper wafted from the dark recesses of his psyche, Tristan forced himself deep into a phone game. One of his old work buddies had asked him to help beta-test it, but that had been before the resurrection of his music career. By the time Tristan finally got around to cracking open Sheep Wars, it was already available on mobile.

Though, the hardened rams in eye patches piloting various space ships and fighting off alien farmers certainly helped distract him. He'd have to give Gemma points for its addictiveness whenever he saw her again. Tristan was happy to fall into the world of battle-sheep, even forking over some of his ramen-noodle-marked savings for more play time, but a pressing need arose.

After rising from the surprisingly comfortable couch, he approached the bathroom door. Fist raised, he was about to knock, when he pressed his ear to the wood.

There wasn't crying—not that he expected any from her stone soul. *Still, best to check when a woman hides away in a bathroom.*

No sounds save the slow click and clack of a keyboard bounced around the echoing room. *What is she doing?* He paled at the thought of her hammering away at the hit piece, her talons sharpening at every adverb to slice him to ribbons. All the while he sat just a room away, pushing buttons on his phone to launch torpedoes at invading chickens.

Straightening up, Tristan pounded his fist thrice upon the door. "How long do you intend to stay in there?" he shouted.

He anticipated that she'd snap at him, perhaps not answer at all, but she called out, "Why? Has it stopped snowing?"

"No, but I need to take a piss." He rolled the words out slowly, imagining her icy cheeks lighting up pink. "And I'd prefer to not do it in the kitchen sink."

Scrambling sounds echoed from inside the bathroom, Ms. Cho struggling to gather up her mass of things. He leaned closer, his ear almost pressed to the door, when the wood flew back. *Caught.* A gulp thudded down his throat into his gut—Tristan was ensnared by not only guilt but the shock of her body standing an inch from his.

She too seemed gobsmacked, her petal-pink lips falling slack. "Well…"

"Well, what?" gurgled from Tristan's mouth. He tried to focus on her, but he kept staring at the little mole perched upon her cheek. It wasn't hairy or oddly misshapen, didn't seem diseased. If anything, it was a cute mole, like one a designer would add out of fear of its creation being too perfect to be believed.

Her flat eyebrow arched to a mountain-like peak. "Do you have to pee or not?"

Tristan mentally pinched himself for his idiotic thoughts. "Yes, I do. If you don't mind."

She'd clearly slammed her laptop closed on the mountain of notebooks. Were those all about him? No way she'd got more than a page out of him in the bedroom, but…there was a lot in his history. *Never mind.* Shoving past the woman, Tristan escaped into the open bathroom.

After alleviating his pressing bladder and washing his hands, he stared daggers at the man in the mirror. Some of the photographer's makeup remained, though it was thinner than what he'd suffered as a teenager. Pimples, which had once plagued his forehead and nose, had required the pancake slather. Now, it could all be magicked away with a little computer graphics.

They probably wouldn't do much about the wrinkles cresting along the sides of his eyes or at the tips of his mouth. Maybe lighten up his eye bags earned from too many long nights in front of a screen, then early mornings beside his guitar. But the wrinkles, the proof that only the good died young, those they'd keep. It was a fitting toggle on his return from the metaphorical grave.

Wiping his hands on his shirt, because the cabin didn't come with a towel, Tristan left the bathroom. He expected to have Ms. Cho barrel past him and return to her vigil on the toilet, but she was glued to the front window. Only her back was evident to him, her pin-straight ebony hair reaching to her elbows as she crossed her arms.

"What's wrong?" he asked on instinct. It wasn't until the words left his mouth that he realized she was hugging herself for comfort instead of in wrath.

"I thought it'd have stopped by now," she whispered to herself. Tristan watched her reflection bouncing off the window, its ghostly form overlaid with the tumble of white snow. It was easier to take than her hard glare watching him both warily and sharply.

Wiping his hands once more across his chest, he walked closer to the window. It was wide, nearly the size of a set of french doors. But even as he stopped an arm's length from her, he could feel her heat competing against the cold draft sputtering between the glass and frame.

"Provided it doesn't last through the night, we should be fine," he surmised, staring across the disappearing landscape. It was hard to tell where the smaller shrubs and saplings had been. *Any more and…*

What are the chances of it being a true blizzard?

"The night?" she whispered as if she'd thought they could just pack up and leave once the snow had stopped falling. *Nice idea, but no.*

"I'm afraid you're trapped with me until the morning. Then they'll send some trucks out to plow the road. Maybe you can even hitch a ride in one if you charm them," Tristan threw out. One part of him wanted to sink a barb in, but another buried and forgotten part wanted to soothe her. At least keep her calm until daybreak.

Eyes narrowed to a pinprick, Ms. Cho snapped her head at him as if she was going to peck. Okay, he'd played that game too long. "And how do you know all this?"

"I've seen far worse storms growing up. They wouldn't even call school for this in Bemidji."

Her wary stance softened as if in surprise. "That's in Minnesota?"

"Yes." He tried to form it as a statement but the rabid curiosity rising in her face caused him to wilt.

Snickering, she cupped her palm to her chin. "I got something personal out of you after all."

Tristan scoffed while the room pushed in tighter around him. "That's hardly uncommon knowledge. I'd mentioned before that...regardless, what do a person's origins mean in the grand scheme of things?"

"Where are you living now?"

That reporter edge he'd foolishly forgotten about snapped back into place. While she didn't pull a pen out from behind her ear and crack open a notebook tugged from her breast pocket, she did tap her foot impatiently, as if he owed her an answer.

"Elsewhere," he breathed. The air spurted from between his lips in a silent whistle.

The face he'd thought of as soft and feminine elongated into that of a ferocious lioness stalking through the grass. He'd stupidly revealed himself to be a gazelle with a limp without realizing it. "Same state, or did you retain residence in California?"

A shudder rumbled through his soul, his gaze shutting tight as he thought back to that small, once-shared house. "I'm in the Twin Cities, since you cannot stop prying," he answered, doing everything to keep her away from digging into his California days.

"Interesting," she said as if she could will the fact so. "Most would have said either Saint Paul or Minneapolis."

It caught him off guard that she knew their names. Using the Twin Cities excuse for people on the East Coast tended to get him a shrug, or question of 'What's the barbecue like?' Swallowing, Tristan scrabbled a chipped nail against his earlobe. "Should it surprise *me* that I don't share much in common with the average sort?"

The tone was so flippant and snotty even he winced, but Ms. Cho appeared unflappable. She hadn't abandoned her vigil over the snowstorm, but she was clearly working through a new angle in her brain. It pained him to find that he preferred the rabid reporter hounding him to the pretty but empty shell staring at nothing.

"What of you?" he asked, startling her from dissecting his life in two thousand words or less. "Where are you from?"

"What do you care?"

What do you care?

Tristan tried to laugh it off even as his inner mind echoed her sentiment. "It only seems fair. You ask me, so I ask you."

"Nowhere in particular," was her guarded answer, instantly piquing his lagging curiosity.

Snorting, he leaned back against the couch, his backside gracing the backrest. It gifted her room to escape should she wish, but to his surprise, Ms. Cho stood directly before him. Her legs were staggered the way a superhero's would be in battle, but she wasn't fleeing to the bathroom refuge either.

"Everyone's from somewhere," Tristan voiced his thoughts.

She regarded him cautiously, her tongue flitting with her thinner top lip. "I was born in San Francisco but grew up everywhere. For the most part."

Army brat? Family of circus acrobats? Perhaps they were in the mafia or witness protection? Tristan's mind played through the possibilities, each one growing more outlandish as his curiosity inflated. Who was this woman he was being forced to spend a snowy night trapped in a cabin with?

"You said something earlier." Beth spoke, causing him to look up from below his heavy brow. "About how you felt as if you were dressed to perform at the prom, but not as someone sent to it."

Tristan grimaced as if it was yet another misstep in his foolish attempt to appear normal. "I doubt it would surprise your readers or your editor to learn that the child star did not in fact…"

"No," she interrupted, a hand cutting through his venomous vitriol. "I know that. I only noticed because I've…I skipped that part of American culture as well."

"What?" He folded his arms tighter to his chest, leaning so far back against the couch he might fall over. "Prom?"

"High school." Her cryptic answer clanged like a bell in his head. Tristan watched the strange woman stare out of the window. They couldn't be more different. He was in the creative side of the world, she the destructive. He came from the frozen Midwest, she the balmy coast of the West. He'd already reached his zenith and grown jaded in the industry he couldn't quite quit. She seemed to be scrambling to make it anywhere in hers.

Yet, there was that one thread. Neither knew what it was to have lockers, and overstuffed backpacks, to throw limp tater-tots in cafeterias, or awkwardly hold someone's sweaty hand while dancing in a gym. He wasn't sure which surprised him more—to have found a common link or to care that he had.

She finished staring overlong out of the window, a resigned sigh rattling in her lungs. "I suppose there's no point in watching. It won't stop just because I stare." Stumbling from her wary stupor courtesy of the weather, she began her march back to the bathroom.

"Ah," Tristan called, leaping to his feet. "Ms. Cho?"

Her steps paused.

"You may use the couch if you'd like." He pointed to the furniture in question as if she was too stupid to know what one was. *Tactful as always, Harty.* "I need to stretch my legs and find it's easier to recline in the"—he tried to not glare at the antler monstrosity—"armchair."

It wasn't warmth that radiated from her, but the black ice melted a few layers down. She nodded. "Thank you." Before he could rescind his offer, her work plummeted to one cushion while she claimed the other.

Tristan nodded, despite her not looking at him. Tugging out his phone, he tried to drum up any manner of distraction, but his mind wouldn't stop toying with that common thread. It wondered how much more could unravel if he tugged harder.

* * * *

That's fantastic.

Beth grumbled into her hands, occasionally peering at the single response from her editor regarding her entrapment. He seemed to be of the opinion that it was a great opportunity for her to get to know the real Tristan Harty. Had anyone ever considered that there wasn't much to report upon him because there wasn't anything below the surface?

Pompous, belligerent coating atop a haughty, antagonistic filling. She'd be surprised if he had any friends outside of those he paid. After graciously allowing her use of the couch, he took to wandering aimlessly through the creaking cabin. Every pass of his thin body on the periphery of her vision startled Beth.

She retyped the same sentence six times, deleted it, then restarted with threats to rip her hair out. At one point, he finally grew weary of playing his own one-man game of ping-pong behind her and walked outside. She breathed a sigh of relief, only to have him rush back in with snow piled atop his waning chestnut hair.

Shivering and stomping his feet at the foolish move, Tristan stood before the door, trying to shake off the snow. It reminded her of dogs running in from the Russian cold and leaping straight for the rug by the fire. She only chuckled at the memory, but it drew his ire in an instant. With his nose in a twist, Tristan plummeted to the armchair.

So that was what Beth faced as the storm rattled outside and night ticked to an uncomfortable ten o'clock. He stared askance at the side of her face, his phone occasionally emerging to entertain him, but just as often not. While she…she stared at the blank page, struggling to find the courage to put him back to the screws.

"Your song?" she whispered more in thought to herself, but Tristan perked up.

"Which one? There've been..." He paused as if to count, but shook it off. "Quite a few," he humble-bragged with a smug grin on his face.

"*My Half,*" Beth announced, watching the scowl slither into place. "Why do you discount it so quickly? It was your number one hit, the first single off your freshman album..."

"I fully well know my own discography," Tristan hissed, his body snapping to the edge of the chair. But he didn't leap to his feet and run away. Not that he'd get far in this storm. Pulling in a cleansing breath as if he had to remind himself he was trapped here with a foolish mortal, he sighed. "It's not the song I hate but the interpretation."

"Interpretation?" Beth snickered. "It's your standard boy meets girl, boy loses girl star-crossed love song."

Tristan's right half was lit by the dancing red and orange flames as he stared her down. The fire crackled and popped to fill the silence of him glaring at her. She wished she could read whatever was drifting through his mind, but he kept hiding in the shadows. Only a sliver of emotion broke through, exhaustion at having to deal with the 'normals' clear, but there was something else. If this wasn't Tristan Harty, she'd swear it was pain.

He broke their eye contact to stare at the fire instead. Scraping at his fallen hair as if it should be longer, he said, "That's what everyone thinks."

With that, he shut off communication again. *Yes, this is just fantastic.* She'd met people without tongues who could communicate better than him. He moved as if the mere existence of humanity was a blight upon him and suffering another person in the room a test of his resolve.

While the brooding ex-singer glared into the fire, an idea flitted through Beth's brain. She didn't have anything locally stored, but a quick internet search found one of those YouTube videos teenage girls made with static shots of black-and-white photos. Watching the moody blue from the edge of her periphery, Beth pushed Play.

Twinkling piano music began enveloping the slumbering cabin in its notes. It wasn't until a guitar joined in that Tristan sat bolt upright.

"You are not..." he started, when the lyrics began.

The voice sounded young, fresh and vibrant, without a world-weary crack to the syllables. Still, even knowing who it belonged to, there was a depth there in the confident bass. He never strayed too high in his compositions, but he stuck every note like a gymnast at the Olympics.

"Me to you, you to me. Stare in the mirror, what do they see? You to me, and me to you. Never imagined that one could be two..."

Tristan sank deeper into his collar, as if he truly didn't want to relive his greatest hit. Was that it? A reminder that he'd already reached his peak and it was only downhill from there? No, that wasn't accurate. While this song was easily his most memorable, he'd had other hits even into his twenties and collaborations with bigger artists. There was something else.

Some reason why he dismissed it out of hand, but still clung to the words. As the bridge washed to the chorus, he closed his eyes. He didn't mouth along, but his cheeks fell hollow and his lips slack, as if he was waiting for the trauma to end.

"Me to you, and... Rain of glass, forever between we. Once there was us, now only me."

The last of the words in the song drifted away upon the final piano refrain held into a fade. All the while, Tristan kept his fingers locked tight together as if in prayer.

She'd been moved to tears attending concerts in both massive arenas and private dining rooms, but Beth had never felt such a trembling rise through her body from a single song. How often had she heard this song on the radio in the past two decades? Discovered it, danced to it, dismissed it? Never before had she felt stricken like an icicle was plunged through her heart until watching the man who'd created it struggle to keep his sheen in place.

With a rattling finger, she shut off the playlist as it cycled for another Tristan Harty song. "Are you..." She coughed. "Will you tell me what it means?"

Her voice had lost all its command. This one pleaded and cajoled for the once ice-man melted before the fire to explain. He seemed to hear it, though whether he'd respect her for it was hard to guess.

"I...I can't," Tristan said. He swept the heel of his palm up over his cheeks, blanketing away the icy blues. He watched his own movement as if unaware his body could do such a thing. In an instant, he sat up, rod-straight. "I doubt you could comprehend it anyway."

A sneer raised her lips and Beth let the growl loose. Perhaps he heard it and snickered, or perhaps his own smug satisfaction clogged his ears. Either way, she dove back into her work. The work she could complete without needing him. Slapping her blinders on, she paid no heed to the other person in the cabin.

He could be laid out on the floor bleeding to death for all she cared. Swiping back and forth between different documents, Beth hate-wrote nearly two thousand words before a crick in her spine caused her to break. No one was sitting in the chair.

A confounding fear rattled in her heart that he'd left, which should have been a godsend. But she spotted him standing before the window. He cradled his chin in his hand, worrying the rising scruff in thought. She assumed he had no idea she was watching him and was about to resume writing.

"It's stopped." Tristan's voice echoed through the cabin.

"Thank God," she gasped, pressing Save and backing her work up into the cloud. At least this place had working internet and electricity. The heat seemed to come predominantly from the fire, but there were a lot of trees around. And all she had to do was make it through the night, then she'd be free of him.

He stared at her from the reflective window, but she wouldn't look up. What time was it? The moment she saw it was nearing midnight, a yawn rumbled in her gut.

"There is the matter of sleeping arrangements," the strange man she'd only met this afternoon declared.

Beth's heart sank. *One bed in the honeymoon cabin. Not a reason for another.* "I don't care how big it is. I don't want it," she babbled, rising from the couch.

To her surprise, and small delight, Tristan blinked in confusion, his brow clouding. "What…what are you? What do you mean?"

"The bed, the only bed."

"Oh!" he gasped as if coming to God. He canvassed the ceiling before landing his sight upon her. "You referred to…yes, of course."

"Why? What did you think I meant?" The moment the question left her lips, she played back what she'd said without thought and the innuendo it crafted. A blush moved to scamper over her cheeks, which she could disguise thanks to the firelight.

"You take the bed, alone," he tacked on quickly. "I'll sleep out here on the couch."

Beth glanced at the small two-seater. She could probably scrunch up to fit, but no way he'd manage. "I'll sleep on the couch. You, Mr. Big-Wig Musician, take the bed."

"Ha," he snorted. "You think I can't hack it out here?"

"Damn certain you can't." Beth nodded to herself, well aware of the riders most celebs demanded just to sit for a few minutes and talk about themselves. No way anyone who'd gone platinum would demean themselves by sleeping on a couch.

"I'll have you know, I've slept on buses in my touring days." Tristan broke from his vigil over the snow, his closed-off body sliding closer.

"Oh yeah? I've done Greyhound."

"Vans, as well. One time, I had to sleep on the floor of an overbooked hotel room."

"Big deal." She prodded at him without touching him. "You ever slept on the floor of a cargo plane? Or a rickshaw? Or the bottom of a leaking boat?"

Her rather colorful background threw Tristan off. The cocky demeanor melted, his arms falling out of their tight cross as he eyed her. "No. No, I haven't."

"Then take the damn bed." She indicated the bedroom, exhausted by his sudden chivalry. "I can handle myself on a damn sofa for a few hours. And no, I won't mention it in the article. 'Musician sleeps in bed.' Hardly pull quote material."

The edge of his stark-white canine emerged as he sneered. Had he perfected that in the mirror when younger or was it simply his face reacting to his soul? "You cannot stop riling people up, can you? Like a scrap of splintered wood rubbed over skin."

Beth moved to rise to defend herself and point out how he knew as little about her as she did him. But the haughty musician spun on his heels and finally trudged off to the open bedroom. Without another word, the door slammed, rattling the cabin's frame until snow plummeted off the roof. A shudder climbed her spine as she remembered she was trapped in a cabin with a stranger.

A near-stranger known to have a temper problem. He buried it under cold scowls and erudite language, but it was there. It was the sixth or seventh thing people thought about when imagining Tristan Harty. And Beth knew better than to ask about it, especially with no one around to pillow his punches.

Twisting in place, she glared at the short sofa she'd vehemently insisted be hers. Sitting up wasn't so bad, with her back nestled against the armrest and her feet up on the cushion. But how was she going to sleep on this thing? She'd have to scrunch up like a child in the throes of a nightmare to fit. And he'd thought he could do it?

Too riled up to sleep, Beth turned her back to the closed bedroom and opened her laptop. The blank page mocked her, the blinking cursor questioning why she didn't get a job in engineering instead.

Because you're awful at math and fear being electrocuted.

At least engineers didn't have to deal with being trapped in snow-bound cabins with fickle, thin-skinned musicians. He'd been so damn insistent she not take her car when there'd been a chance and now they were both stuck together. *Always having to be right, having to throw his intellectual weight around as if it were a ten-ton wrecking ball.*

Flexing her fingers, Beth laid into her keyboard to quickly type, *Tristan Harty is an arrogant know-it-all who cares little for the consequences of his actions.* The cursor flickered at the end of her cruel cut, wondering about the bias and the rather limp lede. Folding her other fingers into a fist, Beth plunged her pointer to the delete key, pressing to vanish every letter of the accurate but inflammatory sentence.

Tristan Harty is...

The sound of the door opening caused her to crane her head around. Instinctively, she closed her laptop as the subject of her non-start barreled out of the room. A blanket curled from his arms down to the floor and a pillow nestled against his chest. "Here," he said, thrusting both at Beth.

She reached for them, confused as to why he'd bothered. Before she could ask, he spun on his heels and marched back into the bedroom, once again slamming the door. Wrapping her arms around the offering ripped from his bed, Beth breathed in a surprising masculine scent. Warmth lingered in the wool fibers. Had he been tossing and turning in the bed before deciding to give the blanket to her? Or had he been holding both blanket and pillow, pacing back and forth, wondering if she'd even accept them?

Despite her annoyance at the man, she wasn't stupid enough to turn down potential warmth in the midst of a snowstorm. Tucking the pillow behind her back and laying the blanket out over her legs, Beth tried to dive back into her work. She stared blindly at the blinking cursor, watching as the document automatically synched up to the cloud with its half a sentence. As she leaned back into the pillow, warmth curled across her weary back and the smell of sandalwood spiced with juniper wafted around her.

Tristan Harty is confounding.

Chapter Six

He tried shaking her first. Not with any gusto, just a gentle shove of her shoulder poking out from under the blanket. Her body bounced against the couch cushions, but her eyes remained obstinately closed. Despite the awkward position of her knees cuddled to her chest to fit her body in a tight space, she was deep asleep.

Rubbing a hand against his chin and frowning at the rising stubble he was going to have to leave there, Tristan stared at the ashen fireplace. Cold swept through the unheated cabin, and his toes trembled inside the only pair of socks he'd thought he'd need for a day. After glancing back at the outside world, he leaned closer to the slumbering woman.

With his face an inch from hers, he began again. "Hey." Slowly, her lush eyelids fluttered. The lids still smeared in dusky shadow fluctuated until an edge of brown cracked from below. "You're going to want to see this," he finished, rising away from the woman fleeing her dreams. Judging by the frown knotted on her lips, it'd been one where they weren't isolated together in a cabin.

Ms. Cho sat up, the green wool blanket tumbling from her pink-bloused shoulders. *Oh, God!* He trailed the movement, from her mostly chaste collar down the full cup of a breast pressing against the tissue-thin fabric. A dark pink nipple strained the shirt further, ensuring that no matter how hard Tristan tried to look away, he was trapped.

"What?" she thundered, clearly not a morning person.

"You…you're—" Finally, he hurled the awe-struck hormonal teenager into a box and ripped his stare away. He raised a hand to try and shield his gaze, but it froze upon his spotting a tan bra with black lace over the cups resting on the armchair. "You're not dressed," he gasped.

Movement told him that Ms. Cho had risen from the couch, though he couldn't watch. "Most women don't sleep in their bras," she grumbled from deep in her chest. A flutter near his body told him that she'd yanked said object of clothing off the chair. *Shit, is she putting it on? Should I turn around?*

"What do you want?"

Dropping his enforced blinders, Tristan found a woman who looked more furious than a wolverine, with a black blazer buttoned up over her chest. The bra was nowhere to be seen. And she noticed he was staring at her breasts. *Damn it!*

With a wince, Tristan pointed at the window. "That. You should go see that."

Scowling, no doubt at his unplanned leering, she stomped away from him to the window. And froze. White eclipsed almost every landmark of the front drive. Tips of trees poked above snow that drifted to three, nearly four feet deep. They looked like snorkelers attempting to make it through the thick white sea.

Ms. Cho's shock snapped to nervous energy. She ran for the window, her nose smudging up the frozen glass as she stared at what he'd already tried to check. The road was gone. Her car remained, but the snow blew from the storm until it hugged all the way up the driver's-side windows. There was no chance of either of them getting into the car, never mind using it as a means of escape.

They were truly trapped.

A guttural curse rolled from her lips, the reporter smacking her forehead to the cold glass as if that would help. "You said there'd be no more snow."

"I guessed," Tristan answered. "Snow can be tricky to…guess." Why was he apologizing? Why did he feel guilt seeping from his pores?

She whipped her head back to him. "Aren't you some snow god?"

That was the first time he'd been called a god, even with biting sarcasm.

"Know all about it from your time in North Dakota?"

"Minnesota." Tristan sighed.

"Wherever it is, you don't know that much about snow!" she snapped. Rubbing both hands to her cheeks, she pushed her rounded face inward while cursing to the heavens. "What am I going to do? What can I do? What the hell do I do?"

He had no advice, having only woken a few minutes prior, taken one glance outside and realized his new fate. Ms. Cho placed all her anger at the situation upon him. "You know what this means?!"

They were trapped.

"We're stuck together for another day," she said

Or longer. Tristan grimaced at the thought of an extended stay in this cabin in the mountains, then frowned at her phrasing. "I wished for this predicament as much as you did."

"Sure," she snorted, her arms crossed under her, uh, unbound chest area. *Crap.* Heat prickled up the back of his neck as her pouting swerved to the man who once again let his eyes wander. Slamming the cursed things shut, he couldn't escape the image his libido was quickly building of her fully topless.

"I have to call the office. And Steff. And Mads. And…" She paused in her recitation of people he didn't and would never know. Placing her palm before her mouth, she breathed upon it and sniffed. That brought a scrunch of her nose and a toss of her head.

"I can at least wash up first," she pronounced. That eyebrow of hers peaked into place as if she was waiting for him to argue.

Tristan extended a hand to the bathroom he had yet to visit properly. "Be my guest," he announced as if the cabin was his. *Shit.* Were they going to have to pay for this screwup? Or did the magazine rent it out? *One more thing to ask Barry.*

A groan rumbled in the bottom of his gut as he thought of his manager hyperventilating over the weather report. Ms. Cho hauled up her bag, including the laptop and notebooks, and carted them all off to the bathroom. He heard the lock click rather loudly into place, as if to remind him to keep himself in check.

That shouldn't be difficult. She was, on the whole, one of the most unpleasant people he'd ever met. Not for her features, or her body. Another image drifted through his mind of her little nose crinkle being kissed away by tender lips. No. It was her manners, or lack thereof. Clearly, she believed that she was the alpha and omega, answerable only to God himself. Assuming she didn't plan to take that job as well.

The gentle rain of water bounding against a tiled floor echoed from the bathroom. In an instant, the picture of her topless flooded his mind. That silky soft-pink blouse sliding off her skin, pinpricks of freckles caressed by the falling water. How her nipples hardened at the chill of the water beading on her skin.

Get it together, Harty.

After banging a fist on his skull as if that would wake up his brains, he dug his phone out of the back of his jeans pocket. He dialed up Barry fast, the click coming as Tristan's finely tuned ears picked up the sound of water bouncing off a warm body.

"Hi," he squeaked, then strangled his voice to a deep baritone, "Hello."

"Tris? Jesus tap-dancing Christ! Are you okay!"

"Yes, yes, Barry. Calm down. I'm fine. A little stranded, but the cabin's standing. We still have power..." And if there weren't any more storms that should keep. He glanced to the fireplace and the waning log pile. That'd have to be remedied or they'd freeze.

Perhaps Ms. Cho would accept the idea of their being locked together in a sleeping bag to preserve body heat. He snickered at the idea and how it was doubtful either would make it out alive.

"This is a disaster, kid. A. Dis-As-Ter!"

God, I knew Barry would be out of sorts, but it shouldn't be this bad.

"We need to get you out of there, ASAP! I'm gonna call nine-one-one."

"Barry…" He groaned, fairly certain his manager had already tried and had been told they couldn't do anything.

"The National Guard. Someone who can dig you out of there!"

"Barry! We're fine. I'm not required to appear anywhere in person for…what, a week?"

"Three days," the manager with the schedule tattooed onto the inside of his eyelids mumbled.

Tristan shook his head, a bounce rising up his legs. "Great. Three days. The sun's out now, that'll take a good chunk from the snow. They're probably clearing highways and interstates. After that the main roads, then finally someone can get up here to pluck me out. Can't be more than twenty-four hours. Forty-eight at the worst."

Silence fell from the outburst of optimism. It lasted so long he moved to check his phone, when Barry spoke, "Tris? Yer still there with the reporter."

"Yes, I know this." Hard for him to forget.

"Just…are you sure you can last twenty-four hours without, ya know…" Barry didn't need to finish the thought, nor did Tristan want him to.

"It was one time…!"

"Uh-huh, and I know, I know, you were in a bad place. I hear that. But she don't exactly seem the kid-gloves type."

Understatement. Tristan glared at the bathroom door. The shower ceased, which meant she was probably trying to dry herself off with no towel in the place. Shaking her hair and causing her breasts to…

"Kid? Kid!"

"What? Yes. I'm here. What?" He tried to focus on the task at hand, except there wasn't really one to properly distract him. Not until they could get a plow to free them both.

Barry took his time, no doubt running every worst-case scenario through his head. *Wonderful.* It was never good when Barry tried thinking. "Look, I know yer not fifteen anymore. Though, God, I wish I was thirty-seven again. But it really ain't smart to sleep with a reporter."

"Don't be ridiculous. I cannot stand the woman! She's arrogant, callous, supercilious, demanding."

A clicking noise rolled over the phone. "As if that don't sound familiar."

Tristan's brow clouded, his hand digging into the phone as he cursed. "Do you have something you wish to tell me?"

"Not a thing, kid. Watch yourself. Keep away from the windows so the glass don't get ya."

"That's tornadoes," Tristan sighed.

"And call me in an hour so I know you ain't dead," Barry the eternal worrier ordered.

After a quick goodbye, Tristan shut off his phone. The studio would be calling, wondering why he was trapped behind the blizzard while Barry wasn't. No doubt they'd expect him to pay for this mess. Or take yet another cut from the measly amount he made on sales. What was it? Every hundred downloads gave him one one-hundredth of a penny? At that rate, he could get himself a bag of marbles back in 1920 in ten years.

Flicking at the silent phone, Tristan picked at the protective case. It was starting to crack at the edges, the plastic printed image rising up. The bottom of a black-and-white photo was tearing into jagged pieces with each call or text.

Twenty-four hours. What was he going to do in twenty-four hours with a stranger? A rumbling in his stomach answered that question. They'd have to take stock of the supplies, ration it out in case of the worst. Not to mention getting wood for the fire. Keeping that dry and…

"May I use your toothpaste?" her voice echoed from the bathroom.

"What?" Tristan was so deep into scheduling he was fully thrown by her intervention.

The door cracked and her head poked out. Without a towel, her black hair clung to her head, revealing wide pale ears poking between ebony waves. Between those and the big brown eyes, she looked almost adorable.

"May I use your toothpaste?" she asked again, the door hugging tight to her naked skin.

"Yeah." Tristan nodded. "Yes."

"Thank you," she said curtly and closed the door between them.

It felt like ages since a woman had borrowed any of his toiletries. The odd intimacy struck a sour note, but as he busied himself checking the cabinets and fridge it twisted into a haunting melody. *Twenty-four hours. Get through that and he never need worry about Ms. Cho again.*

Chapter Seven

Day two of this outfit. Beth frowned at the blazer that was too warm to wear inside, the sleeves too constricting around the upper arms and the wear on her elbows fading to an ashy gray. She could go without, but that'd leave her in only the blouse. Why hadn't she noticed how see-through it'd become?

A gurgle of shame rumbled in her gut as she thought of his sapphire eyes first homing in on her accidental exposure, then whipping away in shock. Was it that bad to look upon?

What do you care?

Because, like it or not, they were stuck together for at least another day. *What if it's more?*

Bouncing her forehead once more upon the steamed-up mirror, Beth prayed that a miracle would rescue her from this nightmare. Good thing she always kept a spare toothbrush in her purse in case of emergencies. Surviving an entire day with cottonmouth while around the pompous twat sounded like a curse from hell. Though, she wished she'd been wise enough to keep her entire suitcase in the car instead of at the hotel. With no towel to dry off on, her damp body quickly suckered to the once loose clothes, pulling them tighter than she wanted. *Ha.* As if he'd care anyway. Or even notice.

Annoyed at herself for being annoyed at an annoying man not looking at her, Beth strolled out of the bathroom with her head held high. Water dribbled down her hair to puddle at the small of her back, but she ignored it all under the mask of confidence. She expected Tristan to rush past her, needing the bathroom himself, but it took scanning the cabin to find him bent over in the fridge.

Unearthly yellow light shadowed through the open door. He looked as if he intended to climb deep inside, his ass stuck far out. The jeans were so tight she could make out not only his phone but had an easy time guessing the make and model.

You're staring at his ass.

"What are you doing?" Beth called. She meant it to be at herself, but it drew the slow shift of the face inside the fridge.

After closing the door, Tristan splayed his hands over the counter and leaned toward her. "Taking stock of our food supply."

Beth grimaced at what had to be bad news, and the fact they even needed to worry about such a thing. "Let me guess, we'll be cooking our own shoes?"

A laugh rolled through his chest that was more reminiscent of his singing voice than his speaking one. For a breath, she returned the foolish smile as if she hadn't been the one to make the biting comment. Tristan rapped his knuckles thrice on the counter. "So far we should be in the clear. There's not much by way of fresh food, certainly no fruit or veg to speak of."

"Veg?" she snickered, approaching the Midwestern boy with a slow saunter in her hips. "Hopin' for a spot of tea there, Guv'nor?"

Where she expected a snide remark or cruel sneer, she got a shocking blush. Digging his fingers through his hair, he admitted a fact about himself of his own volition. "Too much BBC, I'm afraid. You're not a vegetarian, are you?"

"No." She shook her head slowly. *He can't be suggesting we, what, trap rabbits for dinner? Hunt down a deer?* She was in ankle boots and a pantsuit, for God's sake.

"It doesn't matter." Tristan shrugged. "There's no meat in the freezer either. It's mostly nonperishables. A few bags of plain, generic chips, some crackers, a pile of packets of ramen."

"Then we'll survive the nuclear fallout at least." Beth swung up onto the bar stool perched in front of the kitchen. There wasn't much on the counter—a few brochures, the proof that he really had dug through the kitchen cabinets, and a small basket wrapped in cellophane.

Curious, she began to tug on the ribbon around the cellophane. It crinkled with an ungodly noise as she tugged the wrapping down.

"I thought it was only Twinkies that'd last through the apocalypse," Tristan said, seemingly enthralled with her flaunting the rules of the welcome basket meant for another couple.

"Common misconception. Twinkies won't survive much more than a year or two, but ramen...that's timeless." She smiled while finishing her excavation of whatever was meant for the happy newlyweds who sequestered in this cabin next.

Two mugs stamped with the lodge's logo rested inside a pile of shredded paper. Tristan picked up the first, pulling out a foil bag crammed inside the mug. "Hm." He spun the bag around to reveal it to be pancake mix. "I guess breakfast is handled."

Beth fished into the second. "And we don't have to eat them dry." The tiny handle for the plastic jug of maple syrup barely fit around her pinkie.

It was Tristan Harty, famous songwriter and musician, who turned to the array of cabinets and pulled down a bowl. "Real maple syrup seems a shame to waste on pancakes."

After fishing out a whisk as if he lived there, he dumped the powdered would-be pancakes into the bowl. The water was easy enough to add, but to her surprise, he began to crack open an unending stream of coffee creamers to fill in for the missing milk. Beth watched, her legs crossed tightly as the fussy man whisked the dry powder into a pourable batter without a second thought.

"What else is there to do with maple syrup?" she asked while watching a grown man make pancakes as if she was observing a bird of paradise's mating dance. It wasn't even from scratch, but she'd never seen such a feat performed in the wild, so to speak.

Placing a skillet upon the micro-stove and lighting the gas, Tristan shrugged. "Desserts mostly."

"Wait, you bake?" she gasped in shock.

In an instant, the easy air of two strangers trapped in an odd situation snapped away. They were once again combatants staring across a battleground as a storm raged around them. He snapped his shoulders up tight around his head, like a turtle trying to retreat into his shell. Long gone was the easy manner from when he'd stirred the batter.

Cold, harsh movements dumped a pat of butter into the skillet and he watched it melt. That man was the prickliest creature she'd ever met, and Beth had once had a porcupine sleep on her lap. With only the hiss of butterfat bubbling in the pan for sound, the creation of pancakes passed in silence. The stack piled up with Tristan's back turned to her.

She tried to follow suit, keeping her gaze on the living room, or the snow shifting in the winds. But movement drew her to look back and watch as the man shivered the skillet in his hand, gave it a toss and sent a pancake flying into the air. Without any fanfare, he caught it dead center and returned it to the fire. Beth stared in surprise at the perfect flipped pancake while Tristan snatched up the full plate.

"Here." Cold indifference punctuated a plate of surprisingly fluffy golden pancakes being dropped in front of her.

She darted her gaze from the breakfast that her stomach demanded she eat to the man returning to the stove. "Aren't these yours?"

The shoulder slouch vanished, his neck extending as he leveled a frozen glare on her. "Concerned I poisoned them?"

"No," she insisted even while shoving the plate away. After dropping to her bare feet, Beth dashed into the kitchen. It wasn't until she stood trapped between stove and counter that she realized how tiny it was. Tristan had to shift to keep from knocking his elbow into her chest as she moved to pick up the skillet.

"I can make my own breakfast," she said, already spooning a clump of batter onto the pan.

Even as she watched the ivory-tan liquid ooze over the hot silver surface, he remained in place. There was so little room that when Beth tried to shift the skillet to keep the pancake from sticking, she accidentally nudged into his side with her elbow. When her elbow barely sank into his rock-hard hip, the man who seemed to think he needed to do everything finally threw up his hands and left.

Glowering above the perfect stack of syrup-drenched pancakes, Tristan dug into his food. The first pancake Beth babied, relying upon the spatula's help to flip it. That one went onto a plate he'd placed down for her. From behind, she could hear the methodical fork cut, drag across the plate and chew of a man who refused to talk.

They could maintain this unending battle for hours into days, or she could try for a ceasefire. "I asked because I only know how to bake one thing."

"Cookies?" he snorted.

"Nope, I burn them the second I look at the sheet." Beth dumped the next pancake onto the plate, feeling better about herself. "Baklava," she said, staring at him even as she poured the next round of batter.

That caused the man's fork to hit the plate. "You can make baklava but not cookies? Baklava? As in the honey, and nuts and layers and layers of…"

"I know, I know." She waved her hand to try and cut off what she always heard. *'Beth, why don't you whip up a cake for this random celebration?' 'Do you want it to be both over and undercooked, and probably ooze in places?'*

Shaking the skillet, she mused, "Something in the methodical layering compared to 'you'll know when it's done' appeals to me. Or maybe I'm a baklava savant."

"Hm. I'm sorry we don't have any honey and walnuts now."

She smiled at that. "And phyllo dough. I'm not that much of a savant." That brought a surprising laugh from the dour man. Feeling plucky, Beth raised the skillet off the fire and gave it a flip. The second the pancake launched, she realized her mistake. It tumbled haphazardly through the air and struck the edge of the pan.

"Shit!" she cursed, watching one half of the partially cooked pancake flop to the floor like a wet blanket. The rest skidded down the side of the skillet, hissing as it no doubt charred to a briquette.

Embarrassment burning up her gut, Beth was unable to face the look of certain mockery from the would-be chef in the cabin. Leaving the skillet on the cold part of the stove, she bent over to pick up the lost pancake. "As I said," she muttered to herself as the blush rampaged to a level five, "only a baklava savant."

"Uh, here." He thrust a small hand towel at her.

After dumping the scourge of failure into the stainless-steel depths, she tried to swipe up the last of the sticky mess. "It's a shame this is the only towel in the cabin. I could have used one in the bathroom."

"Yes," a wobbly voice whispered behind her. The always certain man sounded adrift. "...a shame."

She risked a glance over her shoulder and found his gaze hooked right on her ass. The one with both her underwear and thin pants plastered to her skin thanks to the shower. *Oh, God.* Tristan walked away before he was called out, resuming his vigil at the bar counter. It was Beth who had to pull in a calming breath.

So he acknowledged she had a backside. It changed nothing of the situation. She was the evil reporter, he the valiant artist defending his craft. Rising from cleaning the floor spotless, Beth returned to finishing the last of her breakfast. But even while she heard the walled-off man slip away to his phone, a smile blossomed. She'd gotten to him.

* * * *

He'd learned how to kill unending hours in his youth. While waiting for a bus to arrive, while riding on said bus, while sitting in a greenroom hours before a show, while reclining between stopovers in airports. At each one, Tristan was a master of falling into any mindless task to keep himself busy. But, sitting in the middle of a cabin trapped behind snow, he itched to leap to his feet and run anywhere.

A tickle formed on his ear, and he lifted the noise-canceling headphones to scratch it. In doing so, he turned his head out of habit. She sat at the same counter where she'd eaten breakfast, her laptop and notebooks oozing across the space as if she owned it. At first, he ignored her syncopated typing, deluding himself into thinking he could work on his song.

The guitar remained curled up in its case, Tristan only pulling it out to check chords. His earlier strumming had brought a glare from the woman at the counter. She'd promptly slammed her own earbuds in to drown his noodling out. It wasn't as if he was trying to serenade her…not that he ever would. But sometimes the melody would slip past him and he'd fall behind.

Ha. Behind. He glared at the nearly empty blue notebook that should be filled with scratched-out lyrics. A handful of words sat there, most pure dribble from staring around the cabin. For about an hour he'd thought he had something with *Fires of Flame* before realizing he was just describing the proper maintenance of a fireplace.

Otherwise, all he had to show for the morning where she'd let him work uninterrupted was a sea of white. A reflection of the ever-pressing outside world, no less. *Will that work in a song?*

Ms. Cho leaned back in her chair, stretching her hands out as if she was trying to scare a cougar. He thought she was about to rise, perhaps take a break, before both hands collapsed to the keyboard to type anew. She'd been at that for a while. A rather long while.

"What are you working on?" Tristan sighed. He'd mostly meant it to be to himself, but he foolishly voiced it aloud.

The typing paused and she tugged out an earbud. "What was that?"

"You seem to be typing an awful lot. More than I'd expect a two to three-thousand-word article about me would require."

A snort rolled her shoulders, which were freed of the squaring black blazer. "You think they'd give you three k? That's getting into in-depth reporting with real pull quotes and conclusions instead of 'Subject does verb at noun.'"

Her derision stung, but he didn't want to reveal it. Tristan raised his chin higher as if he didn't even notice. Without a second thought, she returned to her laptop. "You're not my only interest, you know."

"I gathered that. I was only curious…" Tristan began before sighing. Why should he expect her to explain herself? He certainly didn't wish to. Ever.

A creaking noise caused him to look up. To his surprise, Beth was staring at him. With an arm draped over the back of the stool, she said, "It's a book. Non-fiction, hence the unending sprawl of notes."

"An autobiography?" Tristan perked up. "Going to share all your tips for a perfect skincare routine?"

"Smartass," she muttered under her breath. But she did glance the back of her hand against her silky-smooth cheek. "No, it's a biography, not autobiography. Since you can't stop prying."

God help him, but now he was curious. A blogger for a mid-level entertainment website was writing a biography. He tried to run through the list of C to D-level celebrities who would require such a task for their brand, but it seemed unlikely for a ghostwriter to put so much effort into that.

"Who of?" Tristan asked. His bored feet pulled him nearly beside her chair, his body stopping just before he could easily read the screen to answer for himself.

She craned her head up to the ceiling as if praying for salvation, before facing him. "Just so we're clear, in your mind it's okay for you to ask questions of me, but not the other way around?"

"I haven't stopped you from asking, and I don't require you to answer." He tried to wipe the curiosity from his voice, but in doing so a sliver of hurt warbled in instead. To his surprise, he wanted to know this about her.

She drew her obsidian gaze up and down him as she no doubt weighed the hypocrisy of the situation. Tristan assumed she'd shove her earbuds back in and ignore him. He picked up his blank notebook, when she said, "My dad."

"Your…?" He flinched, instantly hunting over her face for a hint of celebrity or recognition. While it was a surprisingly genteel visage for such a cutting tongue, there was no obvious answer. Her lips were pert, with all the master sculpting devoted to the bottom one. The nose was pixyish and gently turned upward. And those wide eyes—they burned through every damn layer of armor he had.

As Tristan fell silent, trying to drum up an answer to a question he'd failed to ask, she stared at him. "He's a—" Ms. Cho began when an alarm went off from the couch.

He pursed his lips, fearing Barry was trying to get in contact with him, when the date struck hard against the back of his head. *Damn it!* Leaping to his feet, Tristan tugged up his phone and yanked his charging laptop from the wall. The poor thing was struggling and ready to be put out to pasture. It took a few more cycles before it found the Wi-Fi and he opened the browser…

Only to glance over at the strange woman sitting in and watching. "If you will excuse me," Tristan announced dramatically. With the open laptop balancing on his palm, he picked up the guitar, draped the strap around his neck and headed for the door.

"Are you…?" the reporter breathed, but the rest of her question was drowned out in the door slamming shut.

The unending white burned against his retinas, Tristan's eyes trying to bead up tears as protection. Which was when the cold winds burrowed through his somewhat thin shirt. Damn it, he'd forgotten his coat. But there wasn't time.

Swiping snow off the charming outdoor chessboard, he placed his laptop on it and quickly booted up Skype. As it worked through the challenging connection, Tristan tumbled into the rocking chair across from the board. His movement caused snow to plummet off the back and down the gap in his waistband. Yelping, he scurried away just as the other end connected.

A bright pink wall came into focus first, Tristan recognizing the bunny and duck banner behind the bed. The connection cut out, freezing to ungodly streaks until suddenly a little girl dashed forward so fast he feared she might crack her head on the screen. "You're late!" she chided him, putting all the wrath of an eight-year-old into her sentence. When she moved to cross her arms, her mom stopped her for fear of kinking the mass of tubes piped into her veins.

"Morning, Olivia," Tristan called, giving a little wave.

"Where are you?"

Surprise overtook him as Tristan set up the camera for a perfect view of the mountain range. The blues of the skyline blended in with the middle of the craggy rock until a peak of pure white pierced through the sky above. Rubbing the back of his neck, he admitted, "It's a long story. I—"

The squeak of the screen door cut him off, and he glanced up to find Ms. Cho stepping cautiously onto the porch. She glared at the man who'd set himself up to freeze to death. She'd been smart enough to put on her coat. Catching her look, Tristan gulped.

Forget her. Forget whatever truth she might divine from this. Focus on the reason.

Letting a real smile cross his lips, he gazed past the hospital room to the little girl trying to sit up higher in her bed. "What should we play today?" he asked while running his fingers over the strings in a little scale.

Olivia licked her lips and grinned. "The song. I want to hear the song!"

"Really?" Tristan risked glancing up at the woman who had no intention of leaving now. "What about something else? I was thinking..."

"No!" his audience demanded. Ignoring her mother, she crossed her arms, her face twisted into a full-on pout. A nurse tried to get her to both open her arms and rest back, but she wasn't budging.

Giving another dance of his fingers down the guitar, Tristan swallowed a groan. Strumming the chord, he sang, "Baby shark..."

"Do, do, do..." Olivia took over immediately, pinching her fingers together. Tristan tried to keep up, but the girl overpowered his lower range with her exuberant bellow. At the mama shark, she rose to her knees, seeming to forget the pain in her body.

When the pair reached daddy shark, Tristan abandoned his guitar to slap his outstretched arms together as if they were a set of jaws. That caused Olivia to giggle wildly, her tiny body shaking on the bed. "Again, again!"

"Olivia," her mother warned, "I'm certain that he's very busy."

"You'd be surprised," Tristan muttered to himself, but it was obvious both parent and nurse wanted the girl to rest.

"Mo-om!" she whined even while lying back as told. It was doubtful she'd have had enough energy for another round.

"Don't give me that lip, young lady. You can talk to him next time."

"Fine," she agreed, and darted her sunken but shining eyes to the laptop. "Bye, Tristan!"

"So long, Ms. Olivia. Rest up, and please request a different song for our next performance."

"I'll think about it," the girl pronounced, clearly with no intention to do so.

As Tristan laughed at the seriousness in her words, reminding him far too much of the studio failing to ever take his requests, the camera moved. He waited for the blur to calm until Olivia's mom appeared on screen. They seemed to be out in the hall as she said, "Thanks for taking time for her."

"It's not a problem, Mrs. Finchner."

"I'm sure you're busy with all your touring and other music things. Olivia's already got your appearance on that talk show scheduled."

Tristan blanched at the reminder. "Isn't that one only for Boston locally? How can she…?"

"Kids and the internet. Says she's got a viewing party all planned and everything."

Tugging back his hair and swooping down the part, he sighed, "I'll have to actually try then."

Mrs. Finchner laughed as if it were a joke and Tristan joined in. "Thanks again," the harried mom said, "You…you really lighten up her day."

"I'm nothing. Believe me, speaking to her is a delight," Tristan said. Just as he leaned to end the call, the feed cut on its own. Good timing for the twitchy internet, at least. Slowly, he closed the laptop lid and came face to face with the woman who'd watched his entire performance.

Before she could say a word, Tristan bundled up the computer under his arm as if he could pretend that hadn't happened. To his surprise, the jaded reporter seemed lost for words.

"You have a young fan? Friend?"

"It's... Olivia contacted me through an abandoned fan club. Purely by accident, off an old PO box address insert tucked inside a CD sleeve. Even her mother didn't know. But she made mention of how boring her hospital stays were in the letter, so I thought to liven them up." Tristan pulled in the frost-coated air around them. It burned down his pampered lungs and back out his nose. "Please don't mention this."

"Why?" She seemed surprised, as if he would want to brag about such a minor matter. Then the bloodhound picked up the scent. "Why?"

"I know what you believe about this. Musician with a heart of gold serenades cancer patient in the hospital," he said. Ms. Cho snorted at the 'heart of gold' part, but he continued past it. "All it would do is bring potential grief upon the family. In truth, Olivia doesn't know much of my music. I think she only learned I was the one who wrote and sang that song in the popular movie a month back. I am less someone famous to her and more a funny man with a guitar."

"How long have you been doing this?"

Tristan tipped his head in thought. "About a year. Mrs. Finchner emails me telling me when Olivia's trapped in the hospital for chemo, or checkups or other medical maladies. I once had to play *Happy Birthday* for three of her classmates she snuck into the room." There'd been so many squeals, the girls carrying on as if he was a real rock star on par with their Disney Channel heroes. *Far from it.*

Blinking rapidly, Ms. Cho stared from out across the horizon back to him. "But why? Why agree? Why keep it secret if…?"

A snicker rolled through his frozen sinuses, Tristan remembering he was standing outside without a coat. With his foggy breath coiling around his throat like a scarf, he said, "If you need a trite answer, I do it for my ego."

Leaving her jaw hanging at his quick summation of how little she thought of him, Tristan slipped inside. He expected the intrepid reporter to wander about outside, stomp her feet, maybe take a few pictures of where he had been sitting, then come in. But as the minutes ticked by, his thumb and forefinger absently picking at guitar strings that needed to be re-tuned, he heard it.

Swish. Thwunk. Clunk Clunk.

The noise repeated from outside, echoing off the blanket of snow that silenced the rest of the world. Thoroughly intrigued, Tristan remembered his damn coat this time and plunged back into whatever the reporter was up to. He stuffed his hands deep into the pockets, trying to savor the last of the fluffy down that was supposed to survive subzero temperatures.

A shadow loomed from the side of the house, elongating from a stretched-thin woman to one raising something sharp high above her head. With a crack, it came slamming down, splitting a head in half. Tristan gulped, his body shifting to watch another victim being placed upon the headman's stump.

Ms. Cho was reaching behind her into the woodpile. Bark shredded in the wake and dirt clung to her gloves as she placed a cut log upon the stump. After turning it a quarter inch to the left, she raised the ax high and brought it clean down through the wood, making one end of the cut logs tumble to the rising pile on the snow-strewn ground.

"What are you doing?" Tristan gasped.

She'd opened her coat as if the exercise inflamed her body. The crisp air flattened her pink silk tighter to the flexing chest and shoulders, revealing a hypnotic sway to her muscles. Pink scaled her cheeks, brightening her once dour expression as a smile flitted about her lips.

"Getting wood," she said with a laugh.

Way ahead of you.

Dear Lord. Tristan flinched at the crass thought that rose from his brain. She was clearly well practiced in the art—already five logs had been sent to their demise and more were on the way.

"I noticed," Beth said, slamming the ax down fast. The right half of the log shot through the air, making Tristan shift to keep splinters from hitting him. "We were getting low and I thought to restock just in case another storm rolled in. Not that I want it to." She cursed at the clouds, or perhaps God.

"You—" He gulped, in awe of the woman simply chopping wood. "I'm surprised that a city-dwelling reporter knows how to do that. How did you learn?"

"Well..." She jabbed the end of the ax at him for emphasis. "Probably the same reason a rock star musician knows how to make pancakes."

"Because I have to eat?" Tristan shrugged, lost at how one connected to the other.

Wiping her forearm across her forehead, Beth paused as she gazed up at the crystal blue sky. Her sparkling gaze caught his and she winked. "Exactly." The ax swung, severing another log for the fire. "Are you here to watch or do you want to help?"

While Tristan had spent a few of his younger, then older, days splitting firewood, he'd never had the deft precision she showed. And, some part of him didn't want her to stop, nor for him to stop watching her. "I can…" He drew his finger along the pile of cut logs. "I'll carry these inside."

Snow clung to his gloves, the unending powder clumping up inside the log's bark. As he pulled the first pile of split logs into his arms, the heat of his blushing body raced out to melt the snow. Beth rested the ax upon her shoulder, the sharp edge facing outward. She picked up the last pieces of timber he couldn't manage, staring at him. For once it wasn't malice, annoyance or even anger bubbling inside. All he could find was amusement.

What have you gotten yourself into, Harty?

With a bob of his head, Tristan scurried from her, trying to make his way back to the warmth of the cabin. A cabin he had to share for at least another night with this woman. *Barry, is there any chance you did rent that military tank to rescue me?*

"Come back soon," Beth called. "I'll have more for you."

That you will.

Problems. Regrets. The list was endless.

Tristan tried to keep himself steady, focusing on his work, but before slipping inside he risked a glance back as she bent over.

Chapter Eight

The potentially claustrophobic and tetchy afternoon passed into dusk with relative ease. Beth spent it with her feet propped up on her traveling bags, all the logs she'd split crackling in the fire. Tristan took up the armchair, usually with his head buried in his phone. But on occasion, he'd look up, a hint of a smile on his lips, and he would even make a comment or two.

She found herself wishing he'd forgo the hunting lodge chair and sit beside her. And that thought made her frown and dive deeper into her work. Who cared where the prickly musician was sitting? What did it matter if he shared the occasional random thought on the weather with her? So what if he took time out of his schedule to play one of the most obnoxious songs in human history just to make a sick girl happy?

The fact that she couldn't even put that fact down in her notes made her itch. But he did have a good point. If that hit the circuit during a lull when various news crews were looking for a feel-good story to fill time, it might blow up. And very few people wanted the world digging into their life when they were ill. So Beth kept it to herself, almost as if she had a shared little secret about the reclusive Tristan Harty.

When the sun dipped down across the horizon, dooming them to another night together, she moved to the counter while he… That was a sight she still had trouble with. Beth's research claimed most of the eating counter, notebooks spilling out, old newspaper clippings crackling to dust as they found the light. And all while she was head bent into her laptop, Mr. Harty was hard at work on dinner.

He never sang aloud, aside from the baby shark, but he was humming under his breath. It wasn't a tune she recognized, but he didn't seem to be able to get it out of his head. His thin hips rotated to the beat. Knotted into the waistband of his jeans was their lone kitchen towel. It swayed to his attempt at dancing.

Beth cupped her chin in her palm, watching. He wasn't without rhythm, though the dance seemed haphazard and whatever struck his fancy. Still, there was no denying how, with every outlandish move, he had total control over his wiry body. Even the crook of a finger as if encouraging a partner closer was tight and rhythmic. *What else can he do with those?*

Windmilling an arm outward, Tristan snatched up a pair of tongs. With a shimmy in his hips, he spun in place. The utensil flew through the air with a toss and landed safely in his right hand. Tristan reached backward to stir the bubbling pot, catching Beth watching as if in his thrall.

She sat up fast to try and hide her blush behind the unforgiving laptop screen. It had to be her imagination that he smiled on catching her, or perhaps it was her clear discomfort. "I, uh," Beth babbled, "I have to say, I'm surprised at this level of domesticity."

"Expect me to be crouching upon my thighs chewing into a slice of jerky and slobbering all over myself?" Tristan bit back, but there was a lightness in the words, as if he was having fun with her.

"Pancakes are one thing, but this…" Beth extended a hand to the man's mad plan to try and whip up a fancy dinner. It began with the packets of ramen. They had ten in all should the worst come to pass. In her purse, she'd discovered a couple of sleeves of peanut butter sandwich crackers and Tristan had announced he'd formed an idea.

She'd watched from the corner of her vision as he'd ground up the crackers, worked them into as fine a dust as he could then reconstituted it all in the ramen broth. The dry noodles themselves waited for their moment in the sun next to the microwave. Dropping a small pat of butter into his concoction, Tristan smiled at her.

"I learned it on the road. Forever touring with other bands and singers, all of us teenagers and eternally voracious, we defaulted to the usual sorts." His stirring paused as he gazed up in reflection. "I dare say on that Summer Hope tour we ate enough pizza to match Italy's GDP."

After banging the spoon clean on the pot, he cracked the noodles in half and dropped them into the stew. "But eating pizza and burgers at all hours of the day while also being required to have magazine-ready abs at a moment's notice didn't gel. So I learned a few dishes. Nothing special—most of it was salads and wraps. So many wraps."

The reminiscing paused, and his dewy smile snapped to a frown. "Are you writing that down?"

Beth yanked her fingers off her laptop as if she'd been chastised for becoming enthralled with his story instead of doing her job. "Should I be?" she sputtered, truly wondering.

At that Tristan laughed, running his palm over his head and mussing the part further to wherever it landed. "I suppose 'washed-up musician learns the joy of cooking' isn't such a bad comeback angle. I might finally get Barry to eat something other than Hot Pockets, Bud Light and Marlboros." The attempt at self-deprecation, as if he could pull off such a thing, snapped away. "Chewing away at the book still?" He stirred the noodles but even Beth, the microwave chef, knew they needed to steep longer. "About your father?"

"Yes," she said, falling deeper into herself at having to talk about it. Compared to his tale of learning to cook while touring in his teens, her stories seemed trite and pointless. She let the conversation topic fade, trying to focus where she'd left off. 1984, that year was in the notebook…

Beth reached for one of the five and, in doing so, destroyed the fragile containment. The blue one made a break for it, tumbling to the floor. "Ah," was all she got out, watching the poor thing race for the kitchen tile.

In one fluid movement, Tristan dropped the spoon, bent clean over and caught the edge of the notebook. Some of the looser pages slid out, but he let them fall onto his open palm like snowflakes. "You dropped this," he said, eyes bluer than the ocean meeting hers as he placed the notebook onto the table.

"Thanks," she muttered, feeling an urge to hide behind her hair.

"What's this?" Without the notebook in hand, he flipped the old newspaper clipping and Beth's heart sank. A black and yellowed picture stretched across it. Two men in suits stood in frame while a young girl with pigtails and her trusty notebook leaned against the left man's legs.

Tristan pointed at the obvious Korean man in the photo. "Is that your father? And…" He finally caught on to who he was standing beside. "Is that James Arrow?"

Famous news anchor, war correspondent and one of her father's best friends. Beth bit on her lip as she rose on the stool to reach across the counter. Rather than take the clipping from him, she pointed at the man. "Yep. And that's me there. Kosovo. My father was working in tandem with Jim and…"

"You call him Jim?"

"Well, I called him Jimmy Jams, but I was six at the time and I doubt he'd let anyone else get away with that."

The shock on his face turned into the awe usually seen when people learned of her connection to America's beloved James Arrow. Tristan read over the caption. "Are you certain this was you?"

Beth snorted. There weren't a lot of little girls who grew up in news vans and copters.

"Says here Mr. Lee Cho and Min-Ji Cho."

With her blush a full-grade burn, Beth reached over to snatch the paper from his hands. She didn't fold it up or stuff it away but stared down at that youthful old man preserved in newsprint. "Min-Ji is my legal name," she admitted. "I use Beth because it's easier on everything for everyone. But my dad, he's always reverting to the legal one even when in the States because…"

Warm fingers brushed over the back of hers, the tips barely strumming a harmony across her burning skin. "It's beautiful," Tristan breathed. Steam from the cooking rested upon his bottom lip, now glistening as if begging for a touch or taste.

What are you doing?

Beth folded back to her seat, slipping the aging proof of her old life into the folder it should have been in. Tristan seemed to shake off the snow-madness moment and returned to cooking. His elbow swerved and swept as he attacked the noodles head on.

She braced herself for cold words, but surprisingly light ones came instead. "Why Beth? To me, it sounds more like Mindy."

Smiling through the strain of a story she had told many, many times, she explained, "My dad worked with this woman named Liz. Craziest cameraperson you ever met, but she'd always nail the shot. Dangling off a cliff, middle of a militarized zone, fleeing from rubble, she got it. I guess when I was facing a sea of unimpressed faces frowning at my name, I wanted to be like her."

The sound of broth slurping into a bowl drew her attention. Hunger rumbling in her stomach, Beth quickly bundled up her work and the laptop, leaving room for both of them to eat. He placed down the first bowl filled with brown water and white noodles. "Which would you prefer?" Tristan asked softly.

"Beth. Anymore, if I hear Min-Ji I expect to be harangued by my cousins for not having a husband or a new nose."

That caught him, Tristan pausing with his dinner tucked tight to his midsection. "What could possibly be wrong with your nose?"

Pressing the tip of her pinkie to the bulb that wasn't tiny and high enough, she chuckled. "You've never been to South Korea."

He laughed at her dodge and sat beside her. They'd moved the chairs farther apart to give each other room that newlyweds clearly didn't need. But even still, she could feel his presence beside her, and it wasn't off-putting. "Bottoms up, so they say," he said, his spoon hanging over the attempted offering.

"Just, so I know what I'm getting into, what did you make?"

He too seemed uncertain of his Frankensteined dinner, circling the noodles into a knot. "With the peanut butter, I attempted to make a Thai peanut sauce. There's a dab of hot sauce in there from my personal stash..."

"Oh." Beth dug into her purse. "If you wanted hot sauce, you should have asked. Any particular variety?" She had an entire sampler platter of small glass vials to get her through meals. As each one clanked across the counter, Tristan's face lit up. He selected the garlic and ginger-infused one, a favorite, to flavor up his dinner.

She picked the same, dousing hers in twice as much. Even if the peanut sauce was a dud, at least she could burn her taste buds out. "Here's hoping we avoid food poisoning," Beth called, swirling her spoon around the noodles. Tristan was too deep into tasting his own creation to argue. She tried to watch his face for clues, but it was a rock.

What was the worst that could happen? Plunging the ramen deep into her mouth, she tasted the chicken salt of the cheap packets, a hint of garlic blasted by ginger and the clogging, grainy soot of peanut crackers. Beth swallowed it and returned for another bite, this time siphoning the pure broth into the spoon.

"It's, uh, it's interesting," she said diplomatically.

Tristan raised his bowl, stirring the slop around and staring deep into its abyss. "Another failure to add to the pile," he announced, causing her jaw to drop. With a shrug, he said, "I never claimed to be a good cook."

Knocking her shoulder into his, Beth leaned so far over the gap she nearly fell into his lap in the process. "If you pick around the grainy bits, it's almost palatable."

The two laughed together, savoring their unique and mostly edible ramen dinner. Snow tumbled outside in the jet-black world, Beth for once not caring.

Chapter Nine

The one good thing about being trapped in a cabin thanks to oppressive weather was that she had no choice but to write. There were no work requirements to attend, no sudden deadlines to race. Her boss seemed particularly intrigued by the idea of a reporter trapped with their person of interest, for once gifting Beth all the time she'd need. Sure, she had to send the occasional update, but as long as she kept insisting that 'Mr. Harty remains uncooperative' with a sprinkling of 'He's now noodling on the guitar' to whet her editor's appetite, she was free.

Beth sat cross-legged on the couch, her laptop resting in the middle as if it were her egg to protect. To her surprise, Tristan sat beside her, resting his ass on the edge of the couch to fit the guitar head poking into the cushions. But it also meant he had to face her the entire time.

It wasn't his occasional glances and even the rare smile that surprised her. It was that she didn't mind letting someone in close while she was working. While she'd had her headphones on to try and create privacy, he'd started strumming a melody she'd never heard, and she'd shut off her music to listen.

The tune was slow and mournful, very much a breakup or loss song. Yet he played it with a strange smile on his face, as if he was happy with the sad turn of events. Firelight danced against Tristan's face, smoothing away the wrinkles and shifting his blue eyes to a haunting purple. The low flames shadowed his ears poking below the piles of copper-toned hair, elongating them, and he took on an elfin appearance. His stark, almost harsh, features certainly helped the fantastical illusion. The aloof and patrician demeanor he wore from his wide forehead to the tip of his chin turned cold but beautiful.

He was a statue of a beloved king lost in the depths of the snow.

His fingers froze, the song evaporating as he crinkled the once and future proud nose. With the guitar tipped up on his thigh, he fished into his back pocket. A deep sigh erupted at his vibrating phone and he spoke aloud. "Barry, again."

With a clear display of annoyance, he typed a text at his henpecking manager. No doubt it was the same response as before. *Still alive. Still snowed in. Nothing's changed.* They came every half hour, Tristan once asking Beth to respond when he was making dinner. He trusted a random reporter with his phone over the wrath of missing a text from the manager.

Slipping the silenced phone away, he shifted to swing the guitar back into place. Beth shrugged. "At least he cares."

"Yes, and will forever see me as a fifteen-year-old with a snaggletooth, a bowl cut and shoes two sizes too big." It was said with a laugh, but Beth stared anew at the man who'd come onto the scene already polished and buffed into a teenage dream. While he wasn't some stock-photo model for a rocker, it was hard to see him suffering an awkward stage. He looked as if he belonged in those waistcoats and riding boots from period pieces, his features as aristocratic as a duke's. The modern and rather drab attire seemed an anachronism upon his tight body.

With a finger pressing deep into the guitar's neck, Tristan strummed down the strings. The power chord echoed through the cabin and he posed with his hand high above his head as if ready for another. "I'm well aware of Barry's faults," he said. "He's certainly not one of the best managers in the business."

Beth's previous researching of the manager had dug up the fact that he'd been involved with creating some of the ur-boy bands that had plagued the late '90s and not much after that. It was a surprise he'd wound up working with a boy then man who prided himself on creating his own material.

"But he was always overprotective," Tristan whispered as if to himself, "whether I didn't need protecting, or didn't know I did."

Ah. That would explain why the man coming out of retirement had sought the one he knew he could trust, even if the manager was out-of-date, out-of-touch and more hassle than gain. Trust in the creative field was worth more than gold.

Worrying her fingers over the keyboard and leaving a string of gibberish on her manuscript, Beth tried to not think about the exposés that rocked the industry.

Or what happened behind all those closed doors and casting couches people were happy to ignore. "You were lucky," she breathed.

"I was." His gaze shifted inward. "When you're a kid you have no idea how lucky you are because they don't want you to know."

She'd never thought about how the near-misses in those reports would've felt. Lots of people were chewed up by the music industry, but what about the kids? The ones who went to auditions for the monsters in those pieces but never got the contract? Who woke up ten or twenty years later and thought, *'Thank God that wasn't me.'*

"Is that on the record?" Beth whispered. She knew she was bringing up the wall between them. That he'd no doubt, after once again being reminded of who she was, turn insular. But she had to.

Tristan's strumming froze, his head tipped down to glare at the strings as if he'd never seen them before. "That I was never molested?" His voice rumbled deeper, trying to use the hallmarks of masculinity to escape the unspoken fear. "Yes, it is. Though I don't see how a non-fact will assist you."

Opening her file on Tristan Harty, Beth added what little he'd revealed and sent it off to the cloud. "Trying to find any angle I can. You know how reporters are."

She expected another diatribe bordering on a manifesto, but all she got was strumming. Deliberate, contemplative strumming.

Pleased that he wasn't going to call her any number of bottom-dwelling creatures, she moved to slide on her headphones and return to work. Before the strings of a movie soundtrack slipped into her ears, Tristan sat closer. "Do you know how to play?"

"No." She shook her head. "Nothing."

"What?" That shocked the musician. "Nothing? You can't play any instrument?"

Struggling to keep her tone from turning cold, Beth said, "Contrary to the prevailing image, we aren't all born with a violin in hand."

"I…" He blushed bright red across his cheeks, Tristan fading at her tongue lashing. "I only meant because I grew up, where I grew up, everyone…" He faded to a mumbling with no easy answer to being called out. *At least he didn't jump to 'Are you also good at math?'*

With the tension rising in the room, Beth returned to her writing. She was about to dive deep into her father's early years when Tristan asked plaintively, "Do you want to learn?"

A music lesson with Tristan Harty?

God, that sounded like some contest one won by sending in enough box tops or magazine coupons. He extended the cherrywood guitar to her and Beth tried to pull in a breath. Fifteen years ago, girls would have ripped each other to shreds to be in her position. To jockey for his flitting attention, to dream that he'd sing a song just for her, that he'd fall head over heels and the two would go to the prom together.

But she was thirty and well aware of her lagging talents. Beth's mouth ran dry at the thought of playing around him. "I'm not sure if… Okay?" The small part of her that sensed a potential lede in this reached out. The rest was panicking. She was going to make an epic fool of herself in front of him.

Why did she care? Taking the guitar, she folded her palm over the neck, the strings digging into her flesh.

"Ah, that's not how to hold it," Tristan instructed, quickly flipping it around in her lap. Warm wood cuddled around her thigh, Beth got a feel for the alien instrument entrusted to her. It was heavier than she expected and almost too large for her size.

"Feel good?" the musician asked.

No. She nodded, trying to act as if the foreign muscle pulls and arm movements were completely normal. "Is…is this a special guitar?"

"Why?"

"What if I…I could break it?" she squeaked out and a laugh of pure joy erupted from the man.

"As long as you don't channel Pete Townshend, I think it'll be okay. Start by pressing your finger here." He pointed to a spot on one of the neck strings. "And here."

Gently, she placed her fingers over the hard strings, struggling to reach with her ring finger.

"Now, strum with…I don't have a pick but if you scrape down the side of your thumb, that should work."

Scraping my skin over strings? Sounds pleasant. Darting to the fingers hovering above hers, Beth wondered if he'd developed calluses over his thumbs. *What would those feel like rubbed against intimate skin?*

Why am I thinking that?

With a gulp and a prayer, she swung her thumb across the two strings he pointed to. An ungodly whine, as if she was slaughtering an entire village, broke from the guitar. Beth's face cringed inward, but Tristan seemed unsurprised. "You have to press tighter with your fingers up here. Really tight. Don't worry, you can't strangle it."

"What if I snap it in half?" she gulped even while doing as told.

"We check you for superpowers?" was his less than useful response. "Trust me."

There was no reason for her to. He could be setting her up to fail, watching that dim-witted blogger struggle with something he was born to do. The warmth of the guitar hugging her lap spread up her chest and Beth picked at the string.

A single note echoed from the guitar, humming out through the fire-lit air. Beth's face cracked into a cheesy grin. She wanted to leap up and crow about managing one note, but the teacher wasn't finished.

"Here, this is the next one." He guided her finger lower down the neck and Tristan nodded. Giving another swipe of her thumb made a higher note erupt from the guitar in her lap. Before its reverberations vanished, he called, "Quick, repeat the same moves as before."

Beth struggled to remember where her finger went, swiping at the strings in the hope it was close enough. When the familiar note rang through, she glanced up at him. "Am I playing a song?"

"Of course," he snorted as if there was no doubt. "Okay, now you have to move it, ah…" The teacher, her only port in this confounding storm, clouded over. Tristan peered closer to the strings as if he'd never seen them before, and winced.

"Sorry, I…I've never really done it in a mirror-reverse situation. Um…" He popped his lips, trying to buy for time while switching around the moves for her. "Ah! I know."

The hands that'd been fussing over her fingers suddenly wrapped around Beth's waist. Her jaw dropped, but she gave in to him spinning her on the couch. With almost no force, he pulled her between his thighs. She sat up rod straight, uncertain what he was going to do next.

Slowly, warm palms slipped over the tops of hers. No way he could see the strings with her body blocking his view. But he seemed to know where they were even while the guitar was sitting in her lap. "How about I lead?" Tristan's warm words tickled against the back of her neck.

She should refuse. Leap to her feet, thank him for the lesson and return to her work. Keep up that necessary professional distance that'd seemed so easy before. It was just a day back that she'd wanted to pluck out his eyes, and now his body was curled around hers.

Nodding, Beth tried to lick her chapped lips. A single whisper made it through her chattering jaw. "Yes."

Fingers, acrobatic, nimble and toned, smoothed over the back of hers. They outflanked Beth's thinner digits, but Tristan didn't overpower hers. He guided without force, pressing her back to the strings where she began.

The same notes rang out as before, Beth's fingers supplying the music but Tristan creating it. He puffed a single letter to match each note, the warm breath knocking in her hair. "G-A-G-E."

Upon repeating the sequence, Beth's brain overpowered her body lost in the taut muscles pressing against all of her. "Is this *Silent Night*?"

"You found me out." He shifted her hands lower down the guitar which brought out the higher notes. "Did you know that—"

"It was originally composed for the guitar due to the church's pipe organ being broken?" Beth interrupted. The music stopped and he slid his chin across her shoulder to focus upon her. "What?" she said. "Everyone knows that about *Silent Night*."

His chuckle not only puffed against her ear and cheek but rumbled his chest up against her back. "Fair enough, you win the esoteric knowledge crown." All the while his hands kept moving hers, the song reaching its end before returning for another verse. The music glided around them, stripped to its core in the crackle of firelight.

She listened to not only the notes, his G-A-G-E resuming their tumble, but the pop of logs shedding their summer bark to the fire. Heat enveloped her body, his foot curling back in on the couch until his leg fully matched hers. His forearms molded atop hers, Beth watching from below her lashes how his biceps flexed with the musical movements.

"Si-ilent night. Ho-oh-ly night," Beth sang. *Oh shit!* The words slipped unbidden from her tongue, leaving a lump of shame burning up her gut. She'd just sung in front of a professional! A musician who loved nothing more than to critique every little thing he saw.

She slithered her hand from his grip to slap to her mouth as if that could hide away her fumble. A soft chuckle broke from behind her, opening up the pit in her soul. But he wound his fingers around her shielding hand and pulled it back to the guitar. With a steady baritone, he sang just to her, "All is calm, all is bright."

"I didn't mean to…" Beth scrunched her face up even as she continued playing the song with him. "I know I shouldn't sing."

"Nonsense," Tristan scoffed, causing her jaw to descend to the gates of hell. "It's a Christmas song. Every and anyone should be able to sing along with Christmas songs."

"You really…" She tried to peer over her shoulder at him, but she was locked in tight with the music. "Really like Christmas music."

His forehead and hair slid across hers as Tristan tipped his head down in thought. Still, the playing didn't cease, his fingers strumming through the unending silent night. A soft voice so quiet she nearly missed it whispered, "My mother."

"What?"

"You asked why I put out a Christmas album, in rather degenerate terms, I'd like to add…"

Beth winced at the cruel cuts she'd given without realizing. She'd assumed he thought as little of the commercialization as she did. The soul poured into a simple carol playing to no one told her otherwise.

"My mom loves Christmas, everything about it. We used to visit churches, soup kitchens, VFWs, anywhere that'd put up with a little kid holding a huge guitar. Even when I was in New York, trying to get my big break, I'd sit in the subway and play my stable of carols."

That must have annoyed everyone trying to get to work.

"She always asked me to put one out. Slip it into the rotation between all my 'serious work.' I, being a teenager with five Grammys under my belt, thought I knew better." The song stilled, only the trembling strings under her fingers breaking up the silence. But he didn't remove his hands from hers, his body hanging off hers as if he needed her help.

"So, when I decided to return, I knew the first album out would have to be a Christmas one," Tristan finished. "And now you know the deep, dark secret, reporter."

"She must be very important to you," Beth whispered as a painful past banged in her brain.

Tristan's hands broke from hers, sliding to the side to cup to his extended knees. "She is. But that's what mothers are for, right?"

"I…" Dread thudding into her gullet, Beth wanted to tear herself away from him and this conversation. *It's not his fault, he doesn't know.* "Yep," she said, her lips popping the *p* hard.

Pain burning her eyes, Beth stared at the laptop resting on the cushions, the notebooks spilling with the life of her father, of which she'd shared only a small portion. "Did you always want to be a musician?" Beth asked. She could feel the wall bricking itself back up between them, Tristan's heat retreating.

"Yes." His once tender voice froze. "Hence my mother moving heaven and hell to get me where I needed to be."

She didn't want to pick at a wound. Instead, Beth leaned away. The guitar came with her, Tristan opening his hands as if to let her go. But it was the old blue notebook she picked up and she leaned back into him. Tugging the faded newspaper out, she stared at her father in his requisite reporter outfit. She'd rarely seen him in anything else.

"I traveled everywhere I could with my dad. Some places I really shouldn't have. As a kid, I thought the only jobs in the world were reporter, cameraman or dictator."

A snicker rolled down the back of her neck, Tristan scooting forward to take in the clipping. "Your elementary teachers must have loved career day with you."

She'd had to spend her falls and winters in school living with her grandmother and only hearing her father's voice on the phone or seeing him in newspapers. Some days, Beth would wake up at three a.m., just to catch his calls, her feet freezing as she sat in the peeling chair by the phone. But the summers, then she was Beth Cho, intrepid reporter.

"He could get anyone to talk. Dictators, military commanders, people who'd spent their whole lives only saying 'No comment' would sing the second my dad showed up. I was enthralled. I thought it magic. And I wanted nothing more than to do what he did."

The hand that had strummed a full song from hers swept across the clipping. Slowly, it circled around the little girl proud of her notebook full of observations. God help her, she'd even written her own articles as a kid, which her grandmother would proofread before 'publication.' Beth really needed to burn them whenever she was back in San Francisco.

"You don't mention your mom."

She flinched, the clipping falling to the folder. "And you don't speak of your father."

Silence clicked between them, one of nervous energy, of words swallowed and erased rather than being spoken.

"Alive?" Tristan whispered.

"Yes. Yours?"

A deadened voice answered, "Yes."

"I tried to forgive her. To heal that wound all the books talk about. She was sick, she needed help and got it eventually. She couldn't be my mother when I was a kid but wanted to try as an adult." Beth tried to ignore the tears pinging inside her unwanted heart. "I want to go along with it, but then I think about all the missed birthdays, the school plays, the days and days she chose to abandon me and I…I can't."

"My father couldn't even be bothered to cut a check for two-hundred-and-forty-five dollars every month. I get on TV, climb the charts, and he shows up one day. Talks reconciliation, rekindling, regrets." The bitterness oozed from his tongue, Tristan slapping a hand to his thighs with each thought.

"And the second that I vanish from the spotlight, so too does he. Never again. I know far better now than…"

Than to let them back in. To delude yourself into thinking that someone so instrumental in your very being wouldn't break your heart.

Glancing down, Beth realized that he'd scooped his hands not around the guitar with his confession, but her belly. Both pulled her tighter to him instead of farther away.

"I…" She gulped. Frost permeated the window, encompassing the snow-bound landscape. With only the flicker of the firelight to guide them, the isolation transformed into coziness and comfort.

What was she doing? Confessing about her mother like that. Not even her father heard all that. And she just unraveled it all upon this near stranger?

The light softened around her, Beth's head growing fuzzy as she breathed in the scent of juniper and sandalwood. The scent of Tristan Harty.

"I should go to bed," Beth forced out, spinning in place. His hand fell off her, his body locking in tight as she scooted onto her research. She passed the guitar back. Throwing her arms wide, she faked a yawn. "I'm really tired."

"Of course." Confusion crawled across his face as if he didn't also know that maintaining that wall was best for both of them. "Right. As you…" Tristan placed the guitar back into its case and rose on his sturdy legs. "Are you certain you don't wish to take the bed?"

"Let's not start that argument again." Beth interrupted his attempts at generosity. She could understand where he was coming from. First night he got the bed, second night she could. It was even and equal. And the idea of having to curl up under the sheets where his naked body had once been caused her brain to melt.

Tristan took it surprisingly well, nodding once as he clung white-knuckled to the guitar case's handle. "Then, good night, Ms. Cho." He walked stiff-legged to the bedroom, his chin high as if she hadn't just peeled layers from his soul to find a heart beneath.

"To you as well," Beth whispered, watching his shadow eclipsed by the door. "Tristan."

Chapter Ten

Each prick of the staticky stubble rubbing against his palm tugged his frown deeper. Tristan despised his facial hair. It was sparse in the worst of places, uncooperative, climbed higher on one side than the other and was fading to white faster than the rest of him. Why hadn't he put a razor in his bag? He packed damn near everything else to keep tidy before interviews, but that had slipped his mind?

Clean-shaven was how everyone had recognized him since his first chin hair. When he fell slack at keeping his face tidy, he looked less like a rugged man and more like some wild fiend who resided in a shack. No doubt said shack would be littered with animal carcasses and feces from the barbaric ex-accountant turning feral.

"You haven't died, have you?" A melodic voice drifted through the shut bathroom door. It wasn't malicious and it wasn't cold. It prodded with a gentle joke, but concern lingered in the base note, as if she would force open the door if he didn't respond.

"No," Tristan answered, abandoning his attempts at sprucing up. Trying to make himself presentable was clearly a fool's errand. A tiny voice in the back of his head wondered why he cared. Barry'd seen him in worse states, even the dreaded one-month beard that looked like a felt teddy bear with mange.

Once he was free of this cabin, he could properly shave and shake off the salt-and-pepper hairs obscuring his jaw. No reason to be concerned about his appearance at all.

After rolling the three-day-old shirt over his head and arms, Tristan emerged from the foggy bathroom to find her staring out of the window. She'd fully abandoned the black blazer, and he'd swear her pink blouse grew more see-through with each passing day. While her hair obscured the delicate shoulder blades and the band of her bra, Tristan homed in right on the edge of the black curtain.

The scoop of her back, barely shrouded by the pink silk, looked softer than the fabric gracing it. Dotted right at the top of the waistband, before her trousers flared out at the hips, was a birthmark. How deep did it reach down her backside? What shape was it when she rested on her front? Would it taste as cleansing as the rest of her skin?

"Hey," Beth called, shaking Tristan to the core.

What was his problem? Had she seen him staring? What excuse could he give? 'I'm a stay-at-home dermatologist and was concerned about your perfect s-curve.' *Yes, use that one, Harty. That won't send her shrieking into the snowy mountains.*

"Come see this." She indicated the window. Tristan had taken a step when a wave of déjà vu swarmed over him. But instead of the impenetrable night, it was a tender sun streaking through passing clouds. And rather than wearing a look of despair at their situation, Beth's face was bright with joy.

"What is it?" Tristan asked even as he approached to learn for himself. He paused a shoulder brush from her, growing more aware of his clothes washed tight to his skin. Absently, he rubbed his cheek as if that would worry the scruff off.

She didn't point, didn't even open her arms, her breaths shallow as if she feared startling something. Slowly, he turned from her to the wintery vista beyond. Two sleek-haired deer sniffed about the fallen snow. "I've been watching them," Beth whispered so the creatures wouldn't overhear.

Spindly front legs punctured through the snow, trying to dig down to see if there was anything worth eating. All the while, the other deer kept its head up, the ears darting to the sides to pick up any sounds of danger. Both bore a set of antlers, though small and yet growing.

Dipping its nose into the snow, the first deer raked its tongue deep into the drift. When its head emerged, it threw a handful of powdery snow into the air. The pink tongue lagged around, trying to lick up whatever it had found, but it missed the snow perched upon the jet-black nose.

Beth giggled at the image, Tristan smiling as well. "What do you think they're doing?" she whispered.

"Looking for dead grass, or perhaps there's some spilled cooking oil out there."

The second deer joined in once certain the coast was clear, both of them snorting and stomping through the snow's not-so impenetrable depths. Yesterday's sun had really worn it down, most of the car already revealed to them. Beth stared at her ride, her forehead crinkling up in what he recognized as concern.

"You don't think they'd attack the car or anything?"

Why? Planning on leaving already?

Tristan frowned at the accusatory thought as if he could blame her for wishing to return to civilization. Why did he even care if she wanted to go now? He had his own pressing engagements.

As she leaned closer to him, her shoulder grazed right above his heart. "Or does rental insurance cover act of deer?"

A laugh rumbled from Tristan. As he pulled in a breath to speak, he caught her scent. While they'd been forced to share the same unscented soap nub in the shower, a hint of vanilla and jasmine lingered upon her silky skin.

And you sound like that wild-man butcher, Harty.

"I think you'll be okay. It's not mating season and deer aren't known for eating cars."

That answer seemed to smooth out her worries, but she didn't step away from him. Her delicate shoulder glanced against his chest with each breath. "They're beautiful," she whispered.

"Yes," Tristan gulped, staring at her radiant face. "Yes, they are."

Perhaps she heard the unmitigated lust in his voice. Perhaps she sensed that he'd stopped staring at the deer. Beth's hair fell to the side as she stared up in wonder at him.

Step back. Run. Maintain your distance at all costs.

His brain tried to play the warnings on a loop, but Tristan's body refused to listen. Raising his hand, he curled his fingers through her tumbled hair. Each silken strand poured through his grasp like a river of tinsel as he guided it safely behind her ear. A tinge of pink burned up her cheeks and her gaze stared deep into his, but she didn't shift away.

She didn't step back or run. Instead, she began to move closer, rising upon the tips of her socked feet.

A ringing shattered the air and brought with it common sense, both of them stumbling back a step, staring wildly at anything but each other. Tristan whipped around, his brain insisting that that noise was familiar. "My phone," he mumbled, piecing it all together.

Stumbling around the cabin like a drunkard, Tristan found his phone resting upon the sofa. He barely had it to his ear before Barry bellowed out, "Kid! Great news!"

"You booked the Stone Kettle?"

"What?" Barry shouted, seemingly thrown by the rather well-known New York bar, or that Tristan was thinking business this early. "No. I finally got through to Parks and whoever owns that damn lodge you're trapped at. Sounds like, if all goes well, we should be able to get you out of there after noon."

"Oh..." Tristan's lips opened, his jaw dangling without a tether as he digested the thought. They could leave. They'd be free of this place, of suffering cold nights, strange meals of ramen and the mind-numbing boredom. Of watching deer frolicking in the snow not even three feet away. Of listening to the crackle of the fire while sharing truths with each other he hadn't spoken in years. Of feeling her body cupped inside his, fitting perfectly with him.

"So..." Barry prompted.

"That is good news," Tristan pronounced. "We won't have missed any deadlines and should be back on track." He swan-dived back into work, leaving behind the woman by the window. *Focus on the path ahead – it will be long and treacherous. Worrying about some foolish, flitting moment won't help.*

"Well, so, see you after lunch," Barry said.

"Sounds good," Tristan responded without thought.

"And, kid." The voice that'd been bellowing suddenly dropped to a whisper. "Keep it in your pants."

For the love of…

He was about to ream into his manager when the line went dead and the only person who'd overhear was the woman of his interest. *No! The reporter interested in me. As a story, interested as a story.*

"Good news, it sounds as if the plows will be arriving shortly to free us from our banishment," Tristan pronounced while sliding the phone into his back pocket. No doubt Barry would keep him updated every step of the way.

"Oh," Beth whispered curtly as she weighed his words. Was she thinking the same or happy to finally be free of this imprisonment? "How long do we have?"

"Afternoon was what I was told." Four hours left with Ms. Cho as accompaniment. For the first time since he'd walked into that ambush of an interview, he found himself wishing for a little more time.

She swept her soulful eyes across the deer, who'd begun to move on to the next salt lick. "Well," she said, striding away from the window, "we should at least eat breakfast."

A snort erupted from him at her commanding tone. Tristan watched her walk with assured steps to the kitchen. "As you wish," he whispered to himself before raising his voice. "Pancakes?"

She popped up from bending over the counter, whisk and bowl in hand. "I wouldn't want anything else."

* * * *

What have you got?

That was her editor's response to her announcement that she'd be able to leave soon. It was Sunday to the outside world, which might mean less traffic on her way back to the city. Maybe she'd even make it back home before dark and have time to check in with Madeline, who was none too happy about the sudden silent treatment.

What do I have?

Aside from the strangest weekend of her life spent cursing at, then connecting with a confounding man? Their paths never would have crossed without this assignment, Beth was certain of that. If they hadn't been trapped by this snow, they'd have both walked away hating each other. *And now?*

She rubbed a hand up and down her arm, feeling the rise of goosebumps. The fire was on its last legs. No reason to add more wood if they'd be leaving soon. She should be as ecstatic as a prisoner gifted parole, but Beth's shoulders slumped at the thought. There was a ton to do back home. Like Mads and her cats. Or that succulent Beth had thought was plastic until it started to wilt. Those certainly required attention. *Be a shame to miss out on it.*

What did she care?

The chat box from work opened up, her editor typing.

Got an angle?

Every time she thought she had him in checkmate, Tristan would completely invert the board. The Christmas album and his mother's connection? Maybe. His reaction to returning after half of his old studio was named in the sexual abuse investigations a year back? Not a terrible idea, but he wasn't much of a piece in that.

How his eyes sparkled when that taciturn shell cracked off. How warm his arms were when circled around her. How gentle and soothing his voice was as he whispered behind her ear.

No, Beth typed, shaking her head to knock the foolish idea away. Was it possible to be poisoned by testosterone, like carbon monoxide? Maybe she'd breathed in too much due to these close quarters and that was why she couldn't think clearly.

The three bouncing dots shamed her for having failed to strike while the iron was hot. As soon as noon rolled around, it'd be ice cold, Tristan resuming his tour of redemption, she back to the world of glorified blogging.

Give me access and I'll find it.

It was odd for her editor to be this invested, but Beth couldn't argue. Logging on, she opened up her cloud service to include her boss, giving him the opportunity to read every note she'd taken on Tristan Harty. There wasn't much in the TH folder, only snippets and half ideas gathered over the past two days. She skipped past the notes and the single paragraph in a document to the lone picture.

He stood before the tiny stove, one hand raised back, the other thrust out as if he were in a fencing pose.

Instead of a rapier, his weapon was the frying pan. The tan blur flying through the air was a pancake he'd flipped right when Beth snapped the pic. The smile upon his lips was infectious, jumping to hers even an hour after she took it.

Huh. She zoomed in on the photo, noticing that the crow's feet amplified to eleven. So too were the ones framing his lips. They were laugh lines, brought about by the stoic, cold man collapsing into a happy smile when he was safe behind closed doors. She'd assumed they were from the frown, but no. These deep ruts matched a soul that found joy when it could, the exact opposite of who she'd first met all of two days back.

"Beth," Tristan shouted from the bedroom. She hadn't entirely failed to notice his absence, a mug of cheap coffee left cooling on an end table when he vanished. Rising to her legs, she left her editor to scrounge her notes and traced the excited call.

"You'll never guess what I found," he spoke as she eased into the bedroom and spotted him on his hands and knees. He'd crawled his way into the closet, cabin fever quickly taking hold as they both waited for their hour of deliverance.

Placing a hand to her hip, she waited for him to explain. "I hope the answer isn't human bones because…"

"No." He laughed at her exasperation while rising with a long box in his hands. It looked like it could hold a pair of thigh-high boots, though there were no store or brand names on the cardboard. *Odd thing to keep in a cabin, odder to be excited about.* Lifting up the lid, he exposed once-ivory leather cracked and fading to yellow atop silver blades.

Tristan raised the box higher. "Ice skates. Looks like two pairs. There's some old ski equipment and snowshoes as well."

Beth drew her finger along the thin ropey lace, tracing it up to the cracking leather of someone's ice skate. "In case the newlyweds grow bored with sex and need something else to occupy their time?"

Her voice remained flippant, but when the word 'sex' slipped past her lips, a light blush rose over Tristan's cheeks and amplified on hers. Clicking her teeth as a distraction from the heat riding up her body, she asked, "What about the…?" Quickly, the pieces fell into place, his face as excited as a puppy's. "You know how to ice skate."

"I haven't in years, but…" That charming, surprising smile knotted up his lips. "And you don't know how."

"Where have I heard this song before?" she snickered even while picking at the skates.

"The bigger ones are a size eleven. Tight fit but I can manage," he said offhand, as if that wasn't also a way to slip her his shoe size. Her traitorous gaze darted down his legs to the feet in wool socks. She'd never noticed their grand size before and… He was staring.

"I wear a size seven," she sputtered, uncertain what to say.

"Perfect! Okay, these are a seven and a half, maybe eight." He studied the skate the way a jeweler would a diamond and a sinking feeling dropped into Beth's gut.

Tristan Harty wanted her to ice skate with him. She would have to stumble on knives in circles across an iced-over lake while this man of the north watched. Well, that'd be one way to kill this strange tension dead. By the fifth time she fell on her face, he'd want nothing to do with her.

"I can't really—"

"I'll teach you," he said fast, interrupting her half-hearted objection. "Unlike with the guitar, I'm not anything special on skates. But I thought, to while away the last hours we had together, it might be nice to..."

To slide around the ice, hand in hand, his body leading hers in a frozen dance.

You're grinning like a brain-dead imbecile.

"Okay," she said, trying to shake off the rising blush over her back and chest. "Sure, let's...let's try ice skating."

That damn smile was growing more infectious with each appearance. The strength of it nearly banished her rising trepidation as he knotted the skates together and dropped the smaller pair over her shoulder. His fingers curled around her back, the tips dancing up her spine.

"I'll, uh..." The unflappable Tristan Harty darted away. "I'll get my coat."

Beth Cho, you're going to return home with a broken arm.

Yeah, but at least it'll be a story to tell.

Chapter Eleven

"Help!" Beth gasped, her entire leg sinking into the ravenous snow bank. The once biting mountainous air lifted to a breezy temperature skirting just below freezing. It had allowed them easy passage from the cabin to a lake Tristan supposedly knew of. *Mostly* easy passage. He, with his lanky frame, found it straightforward to plow through the drifts while she discovered the snow waiting to snatch at her ankle and pull her under.

A laugh escaped from her panic, the ice skates' sharp blades bouncing against the back and chest of her coat as she continued to sink. At the rate she was going down, her only hope might be to try to swim out of the snow. Snapping through the air, a hand grabbed her wrist.

The strong fingers slid up, enveloping her palm, as Tristan helped to right her from the dangerous quick-snow. With almost no effort, he plucked her up to her feet on solid ground. Beth struggled to catch up, her boots skidding on the powder until she nearly smacked into him.

Eyes brighter than the snow twinkled down at her, the evident concern taking her breath away. "Are you all right?" His body rested not even a hand's breadth away, their skates practically knocking into each other. While the wind whirled around them, Beth felt the warmth radiating off his chest.

She snorted, leaning back to try to pull in a cooling breath of common sense. But their fingers remained entwined even as she did. "Assuming I don't fall into a five-foot hole, I should be okay."

Tristan smiled shyly, his cheeks lighting up bright pink from the cold as he dipped his chin low. Peeking that bright blue through his lashes, he said, "Noted. I suppose if the worst comes to it, you could always ride on my shoulders."

"Well, if you're taking requests," Beth spoke as they resumed their walk to the lake. She could see it now, a vast gray-blue clearing between the white snow and browns of the trees. "If given the option, I'd much rather be carried."

A choking noise caused her to look back. Tristan froze, his long stride stretched nearly to the breaking point as his wind-burnt cheeks turned tomato red. What was he…? *Oh!*

Shit, she didn't mean like… She'd been thinking of those litters and old queens and, and…

Slowly, the shocked man's lips softened and the edge twisted up into a smirk. "I will remember that," Tristan whispered.

Shivering, Beth swallowed deeply, as the chill of winter must have made it through her coat. *That has to be it.* Together they headed to the lake's edge, both staring around at anything but the other. The only warmth in her body was from the rising tension between them, and yet their fingers remained entwined.

The glorified pond wasn't very wide—she could easily see both ends and wave to the trees on the other side if she wished. But that didn't slow Tristan as he approached where sturdy snow became slippery ice. He dropped her hand and swung the skates off his shoulder. Beth moved to follow even while gritting her teeth.

"Hm." Tristan slid onto the patch of scuffed ice and gave a quick knock with his heel. Despite her teeth clenching for fear of his falling or the ice shattering, he remained perfectly fine. "Seems thick enough. Shall we?"

"This is your rodeo, cowboy," Beth said. The tips of her shoes caught on the edge of the ice while her heels remained firmly on ground territory. In general, she wasn't clumsy, but walking out onto ice willingly felt like cursing the fates to their faces.

"Did you know the studio tried to get me to put out a country album once?" Tristan asked while unbuttoning his coat. *Is that a part of ice skating?*

He laid it out on the ice and sat on the down-stuffed nylon. Once he'd kicked off his shoes, he carefully slid his feet—which she couldn't help but notice were well-sized—into the skates. "I wasn't opposed to the idea of branching out to a new sound, but this was the start of the era of trucks and bro-country. Sadly, I didn't have much to add to the experience and had to bow out."

As he moved to the second skate, Beth finally risked sliding out beside him. Sitting wasn't easy, her ass crashing to the ice. She'd swear she heard a crack, but

Tristan didn't react. Her brain was imagining things to excuse her panicking heart. With trepidation, she untied the skates and got to work switching them out.

Tristan finished his work and placed both blades onto the ice. Like a pro, he shoved himself up off the ground. Knees bent, he slid across the still pond, his body rising to its full height as if he'd done it a thousand times before.

There was no way in hell she could do that.

Heat swarmed across her cheeks, the embarrassment trying to take physical form in her body. Forget falling while skating, she was going to trip and chip a tooth just getting to her feet. The man who'd birthed this entire idea didn't skate off down the pond. No, he remained nearby, spinning around to watch her.

You're in it now.

Resigned to her fate of playing the fool, Beth cinched the skates. They were loose in the toe area, but did that really matter? It wasn't as if she was going to be doing anything interesting. *Or skating.* It was highly unlikely she'd even be standing.

"How are you doing?"

"Good, good," Beth muttered to herself. "I can tie shoelaces, at least." With a resigned sigh, she placed both bladed feet before her, knees bent the way Tristan had. And that was as far as Beth could get.

A gentle laugh broke above her and a cool shadow drifted to blot out the sun. She stared up at a pair of hands extended to her. "Let me help," he said. Beth quickly took both in her grip. Like docking a boat, his body slid closer until the tips of his skates bounced into hers.

"Okay." Tristan wafted their grip through the air as if he was counting. "Are you ready?"

Do I have a choice?

"Yes," she said. Her body sprang from the ground, Tristan easily yanking her against gravity. Beth shrieked in surprise, her knees straining as they suddenly had to take all of her.

"Stand up, come on, just like…" He kept instructing, his hands never leaving hers even as the floundering danger lurched toward him. "There you go."

She was standing, she had her legs straight and she was on ice skates. Tristan beamed at her and their locked hands both extended high to allow her body to bounce into his. She didn't slide away when it happened. There was nearly no momentum to allow it. Instead, they paused in the middle of the pond, their chests glancing against each other with every breath, their faces barely a kiss apart.

"Whoa, whoa, whoa!" Beth's ankle slid, trying to take her and Tristan down. But he held firm, a hand locking to her hip to calm her flailing limbs. As the panic ebbed and she didn't go splat on her ass, she stared into the face of the man with his palm over her hip, pressing his fingers into her waist.

Tristan swallowed, his sight rolling far to find anywhere but her face stuck beside his. "It's like rollerblading. One foot glides, then the other." He dropped his hand from her hip, picking up speed backward as he held both of her hands.

"You presume I know how to rollerblade, or skate, or anything else for that matter." Beth gulped even while willing her foot to switch from her usual heel-to-toe walking to the preferable option. Her steps on the ice were erratic and fast, an allegro tempo to his adagio. But even with a flailing charlatan in his grip, Tristan didn't bat an eye.

The presumptive man who she'd assumed had no time to suffer fools slowed to match her serious learning curve. Gently, he tugged her around the pond, not seeming to be bothered that he couldn't see behind him.

"For not knowing how to skate, you're picking this up quickly," he said, cresting her into a turn Beth was not ready for.

She didn't slam her eyelids shut, but it was a fight not to until she was safely on the straightaway once again. "You, sir, are a terrible liar," Beth gasped.

A laugh rumbled in his chest, Tristan smiling as if it were a compliment. "Would you prefer I be an excellent one?"

"No." She shook her head, surprised to find she cared about such a trait in him. "No, I would not."

"Good. Now, how about I let you on your own?"

Launching her panicking hands, Beth gripped his wrists for dear life. "Don't you dare!"

"I won't go far, trust me."

God save her, but staring into those sparkling blue eyes and patient smile, she did. Still, the fear of a cracked coccyx was hard to overcome. Biting into her lip, Beth nodded while trying to unhinge her vise grip on him. It took a while, Tristan still skating backward while waiting until he was finally free.

She expected him to flip around and dash off on his own racing adventure, but he skated closer to her. A breath caught in her throat, her hands dangling limply down. What was he doing heading for her? Was he going to push her along? Wrap a hand around her waist?

Kiss me?

Slowly, she pivoted her head to follow Tristan skating behind her. He glanced one hand over her shoulder as if he needed her to keep him in place. "Here, this way we can both see where we're going," he said. He rested his left hand upon her hip, the fingers chastely touching nothing more scandalous than her coat. Why was she disappointed at that?

"Give me your hand," he instructed and Beth extended her right. Quickly, he took it, calming the panic in her blood. At least if she went down this time, she'd take him with her. Which maybe wasn't such a good thing after all. Who would get him up?

"We'll start with the left foot first. Glide it out. Imagine yourself in your socks sliding over the kitchen floor." His warm breath tickled her ear, the hand on her waist gripping tighter as Beth slid her foot out. The pair of them moved as one, Tristan asking for the next foot.

After a kick of the right sent them farther on, brightness rose in her chest. "I'm doing it, I'm actually skating," she cried in shock. They weren't moving quickly, but it was real gliding with a gentle breeze glancing over her cheeks.

"Indeed you are," Tristan said. His warm words swaddled her ear, reminding her how close he was. How he was cupping her hip, pressing his fingers into her lower abdomen to keep her safe. How there was a body of no-doubt sinewy muscle directly behind her. Okay, so her coat was in the way and he was wearing a shirt and sweater, but…

"What do you think of this?" The voice sang through her, the words carrying back on their skate-induced breeze.

Beth pulled in a breath, her heart beating faster even as they sailed over the silent pond at a walking speed.

Rolling her fingers to grip back onto his, she said, "It's exhilarating."

As Beth glided to the edge of the pond, a dusting of snowflakes began to fall. She glanced up at the muddled clouds bringing more of the light powder to cover the world, but only for a moment. Once freed of his helpless passenger, Tristan took command of the ice.

Long, lean legs effortlessly switched, one to the other. Blades sliced apart the icy top layer, sending Tristan's tight body faster and faster in concentric loops. He kept his hands tucked behind the small of his back, his face leaning forward to compensate for the center of gravity. It reminded her of old professors too vain to admit they needed glasses.

"Can you do a flip?" Beth called to the man flying across the pond.

"Flip?" He didn't cease his looping, but he raised up from the partial lean. Even at the distance of half the pond, even with the shadows of the clouds passing overhead, the luminescent blue of his gaze sent a shiver down her spine.

"You know, that spin thing that ice skaters do," she mumbled. It'd begun as a joke, but as he kept his raptor-like gaze upon her, her insides churned. And it had nothing to do with the strength of the calves and thighs propelling him over the ice. Not at all.

Tristan resumed staring at where he was going instead of her even as he addressed her. "An axel? That seems unwise. I have been out of practice for many years."

Oh, well. Beth shrugged as if she didn't care to watch the ex-teenage heartthrob now all grown up launch his taut body into the air. Despite the cool air circling them,

Tristan left his coat upon the ground. She wondered if he was cold, the tinge of pink upon his cheeks and forehead a warning sign. But there was a comfortable ease across his brow, his lips fully slackened from their hard purse.

It was intoxicating, enthralling to watch a man know his body from the tips of his toes up to the ears. She wanted to say his moves, simple as they might be, were graceful, but that wasn't accurate. They weren't forceful either. It wasn't as if Tristan was trying to beat the ice into surrender. No, he skated as if he knew where he needed to be and knew he could get there.

Confidence. Warm, oddly comforting and intriguing confidence.

Beth licked her lips. A thought struck her and she fished out her phone. Twisting it to landscape mode, she hit the Record button. On the thin screen in her hands was a tiny flat version of Tristan Harty. When she glanced down at it, it reminded her of those little village models for Christmas with the figurines on magnets to skate across a mirrored lake.

But when she looked up, when the light the phone couldn't catch lanced against his chestnut hair, reviving the copper highlights, her heart caught. The figurine on the phone moved with technical prowess while the man before her exuded a serenity that reached down into her soul. *Is this what it was like to attend one of his concerts?* She'd looked at old footage online but had thought little of it. The difference between the screen and the person was spellbinding.

Stopping the recording, she dropped her phone into her pocket. The footage wouldn't be useful for an article. It was doubtful anyone would even care. She wanted it for herself, a tiny memento of the man she'd got to spend a weekend with.

Had to.

Tristan skated closer to her. "Do you want to try again?"

"I'm not certain if that's wise," Beth admitted. She'd lucked out surviving before without humiliating herself. Giving it another go seemed like asking for it.

Tristan extended his hands, palms up, for her to hold them. "I'll hold you."

His hands holding hers. No, her hips. Hers clinging to his shoulders as the pair of them skated in an intimate dance, Beth lost in those endless cobalt fields as he bumped the tip of his skates into hers. His tempting lips drifting closer and closer, igniting a spark between him and her.

God! Beth threw a hand up to her cheeks, embarrassed at her imagination going off track so fast. If she'd been on solid ground, it wouldn't have mattered how quickly she moved, but the burning shame threw off her common sense. As she flew her hand up to her face, her entire center of gravity tipped backward, taking her down with it.

Everything whipped past her. First, a blur of Tristan's face dropping in shock. Then the impenetrable mountains of Vermont streaked past and finally the blue-gray skies above.

Flying with the grace of a one-winged goose, Beth's body smacked straight into the ice. Hard. When her head hit, the gray sky streaked like a painting in the rain. Pain lingered in the shadows around her vision, waiting to strike.

But what caused the breath to leech from her lungs wasn't the impact. It wasn't the fact she'd fallen in front of him. It was the sound that echoed around her and up to the snowy skies above.

Crack.

Chapter Twelve

"Beth!"

His gut somersaulted with her body. Tristan was helplessly pinned in place while she tumbled to the ice. When her poor back struck, her head jarring from the impact, he raised his skate to race to her.

Then he saw it.

Cracks spidered out from her fallen form, the ice splintering with white veins.

"Shit," he gulped, slicing both legs to the side to stop himself. He did it so quickly he too nearly fell to the cracking ice. "Beth, can you hear me?"

She mumbled, telling him either she was in the midst of a swoon from the head trauma or out of air. But she wasn't dead. Not yet, at least. The ice under her though, if it shattered…

Without a second thought, Tristan dropped to his stomach. Wet snow and melting lake water smeared across his chest as he crawled his way to her. All the while, he kept watching the white cracks spidering farther and farther out to consume the entire lake.

"Please be okay, please be okay," he whispered to himself as he scrabbled on his elbows. With his chin nearly planted to the ice, all he could see was the blade of her skate and the shadow of her pants. The rest of her body was blocked as she didn't move.

She shouldn't move! "Whatever you do, stay down," he instructed, uncertain if she could even hear him. On the one hand that was good, less likely for her to flail in pain. On the other, she needed to not be hurt. "I'm coming for you."

The skate tipped to the side, smacking into the already fragile ice below her.

Stupid! What were you thinking? Why did you do this?

Cursing at himself, he banished the unhelpful thoughts. Tristan eased closer to her fallen form, and he felt the ground shudder below him. Whipping his head down, he stared at the once sturdy ice breaking into pieces. If he went any farther, it could set off the cascade.

He had to stay in place or he could take them both down. With his bare hand skirting above the wet ice, he reached out for her. The tips of his fingers knocked into the fallen skate, but they couldn't get a grip. *Damn it!*

Relying on his abs, Tristan scrunched his back half up and slowly pushed the front part ahead, crawling like a caterpillar. The ice shuddered but remained intact. It got him another inch. *Please let that be enough.*

With a breath bottomed in his lungs, he skirted his hand out. Freezing cold glanced against his palm, trying to throw him off, but he hooked a finger onto the blade. He had no choice but to risk it and pulled with just that finger.

Tristan moved to her instead of the other way around. Cursing at the foolish action, he wrapped the rest of his fingers around the top of the blade. With his left hand lashed behind him, hoping to find anything to work as a grip, he began to tug. Her body shifted, but not enough.

The ice crinkled like a cat in tissue paper, the sound draining all the blood from his face. He needed to get her in his arms. He needed her off that ice. He needed both of them off the ice.

Not caring about the consequences, Tristan wrapped his entire palm around the bottom of the blade. The edge sliced through his flesh, pain bubbling along with the warm drops of blood. Biting on his tongue to keep the screaming at bay, he ordered all his strength to his arm and started to pull.

With the extra leverage, Beth finally began to skirt away from the crumbling ice and closer to him. He had to stop, inch his body back, then pull hers, but it was working. Slowly—so mind-numbingly slowly he wanted to scream—they both left the cracks behind.

Tristan didn't let go of his grip on the skate's blade, fearful that reaching for anything else could doom them. And he didn't stop until the last of the white cracks faded past not only his body but hers as well. A trail of crimson dots streaked across the ice, the warm blood dribbling off his palm. He grimaced at the gore, but there wasn't time to stanch the wound or wipe it off. Instead, he gripped her ankle and finally pulled the unresponsive woman almost to the other side of the pond.

Once they struck snow, instinct took over. Her eyes were open, tears bubbling from the pain of the rising bump to her head. She moved to tenderly touch the back of her skull as he was already rising to his feet. Without a question, he pulled her off the ice and into his arms.

It caused the tears to pause, but she didn't chastise his foolish heroics. The rescuer who inhabited Tristan's body took two steps before realizing he still had the damn skates on. Like snapping a finger, the cocksure light evaporated to sinking darkness.

His hands opened, Beth's own skated feet landing in the snow. *Don't smell it. Don't think about the pale, mummified fingers prodding above the waterline like a stripped skeleton.* He tried to pull in a breath, but it stank of bleach and stomach acid matted into a carpet. *Damn it!*

Focusing on his feet, Tristan yanked both of them clear out of the skates and walked through the snow in his socks to find his shoes. With his hands wrapped so tight around the laces that blood couldn't reach his fingers, he knotted on the old boots. A whimper shattered the grip he had, coming from the woman left teetering upon the edge.

Her cheeks were flushed bright red, her eyes crumpled as she tried to swallow down the pain while skirting her fingers over the welt. It cracked his heart to find her in such dire straits. But her trying to hide from him the fact she'd broken down stung deeper. "I should," Beth whispered, glaring down at her feet. She moved to bend over, but Tristan grabbed her shoulder.

"No," he said, shaking his head.

Wary concern looked up at him as if he expected her to walk back to the cabin in the skates. "I'll carry you," he managed from between clenched teeth.

"Why?" Her question was emptied of malice, only curiosity singing in it. Why did he insist on carrying a woman who could clearly walk?

Slinging her shoes up over his shoulder, Tristan picked her up into his arms. She didn't fight him, but the question lingered even as Beth slotted an arm behind his neck and held on. Why did he pick her up? Why did he insist upon taking the brunt? Why did he care?

"It isn't smart for someone with a head injury to bend over," he said, striding for the cabin. It wasn't until he was a hill away that he remembered his coat left resting upon the mutilated snow. He could return for it later. All that mattered was getting her safe inside.

She didn't speak while nestled in his arms, though she had to shift so the back of her head didn't strike his chest. It left her welling tears up onto his sweater, her lips whimpering against him. Tristan tried to walk past the pain, but it was radiating from his arms, and it was all his fault. Again.

The picturesque snowfall increased, fat flakes tumbling to obscure his vision, but he spotted the cabin and followed the red and green building poking through the white. With a lash of his foot, Tristan kicked himself into the warmth of their refuge. He made it as far as the couch before his knees collapsed.

By some last remaining dregs of energy, Beth landed on the sofa cushions, while his knees—worn as they were—struck the wooden floor. With the release of his charge, his arms dropped. The muscles not used to that form of a workout cried in anger at the misuse, but that wasn't what kept his hands dead to the ground.

He felt like a convict awaiting subjugation, head bowed, palms open, body broken and collapsed before yet another woman brought to danger's edge. *Why? Is it my curse?*

"Can you see my purse?" Beth moaned as she stretched out on the sofa, her fingers pinching into her nose to stymie the pain.

"I'm sorry," Tristan whispered.

She didn't understand his words and tried to sit up while looking around the room. "Maybe I left it on the counter…?"

Stop castigating yourself! Rise and help her! At least she's alive.

"What do you need?" he mumbled, his creaky joints pushing him back onto his feet.

"There's an aspirin bottle in there." She winced, bending over, cupping the sides of her face.

It drilled deep into his marrow to watch so much pain flood her so quickly. But that wasn't helping. Shaking it off, Tristan found the wayward bag hiding on the chair. "I found it," he said, lifting the teal leather into his arms.

"Side pocket," Beth gasped, "just bring me the whole bottle."

"You want me…?" She wanted him to go through her purse? A man she barely knew. A man who had almost sent her frozen body to the bottom of a lake. Pinching into his leg, he unzipped the middle of the bag.

"No, no," she interrupted, "on the front. There's a side pocket on the front."

That made no sense, but he closed the zipper and undid one of the buckles on the front. Feeling like he was rooting through someone's underwear drawer, Tristan kept his gaze on the ceiling while reaching inside. There were wrappers to something long, wrappers for something flat, and… *Yes! A bottle.*

When it pulled out into the light of day, he glanced down quick. The sight of medicinal green assured him he'd guessed right. But in his haste, as he pulled the bottle free and passed it to the aching woman, a small scrap of paper fluttered free from her purse.

"Shit, shit, shit," Beth hissed to herself, quickly downing three of the aspirin dry. She flipped over onto her front, burying the rest of her cursing into the couch cushions.

Numbness flooded Tristan's body. The immediate danger was over. They hadn't fallen through the lake and she didn't require medical assistance or CPR. Though… "Don't fall asleep."

"Wha…?" her voice mumbled from the couch.

"You might have a concussion. You cannot sleep." He tried to keep his tone level and certain, but it cracked under his pseudo-control.

To his surprise and partial relief, Beth raised up on her hands and her glare struck him. "I know that," she said and flopped back down to hopefully not nap.

"I should call Barry, see if they have any medical units, a way to a hospital," Tristan mumbled to himself, trying to dig out his phone while also balancing her purse in his arms. As the line rang through, he realized the foolishness of holding the bag and put it down.

Which was when he noticed the forgotten scrap of fallen paper. Crouching down, he reached for it when Barry picked up. "Tri—"

"There's been an accident," Tristan interrupted, spitting the words out like a machine gun. "We need you to send someone with medical expertise when you get through. Head injury. It's not fatal but—"

"Whoa, kid. Hold up. I was just about to call you…" The dread in Barry's voice sank Tristan's gut even lower than he thought possible. "With the new snow coming, they called it off. All the trucks are back on the main roads again."

"Damn it!" Tristan cursed, pinching his fingers into the scrap of paper. Slowly, he began to turn it over.

"I'm not happy either, but they're giving me reports about fears of avalanches and other dangers. Look..."

Barry's voice faded as Tristan stared at an old-fashioned polaroid barely bigger than a coupon. It was of Beth wearing a pair of novelty glasses along with another red-haired woman and a kitten in between them. Beth's smile was bright enough to melt a mountain's worth of snow.

His manager's whine phased back into a speaking voice. "We'll get you out soon. I swear. Just put up with her a little longer."

"What?" Tristan shook his head, trying to focus.

"The reporter. Keep away from her for a few more hours, a day at the most, and we'll pry you free."

He nodded, then remembered he was on the phone. "Right, yes, I'll...I'll stay away." Quickly, he slipped the photo back into her purse, but he lingered over the woman prostrated on the sofa. *In pain because of me. Could have died because of my choices.*

Bleach ripped through the archive of his memories, the acrid stench obliterating the comforting smell of a crackling fire. Tristan tried squeezing his eyes tight, willing himself to be anywhere other than that bathroom, but it wouldn't vanish. As he opened them, the bleach crawled along his vision, spots of ivory burning apart his view of the living room.

"I have to go," he said to Barry.

It was Beth who twisted up, her voice raw and ragged. "Where?"

The air filling his lungs tasted of copper and bile, Tristan struggling to breathe around the stench. He caught the ghastly glare of crimson and froze before remembering it was his own sliced hand. Bundling it tight to his chest, he muttered, "My coat. I left it in the snow."

Before she could argue that it would wait, he dashed back into the rising snowstorm. His steps clattered down the stairs until he reached the rising drifts and collapsed. Wrapping both hands into the freezing snow, he tried to ground himself, to remember where he was.

Mountain. Vermont. Not a bungalow in California.

With a reporter and not your ex.

Even if she's hurt because you weren't there.

Even if you failed again.

You. Tristan Harty. Alone.

Forever alone. It's what's best. What you want.

What you deserve.

His hand opened to drop the snowball with a bloody streak carved across its face.

Chapter Thirteen

Fuck!

No, that four-letter curse wasn't enough to encompass both the pain and utter humiliation that charred her soul to a crisp. She wanted to bury her face into the couch cushion and scream murder, but a wary guardian was watching from the kitchen.

When he'd returned from his winter sojourn, Tristan had dashed to the bar stools, his coat soaking from the snowstorm. By that point, the aspirin had kicked in and Beth had staggered up to sit on the couch. Her back ached, her ass wasn't wild about existence, and her head was sporting a dime-sized welt, but it was her pride that bore the deepest wounds.

It'd have been one thing if she'd fallen, laughed, he'd extended his hand to help her up and they'd skated until she could forget. But no. She had to fall so hard she'd damn near cracked the ice under her. When the shock had worn off and air had gushed into her lungs, she'd felt Tristan tugging her body to safety. Cold had seeped up her back as her coat and shirt had ridden up, exposing her skin to the ice below. While uncomfortable, it was the cracking under her with each breath that had sent Beth's heart racing.

But she was here, alive, unfrozen, and watching the fire chew through a log, all while the hair on the back of her neck stood at attention. Was he that disturbed by her *kersplat*? Did it put him off for her to shed tears of pain and also frustration after escaping a possible death by lake? Or was he simply letting the judgmental ass out once more?

Beth gulped at the kaleidoscope of emotions shattering in his eyes. No, whatever Tristan Harty was thinking or feeling, it didn't seem to be passing judgment. This...she wanted to say pain while looking deeper, but couldn't grasp what was churning inside. And he wouldn't cease staring like a starving owl either.

"Any chance you have something better to cure this throbbing headache?" She spoke up, pivoting on the couch to stare at him.

It took a moment for Tristan to respond, his face blank as if his soul had fled his body. "Beg pardon?"

"I'm not gonna narc on you," she said, trying to raise her voice to a laugh, but the curtains drew across him. Long gone was the open and friendly Tristan. All that glared at her was Harty.

"Sorry, Ms. Cho. You will have to look elsewhere."

She snickered, but not at his lack of drugs. "Ms. Cho? So you're back to that."

The walled-off man rose to his feet, his chin held high. "Is it not your name?"

What in the hell is his problem? Sure, her fall had been anything but graceful, but Tristan was acting as if she'd unlatched her jaw and devoured his manager whole. "I heard we're stuck here for longer," she said, rolling her foot on the carpet. She hadn't risked standing since he'd dropped her off, but found that she couldn't remain on the constricting sofa much longer either.

"That is the un-new news, I'm afraid." He spoke as if she was a stranger on a train. Just another face passing in the night amongst a sea of them. As important as a single snowflake in the midst of an avalanche.

Fine. Whatever. My fault for even thinking that he might…

What, Beth? Did you honestly believe for a moment that Tristan Harty, a platinum-selling recording artist, had any interest in you? He made his disapproval of your existence clear from the second you met. Why would that change just because of a few moments in a claustrophobic cabin?

Cursing at herself for letting her imagination traipse off into fairy princess territory, Beth snatched at her laptop. She opened up the mostly blank Tristan file and glared at it. The line of questions he'd deftly ignored hovered on the side, waiting for answers.

"Why did you wish to be a musician?" she asked, her voice disinterested and her tone colder than the ice across a pond.

Tristan glared, but Beth wasn't backing down. He wanted to play this game, then so could she. After gliding the tip of his tongue over his teeth, he asked, "Why are you a gossip blogger?"

"What?" She wasn't, and what did he care anyway?

"It is clear that what you want in life is to be a reporter, a proper one, not someone who asks meaningless questions to barely above-board celebrities."

Beth snickered at the man owning himself, but he didn't blink. No, he seemed to want an answer. To demand more from her when he couldn't bother to give her the barest courtesy of the same. *Very well.*

Snapping her notebook shut fast, she shot to her feet. Alarms rose in Tristan's face, the man standing as well. While Beth teetered a moment, her head swimming from the knock to it, her sights were set fully upon him. "I am a 'glorified blogger' because that's the job I can get. Because when I graduated J-school, I stepped out into a world that was obliterating every proper reporter job it could. A world where the news came from some kid's Twitter account and no one bothered with sources or in-depth reporting."

A snort rolled down the musician's nose as if he hadn't expected her to respond. Bouncing his leg, Tristan finally asked, "So you settled for less than?"

"Yes, because I have to eat. It's not what I want, but it keeps me off the streets and it's writing. And, unlike you, all I have to fall back on are my student loans!"

"So that, that unfair world, that ever-shifting climate, is why you're in the position you are. Why you're wasted chasing after minor musicians and reality stars pimping their diet water brands." He snapped as if angry at her for failing in her potential. As if he had any right, any notion how hard she'd worked to get where she was! As if he was her goddamn father!

"How dare you," Beth said, stepping closer to the man hiding away in the kitchen like a coward. No, she wasn't letting him loose now. He was answering every one of her questions, she was writing a fucking article about him then she was purging Tristan Harty from her memory forever!

"How dare I?" he mocked, laying a hand to his chest as if she'd wounded him. "'How dare I, you say, when you were the one to ambush me about her."

"Her?" Beth scowled, "Her who?" *His mother?* She hadn't asked much beyond a few Christmas tales. *What is he…?*

The fury and thunder faded to a crackle as Tristan dipped his head. When he spoke, his voice barely raised a breath. "Sasha."

Sasha. No last name needed. A rising star on the music scene, burning brighter even than her fiancé, one Tristan Harty. Her life had been tragically cut short at the age of twenty-six by overdose. After that, he'd vanished from the spotlight, leaving behind many questions and no answers.

"You wish to know of her. Of what happened. Of why I…" He pulled in a breath, tears rising. The emotion was so overwhelming that Beth became winded, her hand shaking as she dug for a pen.

With a shudder, Tristan faced the kitchen, unable to look at her. His hands slapped to the counter and he said, "It was my fault. All of it."

God! People whispered conspiracy theories about the less-famous boyfriend growing jealous. She had died in his house, though it was technically shared between them. Most had been sympathetic to his loss, the world's loss, until the pictures had hit the papers. Until he had begun to lash out.

"We'd…we'd been broken up then. Three months, maybe four."

"She still lived with you?" Beth asked slowly.

Tristan's head dangled lower, his fingers knocking a beat against the counter. "I'd loved her since I was eighteen. I did still love her, but I couldn't… I wasn't enough for her. I couldn't save her. So she stayed in the house, I found an apartment to rent because it was easiest. And we carried on always saying one day we'd figure out how to end it all. To unravel it all. Then the paparazzi happened."

His voice roughened from its natural honeyed state. "There were pictures of me cozy with a backup singer, and since we didn't announce the breakup, they were going to publish them as proof of my infidelity. Sash and I..." A choked sob escaped after her loving nickname. "We wrote a press release from both of us. All formal and official to tell the world that we were parting ways, it was mutual, give us space. So on and so forth."

Tristan paused in his story, taking a hand from its grip on the counter to swipe over his eyes. "I was always there for her. When we knew bad news was coming. Bad reviews. Flops in album sales. Just the press...being assholes. I knew I had to be there. To sit with her. To keep her..."

Clean.

"Occupied. But that night I didn't. I thought, 'This is it. This has to be the clean break.' I couldn't keep going back to her, to babysit her. What were a few beers out with my friends?"

The man shattering from old heartbreak turned from his vigil upon the stove. He wanted her to answer, to explain for God or death why it had to happen. Like a coward, she buried her face in her notebook, pretending to write even as her heart leaped into her throat.

"I found her," Tristan confessed.

"But you're not..." Beth began before wincing.

He picked up on her macabre train of thought. "Not listed in the police report. I know. That was Barry's doing, or the studio's, or whoever didn't want to lose all the money with both of us wrapped up in that mess. I sat in that bathroom for what felt like an eternity with her. Screaming at her to wake up, promising her whatever she wanted, begging for her to breathe. But it didn't matter. I couldn't save her."

Jesus Christ. Beth had seen death up close. Not the polished-up, rose-scented formaldehyde and sewn-shut eyelids of a funeral parlor death. The ripped-off flesh, the joints and bones cracked at horrific angles, the eternal unseeing gaze of death. It had sent her scampering under her bed for days and she didn't even know the people caught in the middle of two bureaucrats' war.

"Tristan." She reached out a hand for him.

"I should have been there. Why wasn't I there? I was always there for her. I knew I kept her clean, at least stable. Sober most days. It's my fault."

"No." Beth shook her head, shocked she was stepping into this. He glared at her invading his painful past, but she couldn't stop. "No, it isn't."

"You don't know me."

"I know you can't save people with love. I know you can't… You can't love them enough to get them help. To get them to stop hurting you, hurting themselves. It has to be them. Their choice. Love won't bring them back unless they want to!"

Oh, God. Beth tried to slide away, her heart thundering. Images flitted through her mind, barely developed photographs of a woman skipping out on phone calls, meetings, just taking her sick daughter to a doctor's appointment. Her father insisting that one day she'd come home, one day she'd realize what she was missing out on. One day she'd magically get better.

A warm hand wrapped around hers, Tristan spinning to face her as he held Beth in place. Slowly, he drew his thumb to her cheek. She held her breath, uncertain what he was doing until she felt the cool slick on her skin as he wiped her tears away.

"It's my fault you fell," he breathed, his hand not falling from her cheek. It remained, the thumb folding into her laugh line as he held her safe.

"No, it's my clumsy body's fault."

"I took you out there. I didn't test the ice. I…"

Beth reached out with her finger, placing it tight to Tristan's lips. The ones that'd serenaded countless teenagers across the years, the ones that'd pursed and sneered at her, the ones trembling to hold in his tears. "It's not your fault," she repeated.

Slowly, he swallowed down the unending insistence that it was his duty and doing. She waited to make certain before sliding her finger off his lips. Just before it left the scruff of his chin, Tristan said, "It's not yours either."

They weren't talking about the ice. They'd never been talking about the ice and they both knew it. "I know," Beth said slowly, "but I forget too."

She watched the pain soften, his gaze caressing down her face until he reached her cheek. In an instant, the panic returned and he yanked his hand away.

"I'm sorry, I got…" Tristan babbled as Beth drew her fingers to find a drop of blood lingering upon her cheek. Flexing his palm, he stared at the wrathful line gouged into his flesh. "I must have opened it up on accident."

"Here." She cupped her hand under his and pulled it closer. From the one pocket in her pants, she unraveled a tissue and pressed it to the dribbling wound. "It must hurt terribly."

Tristan gulped, his voice as soft as a whisper as he watched her tend to him. "Not as much, no."

"And it damaged you, your…you need your hand to play. For all those concerts and…" Why did she care? Why was her mind flashing with headlines about how his career had stalled out on relaunch because of her? All because of her inability to stay upright.

"Hey." He swept his other palm to her cheek. The cold, indifferent veneer was shattered. Only warmth pressed to her skin, kindness radiating in his sapphire blues. "I'm all right. It will heal. I've done worse in the past."

Beth began to shake her head but paused as she didn't want to pull away from his hold. "Why? Why risk it for…for me?"

The pursed lips fell apart, Tristan blowing a breath softly between them as her question whipped about in the cabin. Only the howl of the storm filled in the silence and it bore no answers.

"Because," Tristan whispered as he bent to her. He gently caressed the bare edge of her lips with his as if he was prepared to turn it chaste should she react poorly. Closing her eyes tight, Beth launched up on her toes until she and Tristan were ensnared in a proper kiss.

Warm as a mug of hot cocoa, softer than a down blanket, the taste and temptation of his lips sent shivers dancing down her spine. Beth gasped at the thrill invigorating her skin, but the noise caused Tristan to break off. Not far, the tip of his sharp nose crested against her cheek as he moved to lean back.

Reporter. Her job was to interview him. Not get close to him. To learn of his past, yes, to know his wants and hopes in life, but not discover that he smelled of juniper berries and tasted of heart-racing sunshine. This wasn't right. This should never happen.

Beth drew her hand back through his hair, the copper strands knotting around her fingers as she pulled him down into the abyss with her. The calm heat of the first kiss rampaged to a forest fire, Tristan parting his lips for a meeting of tongues. His was amenable, even gentle as it touched Beth's in a greeting of familiarity. Feeling as if her belly was on fire, she tasted deeply of him and tugged his lip into her mouth.

The wounded paw slipped from hers to grab her hip and haul her deeper into his kiss. She moaned at the thought of it rolling across her naked curves, tugging free her panties and nestling between her thighs. Beth flitted her tongue with the edge of the soul patch sprouting below his lip, tousling the sharp hairs to cause him to groan. As Tristan gasped, he tipped his head back as though he wanted her to nuzzle and kiss up and down his neck. She slid her hand along his thin hips. Slowly, she trailed her fingers to his belt, about to send herself and Tristan down a path they could never come back from.

A clicking noise struck twice through the whole cabin. The lovers paused, both glancing up to watch as a final thud brought the cabin's generator down. Like snuffing a candle, the lights and power failed, leaving the two of them illuminated only by the storm.

Chapter Fourteen

Well.

Tristan's hands remained enveloped around her, his senses aware of perfect breasts pressing to him, the roots of his hair tingling from her tousling. But the numbness in his brain could focus only on the lightbulb above their heads and its impotent state.

Growing aware of a tight pinch rising in his jeans, he flinched. Perhaps impotent was not the best choice of words at the moment.

Slivers of light rolled from the windows to let them view a gray-scale version of each other, but it couldn't pierce deep inside. Only the lingering tufts of fire gave them any real color, and the flames had been on a downward slope.

He was focusing on the light in the room to keep himself from the real truth. *You kissed her. You, foolish man, kissed the woman you were explicitly told not to. By many people including yourself.*

Those big, soul-touching eyes met his and he ached to kiss her again. Beth seemed to have a better grasp on her hormones as she turned to business. "Do you think this outage will last?"

"Hard to say. It could pass with the storm moving on," he began. At the same moment, they stepped away from each other. It was a clean cut and it unnerved him how empty his arms felt without her.

"We need… Ah!" She dashed from his side to her laptop and quickly powered it down. "Best to save all the battery life we can. Oh, and my phone." He set his to airplane mode to conserve the limited juice at the same time as she did hers.

"Wood," Tristan threw out. When her gaze snagged his, he winced and spun around to stare out of the tiny kitchen window. A sea of white waited for them outside, a reminder that it was going to get much colder soon. "Firewood, I mean. Logs. Kindling."

"There's some left on the porch under the tarp. I can bring it in." She began to inch toward the door.

His manners rose from their stomped-down depths. "I should be the one."

"Not with your wounded hand," was her answer, Beth slipping out into the storm.

Tristan marched into the kitchen, bent over and banged his forehead on the Formica. *What. Were. You. Thinking?*

How sweet her lips looked parted in concern. How tender her words were to him. How she cut to his quick without a second's hesitation and pulled him back to his metaphorical feet. He saw it in her beautiful face, the same unending tug of wanting to fix someone and failing endlessly.

So he'd kissed her. As thanks. A gratitude for her mercy.

And God it was good. Great. Perfect. No knocking of the teeth, no slobbering tongue. A harmonious melding of lips that soothed his ache and opened up a hunger he feared would never be filled.

What now?

The door knocked open, Beth's black hair coated in snow as she stumbled in with her arms full. "This should keep us for a while," she announced, letting the logs fall on the stone slats before the fireplace. Slowly, she picked each one up, placing them one at a time on the log holder, as if she too needed time to think. To weigh whether to lock herself back up in the bathroom to keep away from his advances or…

Why do you think there's an or?

"A flashlight," Tristan babbled. "I saw a flashlight in, uh…" He scrambled through the drawers, trying to remember what held nothing, what was silverware, and where was the… *Yes!*

A beam of yellow light streaked across the floor. Beth smiled as if he'd performed heart surgery. "Well, that should help some when night falls."

"Hm." Tristan placed the flashlight upon the counter and pulled on the handle. It tugged upward, revealing that the light could also double as a lantern. A haze of comforting yellow formed a corona around him. All the while, the second of a seeming cascade of winter storms raged outside.

Beth rose while trying to pat her pants clean with snowy hands. She was beautiful. As hard as he tried to deny it, to hide it under exceptions and excuses, her face was inviting, her smile warm, and her body… *Stop thinking about her body unless you want to make it worse for her.*

Absently, he knocked his folded-in knuckle to the counter. It kept beating against the Formica as if he could force all the wanton lust from his body that way. *Didn't work in your teens. Why would it work now?*

Clearly hoping to cling to the light, Beth stepped over his guitar and past the now dead Christmas tree. Odd, he'd stopped seeing the twinkling lights before, but there seemed to be a hole in the cabin without them. And Tristan was staring contemplatively at the tree because he had no idea what to say to her.

I'm sorry that I took you in my arms and forced my affections upon you?

It was an accident, a moment of confounding weakness?

It will not happen again?

Or do you want it to happen again?

Of course she doesn't. She'd made it perfectly clear from their first meeting that she found him pompous and conceited. Why would that have changed in any way now? Even knowing he was on the thinner side of being a man, Tristan was no fool either. He tried to hunch down and make himself look smaller, less intimidating to the woman trapped in a cabin with no heat, no electricity and the man who had kissed her.

"So," Beth said, rolling the tips of her fingers over the counter. "Power's out."

"Seems to be. Since it's not a hiccup, I'm fearing a downed line or worse." He could focus on the dire news, barely flinching at the fear of potentially freezing to death if they weren't found in time. The other option was to watch the woman lit by firelight, her cheeks tinged pink from her jaunt into the snow. And the latter was no help.

She twisted her chin to the fridge. "That should be fine, no perishables inside it and the freezer as well."

"No stove though," Tristan whispered as if he'd had plans to whip her up a five-star dinner as recompense.

Beth shrugged, seeming rather accepting of the whole mess. Her fingers skirted across the counter, Tristan watching them as if they were fish on a coral reef. Beautiful, exotic and impossible to touch.

"My concern—" she said, grazing those impossible fingers against the back of his forefinger. One after the other in a straight line, softly caressing him in a loop. "—is the shower."

"Shower?" He gulped, fully lost and unable to find his brain.

"I doubt the water heater will stay hot for long in this weather, and with no electricity to reheat it..."

What is she suggesting? What is she saying?

No. No, it can't be.

Brown eyes stared so deep into his, he watched the flint strike fire. "Perhaps we should share one."

* * * *

Yellow light from the makeshift lantern danced off the shower's slate-gray tiles as Tristan placed the flashlight on the counter. There was no tub lip to trip them up, opening the entire shower so anyone could walk directly into the spray of water. No pesky doors or curtains to get in the way of anyone wanting to watch. And Beth was staring at the empty towel rack rather than coming to terms with what she'd started.

Slowly, she glanced to the man who'd entered behind her. He moved to close the door before they both winced at the puny light coming off the lantern.

"Probably best if I..." Tristan jerked his head to the door that let the few gray cloud-rays pierce into the darkened bathroom.

Was he nervous? Was she?

Catching the trembling in her fingers as they kept tugging on her blouse, she nodded. Yes, fine. She was incredibly nervous. Screwing her eyes shut, Beth undid the buttons that'd put in far too much work these past few days. When the blouse hit the tile, she glanced over her shoulder to find him staring longingly down the swoop of her back.

A thrill rode up her spine, bringing with it a smile. Tristan raised a shoulder as if in a toast and, grabbing the collar of his shirt, hoisted it off his body. *Oh, God!* The blush threatened to consume her whole when her plan fully hit her. *Share a shower. Just jump right from a foolish little kiss to naked bodies pressed together under steaming water, as if that might...*

The tell-tale zipper-pull sound silenced her brain entirely. Beth remained turned away, but she risked a sneaky peek in the mirror. If men were horses, Tristan Harty would be a thoroughbred. Sleek and wiry, there wasn't an ounce of fat on him. His muscles were trim and tight with a hint of veins rising off his biceps as he worried out of his jeans. A neat pile of hair formed at the middle of his stark, flat pecs. It vanished down the center of his body but picked up around the belly button. Beth flexed her fingers, wondering how soft its dark waves had to be.

"So this shower idea..." He spoke, causing her to whip her head away as if she hadn't been dissecting every inch of available skin.

"Uh-huh," Beth mumbled, finally unbuttoning her own slacks and slipping them off. She stood in her bra and panties, neither particularly fancy lingerie, in a dark bathroom with a man she had met three days ago.

Should she take more off? Beth brushed her hand over her hip, toying with the strap of the bikini cut underwear while facing Tristan Harty. No doubt he'd been with models and actresses in the past, women whose job was to keep as thin and acceptably in shape as possible. Every cruel cut to her self-esteem, every braying advertisement to get her to buy their product, every swallowed hatred at her eyes, her breasts, her legs, her thighs came screaming at her at once.

She watched his jaw drop.

"Do we, do you want, should I?" That cocksure, patrician mask cracked, leaving Tristan babbling. He rustled through his hair as if that'd save him, his other hand tugging on the band of his underwear.

Okay. That might be a step too far.

"I'll start the water," Beth announced as if he had no idea how a shower worked. The nod she received seemed both grateful that she planned to shower in her underwear, and perhaps a touch rueful as well.

Fumbling due to the overwhelming shadows, she patted along the wall until finding the silver handle and twisting it far to the left. *Moment of truth.* Water spurted out, cold drops landing on her shoulders and arm. Beth shrieked, a laugh bubbling up as she tried to dash away from the freezing onslaught. But in doing so, she nearly ran over the man who'd slipped in behind. Tristan placed a comforting palm to her back, and she fell into those blue eyes laughing at her reaction.

"It's cold," she needlessly explained.

"That's to be expected." He shrugged as if unsurprised by anything, but then he paused and impishly stared down at her. Water spurted out of the showerhead, picking up steam as it bounded about in their cozy tiled grotto. Beth's shoulder took some of the brunt, her poor arm serving as the thermometer, but a few of the drops beaded up on his face. The stern expression softened, the tension across his cheeks and forehead fading to a surprising tenderness in the hot steam.

"Ah," she called, having to drag herself away from tasting the dew on his lips. "It's getting warmer." Walking forward, her hands extended until the palms pressed to the wall, she gave in to the siren's call of the shower. All the sweat and fear from the ice skating debacle washed down the drain. Her skin—frozen by the lake and the terror of shattering through ice—heated as the water kissed her body.

Beth rolled her hands back across her face, dousing her hair in the shower's stream when she heard a choking sound. She found Tristan paralyzed where he stood. While the water beaded up across every curve of her exposed skin and saturated her bra and panties, only a few drops struck his underwear. And…he was certainly not lacking in the shorts-filling department. Giddiness surged through her veins and Beth snapped her sight to his feet.

Oh, come on, stop blushing and darting your gaze away. When are you ever going to see him again? That fact drew a sour turn to her stomach, but she couldn't run from the logic either.

"Here." Beth reached out to pick up his hand and tugged him closer. Tristan skidded on his toes as if he really expected to just stand inside with her without getting wet. In pulling him closer to the shower, Beth forgot to step away. Tristan smacked his right palm into the wall, his body pinning hers directly under the fall of water.

Bending his head to become her personal umbrella, he took the brunt of the spray to his back. Rivulets streamed from his scalp down the sides of his face as he stared, eye to eye with her. So close, her skin warmed from him and not the last vestiges of the hot water. His forehead nearly crested against hers, Tristan pressed his free hand between their bodies as Beth let it go.

"You are..." Tristan grappled for words, his breaths scrambling like a man straining off a cliff's edge. Raising his fallen palm, he hovered it less than a centimeter above her drenched body. As he skirted around her hip and trailed deeper to her waist, she shivered at the electricity sparking between them. He didn't touch her, but the heat of his body, the rising scent of his masculine form, the beading of water against their skin set her off.

Panting and shivering, Beth clenched her toes in anticipation of his palm touching her. Of it parting through the fall of rain to grip her arm, the hand tugging her to his lips. But Tristan held off, his gaze never leaving hers, and she returned the laser focus as he circled up around the edge of her bust.

"I can't stop," he whispered, ignoring the nipple straining through her waterlogged bra. Swerving along her shoulder, he slowly walked the tip of his fore and index fingers across her narrow collarbone, every touch of his finger matching her rising heartbeat.

At the hollow of her throat, he rested his fingers before they began to ascend her jaw. From the tip of her wide chin, he glided the back of his forefinger, slicing off every water droplet on the way. "Tell me to stop." His paused his finger. "And I will."

Launching on her tiptoes, Beth circled both her arms around the back of his neck. "I can't do that," she said just before guiding his lips to hers. This was no sweet and uncertain kiss. Tongues spun in time with one another, lips sucked upon lips, and they drank of each other as they abandoned all pretense of civility.

Tristan surged forward. With the imaginary forcefield broken by her consent, he wrapped his hand around her hip. Where on the ice it'd been cautious and chaste, now it was a lascivious massage. He pulsed his fingers deep into the side of her buttock while his thumb wrapped the band of her panties around itself.

God! When he tugged on that elastic, Beth gasped into his mouth. Water struck the intimate skin exposed to the world, sending her heart racing. He paused, darting his gaze to her out of concern, but she knotted her hands through his hair and tugged him tighter to her. They slipped in the rising water but landed against the shower's wall. Tristan spun with her, placing them both on equal footing into the water's path. When Beth's back bounced against the shower's tile with no faucets in the way, Tristan's hands landed on either side of her head for balance.

Both pulled in a cleansing breath, only the sound of their panting and the soothing fall of rain filling the bathroom. Tristan was vulnerable, all his weight in the palms spread across the tile. Most was in the left hand to protect his poor damaged right palm. The one he'd cut in saving her.

Water pulsed against Beth's side, the steaming heat drenching her hair and his. It pressed flat to his forehead like dark copper ribbons, rivulets of water streaming down his cheeks. Tristan's mouth fell agape to aid him in breathing air instead of water. Every gasp and sputter puffed against Beth's cheeks, her body delighting in the sounds of the man turning primal.

Slowly, she reached out to place her palm on the pale chest before her. Hotter than the hearth, the heat radiated up her arm and straight down to her thighs. With Tristan running his forehead against hers, she drew her fingers downward. They tumbled in and out of the ribs, his spry body revealed in its near fullness to her. Almost no fat touched his midsection, the abs of a naturally skinny four-pack.

Tristan gulped when she circled her finger around his belly button, Beth finding delight in the downy treasure trail. Hungry for more, she drew the tip of her finger clear across the straights of his waistband. At the sharp hipbone, she knotted the elastic in her hand and tugged it down. Not far—only an inch of stark white skin was revealed—but Tristan moaned.

As he pressed his hips closer, the engorging bulge glanced against her belly as he tipped her head back. Water tried to leech into her mouth, but he cut it off with his lips. Rolling his hands around the back of her chest, he grabbed the fussy bra band. The pads of his hands dug into her spine as he fought against the insipid thing. When the taut elastic gave, Tristan released a small whoop of triumph and he tugged the freed bra off.

Water beaded up her small bust, the falling shower quickly finding the skin freed to the world. Beth pulled in a breath, well aware of what she lacked up top or below. As Tristan tossed the unwanted bra to the bathroom floor, she stared down at her empty cleavage, every mole and freckle amplified by the droplets.

This is me. Do you accept it?

Beth gazed up at him and he cupped both palms over her tiny breasts. When he suckered his lips to her neck, Beth gasped as every tender flutter and nip of his teeth drove straight to her core. When his gentle kneading of her breasts became a stroking of her nipples, she moaned in his ear.

Tristan shuddered, no doubt overwhelmed by her accidental shouting, but he smiled. "Good?"

"Beyond," she gasped, uncertain if full sentences were possible.

Every slick of his fingers against her soaked skin ignited her desire. Tristan's wry lips, once so solemn and curt, softened. Climbing up her neck with his kisses, he worked his way to her ear. All the while, he drew unending pleasure from her breasts with his hands.

Beth's toes curled, her breath trapped in her lungs as she ached for his touch. He found his way to her earlobe with his lips, and, as he pulled it in between his teeth, he rolled both her nipples between his fingers.

"Holy shit," she gasped. Both her hands launched out to grab on to a lifeline as her body revved up from his expert ministrations. It wasn't the screw-cap approach of a young man, but the graceful strokes of a maestro. A whimper rising up her throat, Beth ached for him to never stop, while simultaneously fearing she could take no more. She curled her hands around his back, at his boxer-briefs' waistband, and dug them deep.

Tristan's tight control snapped, incoherent gasps sputtering into her ear. While he prayed for salvation, Beth kneaded against the taut butt cheeks below her palms. Each reach slid his underwear lower and lower. With every stretch of her toes, her belly bounded into the powerful instrument concealed below his soaked gray briefs.

"Please," the once-taciturn man begged her, "take them off."

Smiling from her lips clear down to the center of her being, Beth tugged the clingy underwear down. The boxer-briefs didn't fall far, but they didn't have to. In an instant, his dick was freed. It surged out of the gate fully cocked, but quickly nestled safely against her lower belly. When the head and half of the shaft glided across her water-soaked skin, Beth gulped. How fantastic would that feel where it belonged?

Tristan shook down the errant boxer-briefs, leaving them to float on the rising shower water. Grabbing her hips, he tugged her to him, Beth shocked at the hunger and force. "Your turn," he growled, the look in his eyes telling her he'd shred her panties with his fingernails if he could.

Nodding vehemently that he'd best get to it, Beth placed her hands on his shoulders as Tristan pulled her drenched panties off. He kept one palm on her hip, flexing his pad against the curve, while the other tugged the clingy cotton down.

Slowly, he dipped to one knee while pulling on her underwear. His gaze never leaving hers, Tristan placed tender kisses first between her breasts, then down her midsection.

"God," Beth gasped, flexing her palms through his hair. She rustled the damp locks apart, prepared to guide the man at her feet when he reached the edge of her pubic hair.

The kisses pausing, Beth gulped at the realization. Was he put off by her not shaving? Should she have told him to keep the underwear on and shove them aside?

He planted his chin into the sparse but coarse black hair and beamed up at her. Like the fairytale of Cinderella, Tristan helped to lift her foot, freeing her of the drudgery of underwear.

"That," Beth gulped, wiping off her face, "that's both of…"

Tristan launched to his feet, grabbing her ass, hefting Beth clean off the tile. She yelped in shock, slotting her legs around his thin hips as he took her in his arms. When her back splattered against the wall for leverage, he plunged his lips to hers, scattering kisses across her mouth. Beth's mind fogged as she savored his cock passing against her stretching opening. He didn't force himself in, nor was she in a position to guide, but that hot, smooth crown kept gliding against her lower lips. Every pass drove her wild, her hips straining to try and extend her legs as far as possible.

God, she wanted him in her.

"Are you…?" Tristan gasped, his forehead crashing to hers as he steadied himself.

Was she what? *Ready? Yes! Wanting him? Fuck yes!*

Oh. Birth control. Right. The commonsense fairy tried to bean Beth in the head. She swallowed, her flushed lips opening to tell him when icy rain sizzled down her breasts. Gasping at the intrusion, Beth flinched as the freezing water fell from the shower head. Whatever last dregs of heat they'd had had been long stolen by the blackout, leaving them twisting to avoid the assault.

Her feet slipped from his hips, splashing the lukewarm water up their bodies as both Beth and Tristan reached to shut off the jet. They haphazardly slapped at the dial, one of them finally silencing the freezing attack. Drenched, panting for breath, and naked, they stared first at the dribbling shower head and slowly turned to each other.

What am I thinking?

What's he thinking?

We shouldn't do this.

We can't do this?

Both of them leaped together. Tristan's lips found hers at the same moment as Beth moved to him. He tumbled his wet and cooling hands around her waist, trying to pull her body flush to his. She scrabbled onto her toes, attempting to keep the hot kisses coursing down her body while also moving with him.

They slipped out of the shower's standing water into the dry bathroom. Beth's toes tangled in that workhorse pink blouse while Tristan kicked into his jeans. She heard the jangling sound of keys not needed in the past three days, and he broke from their kiss.

With a smirk, he bent over and fished around in the pocket of his pants. Beth quirked her head, watching at first in curiosity, but then the light striking his body drew her in. Those strong thighs hardened to granite as he squatted, his pale skin shining like diamonds from the lingering shower. After securing something in his palm, Tristan beamed up at her and rose to his towering height.

Kissing Beth with a volcano's worth of heat, he grabbed her hand with his free one and led them into the bedroom. The chill tried to strike her wet skin, but Tristan wouldn't hear of it. His body enveloped hers even as they stumbled backward through the open bedroom door. He swept an arm over the small of her back, pinning her chest to his while he pivoted.

Their lips wouldn't break, both kissing as if fearing what stopping could cause. *Questions. Discussions.* A long litany of reasons why this couldn't proceed.

"Gah!" he gasped, his shock at running the bottom edge of his ass into the bed sputtering against Beth's tender lips. She snorted a laugh at both the surprise in his voice and the rising smile as he too realized his error.

"We…" Tristan drew his palm to her cheek, the same one he'd sliced apart in saving her. She winced at the vengeful line of red but curled into his sweet hold. "We could stop."

"I suppose so." Her voice was devoid of all emotion, Beth draining it for fear of the vulgar want rampaging through her body. She breathed in the scent of the man wrapped around her. Beyond the soapy sandalwood and nervous coffee was a musk so delectable she could almost taste it beading on her skin. *Desire.*

"Do you want to stop?" he asked, his words calm and collected even as his engorged dick pulsed against her belly.

Pulling in a slow breath, Beth tried to weigh every possibility, to stare into the future as if she was some goddess gifted with prophecy. There weren't many roads leading to this being wise. Almost none, she'd guess. *Agree to end it. To walk away with a nervous jitter to your legs, a pounding ache in your loins, and questions of what might have been. That would be best.*

Smirking, she stared through the gray-white shadows of the darkened bedroom, directly into Tristan's deep blues. "No," Beth declared, diving for his lips.

Tristan clamped onto her ass, clinging tight to the flesh and lifting her higher and higher into the air.

Reaching out, Beth was about to hook a knee to the bed when Tristan spun fully in place.

She twisted through the air, revolving until she was the one with her back to the bed. Opening his hands, Beth fell to the raised mattress, her body bouncing along with her laugh. "You gave me an axel," she giggled.

It took a moment for the reference to strike through Tristan's hunger, but he too smiled. "And it's much easier to do in the bedroom than on the ice." He burrowed his hands into the mattress beside her hips, pushing Beth's forehead back with his to accommodate his feverish kisses.

She began to slide back on the waiting bed, but when Tristan remained in place, Beth drew her fingers up his wrist. Tugging, she thought he'd follow suit, but the man remained a stone guardian. Abandoning her mouth, he whispered in her ear, "I want you here."

Burning his gaze into her, Tristan abandoned the mattress, leaving behind the silver wrapper he'd excised from his jeans. *Smart.* But Beth didn't have time to consider the luck of a prophylactic being in reach as he drew both hands along the outside of her thighs and took a knee.

A gulp rose in her throat as she realized he wasn't planning on screwing her while standing. As Tristan fell to his knees as if in obeisance to her, he circled a slow strum of his fingers from outside her thighs, down her calves and around her ankles. All the while, he watched as she struggled to funnel air to her lungs.

"Do you—?"

Beth parted her thighs open wide, bringing a laugh to the man before he could finish his question. As he nuzzled his cheek against the right side of her inner thigh, a static charge rose from his patchwork scruff. Not against her skin, but the sparks carried up through her body. The lightning struck deeper and deeper into her core, causing Beth to tremble in anticipation. He drew closer, trailing kisses up her leg to the crease of her thigh.

With his tongue, Tristan lapped from the bottom of her folds clear to heaven. Not expecting him to leap forward so fast, Beth cried out in shock, digging her fingers into his hair. Reading the signs correctly, he lapped that acerbic tongue in figure eights all along her clitoral hood and down her labia. Each turn of slick heat washed another wave of pleasure against her core.

Where before her orgasm had been sparking to go off at a touch, now it was ebbing and flowing like the tide. When Tristan rose to tap the point of his tongue directly on her clit, Beth gasped, trying to clench inward, but the orgasm slipped away. Aching for more, she hooked her legs over his shoulders. All the while, he curled his fingers around her ankle, forming a cuff with his wide hand.

The orgasm tide returned, its crest rising higher than ever before. Clenching her toes, Beth leaned back as her heartbeat thundered all the way up to her hair. But once again, it wouldn't break, the wave slipping away to the tantalizing kisses licking her closer to heaven. To think, those lips that had serenaded countless girls in their bedrooms, that had thrilled arenas and rocked charts, were licking and sucking her to bliss.

Squealing at the mounting pressure rising in her body, Beth tipped backward to lie on the silky coverlet. Breath panted down her throat, but not enough to quench the flames rising through her veins. A moan rumbled from Tristan's lips, causing her to buck against him.

Quickly, he hooked his arms around her thighs and tugged Beth to him. As she felt herself slipping, the duvet sliding to the floor, Tristan suckered his mouth around her. He flitted a patter song against her clit while his lips spread a warmth across her entire being.

Rising from her depths, the orgasm wave towered thirty, forty, fifty feet high. She clung by her clenched toes, arms outstretched to claw for a handhold as it reached its aching crescendo. All the blood rushed to her ears, blanketing away the sounds of sex. Spots of gold glittered across her vision, blinding her to the sight of Tristan on his knees. All Beth knew was the rush of pleasure reverberating across her body. She wanted to stay in that cocoon, to swaddle herself in the flying freedom of her body.

The power chord struck hard, Beth gasping incoherently as she folded in on herself. Her hands dug tight to Tristan's head, holding him prisoner between her thighs as she clung to the orgasm. God, her head was floating, her lips numb from the panting. She couldn't think, Tristan forced to dig himself out of her crumpled-in ball.

There was a quirk in his eyebrow, his gaze stripping her. As he rose from the depths of her thighs, all she could focus on were those sapphire blues and the fallen mahogany hair clinging to his forehead. "I'm guessing that was…?" he began when Beth grabbed his cheeks and kissed him deeply.

Her own arousal smeared across her chin, the taste quickly replaced by Tristan's tongue as they tried to scurry back onto the bed. On the trip up, Beth snatched the condom as if it were a holy relic. All the while, he kept kissing her, cupping her face as if he feared she might vanish.

When she struck the pillows, Beth paused, both of them leaning up, Tristan on his knees astride her hips. She glanced at his cock, which had grown even larger from his eating her out. Dipping his chin down, Tristan worried a hand through his scruff and confessed, "I should warn you it has been some time."

Tugging apart the foil with her fingers, Beth met his gaze as she fished to sheathe him in a protective layer of latex. "I should warn you—" she said, rolling her hands up his back, her nails evoking a gasp. When she gripped his shoulder, she tugged the both of them down to the bed. "—I don't care."

Tristan knocked her thighs apart. Thrusting once, he slipped partially inside her, Beth gasping as he filled her fuller than she'd been in months. Tristan gripped her thigh, guiding the leg to circle around his hip as he leaned down. He crested his forehead over hers and his trembling lips spoke sacrilegious prayers as he gently worked his way deeper inside.

Latching on to the nape of his neck, Beth tipped her head to kiss him and hissed in pain. That damn lump she'd put on her skull struck the pillow's edge. Tristan paused, his face twisting in concern, but she smiled wide and adjusted away from the bump.

Even buried nearly to the hilt, Tristan waited. He kept stroking the leg she had wrapped around him, Beth lifting the other to envelop that tight waist. His sharp hips prodded into her thighs and her heels rested on the buttocks she wanted to feel flexing. But he remained holding himself upon that cliff.

Rising off the pillow, Beth breathed in his ear, "I want you to fuck me until I see stars."

A solitary laugh broke from his lips and he turned them to her. His hot breath curled across her cheek as Tristan whispered, "Gladly."

In an instant, the shy, cautious man transformed into a ferocious Casanova. Tristan thrust a steady beat, each push of his hips reaching deeper and deeper. Beth happily grabbed on for the ride, her sight slipping closed as she savored in the rising swell of another buried orgasm. Each pulse drove her closer to release, her spine arcing to meet him as her legs tugged her onto him.

"Damn it!" she cried, flinching at her cursed bruise once again thrusting into the pillow.

"What?" Tristan swallowed, his breath panting as he struggled to keep himself coherent and also pounding her to the stars. "What's wrong?" The answer came to him from Beth trying to rub away the bruise. She didn't want him to stop, but the constant jab of pain wasn't exactly a turn-on. Not that kind, anyway.

"Here." He bent down, that glorious cock trying to slide free of her hold. Grabbing her shoulders, Tristan hefted her up. Not far, perhaps a forty-five-degree angle from the bed and his still pulsing penis. With one hand wrapped around her lower spine for support, Tristan leaned back. He reached to keep himself steady, the thrusts faster but shallower by default.

Sweat dripped down Beth's breasts, her face heating to a thousand degrees from the passion rising between them. She watched his face struggling to maintain composure as the pleasure of her body swarmed his. A flush burst across his cheeks, reddening them to sunburn levels as he increased his thrusting.

"Damn," Tristan gasped. "Damn, damn, damn it!" The hands switched, his left cupping her back and the right...

She caught the small trickle of blood welling up from his wound. Even bleeding, he wouldn't stop. It was Beth who reached out to hold his hips and still him.

Fractured blue eyes snapped open, hunting wildly for the cause of his abrupt halt. When Tristan focused on her, she smiled almost sarcastically at how foolish both of them were. "My turn," she said, lifting off him. A gasp erupted from him at the loss, but she was fast to flip him onto his back and climb over his reclining body.

"This makes far more sense," she explained, even as the wounded look grew to a knowing smile. Tristan swept his palm over her hip, gliding his fingers against her glistening belly. With certainty in her veins, Beth straddled him and began the rhythm herself.

She was no musician. Beth couldn't keep a beat to save her life, but Tristan didn't seem to mind. His head tipped back into the pillow, no goose egg to stop him. Quickly, both palms swept across her bounding tits. Tweaking her nipples, Tristan sent shudders of electricity racing down Beth's spine as he met her thrust for thrust.

"Take me," Tristan whispered between his moans, his hips rising off the bed. Reverse planking, he tried to burrow deeper into her, deeper than even Beth thought she could manage. But fuck, was it good.

"Take all of me." He slapped his hands to her hips, raising and lowering her to his hungry beat. Beth scrambled to hang on, her body quivering down to her knees as she leaned back. In an instant, that thrusting cock pulsed against her G-spot and she was gone yet again.

Sound remained, thank God, as she could hear both her cries of joy and Tristan responding with a guttural moan of satisfaction. But her vision grew white as the orgasm racked her body, Beth gripping to the man still thrusting patiently into her. He had to know she'd succumbed, her cunt constricting around what brought it such pleasure.

"Gladly," Beth whispered. Her sight returned just as Tristan tipped over into his own orgasm. His face shuddered, the lips lifting into an almost sneer-smile while his eyes rolled clean into the back of his head. Beth's heart quickened at his pleasure-filled face, at how undone he let himself become in her presence.

The wild sight slowly softened to that of the cultured man she knew. With a laugh, he abandoned her hips to swipe the sex-sweat off his forehead. Wincing, he asked, "You're… Your head?"

She winced, brushing back her soaked and mussed hair. When she touched the bruise, a burst of pain knocked into the back of her head. "I don't know why I did that," she chastised herself, before glancing down to the right hand cupping her. "Your hand?"

Tristan tugged it off her. There was no bloodstain left behind, but he still frowned at the wound that really needed a Band-Aid. "Well enough," he answered.

Rising to her knees, Beth slid herself off him. It wasn't easy—even with his orgasm, he didn't seem to be wilting anytime soon. Tristan sat up, using his elbows for leverage. They gasped together, Beth trying to breathe in air that wasn't bulging with sweat and sex. But try as hard as she might to ignore what had happened, neither could deny it.

"So," Tristan whispered, pushing her fallen hair back behind her ear. His palm lingered, curling down her shoulder, his fingers kissing with a light touch. Did he regret it? Did he despise himself for giving in? Did he despise her for not stopping it?

Straining his neck in a stretch, Tristan asked nonchalantly, "How was it?"

"Encore," she called, raising both her hands to clap. "Encore!"

Laughing, Tristan nuzzled her neck, his breath whispering against her skin. "Happy to oblige."

Chapter Fifteen

Don't sleep.

It'd been an easy order to follow when pain thundered up through her eyeballs. But curled under the warm blankets against the furnace of his body, Beth kept drifting away. She'd be awakened by a gentle shake each time, Tristan staring down at her as the afternoon slipped to nightfall. Shadows crept across the dark bedroom, attempting to lull her down into their depths, but he wouldn't let her fall.

They had left the bedroom at one point, rummaging for that box of crackers as sustenance. It was no strawberries and cream, but the energy helped tremendously as they somehow found their way right back to that oversized bed. Afterward, Beth tried to dig in to her research books, regretting not bringing some light reading for herself, while Tristan had to stretch his legs. His taut and overworked legs.

Huddling under the blanket to try to escape the draft whistling through cracks between the logs, Beth glanced to the chair at the vanity. The one where she'd put the screws to him. *Hm…screwing on that? Put a pin in it.*

Piled at the top was Tristan's sweater, torn off long before their shower began. Heat burned up her cheeks as she thought back to those earlier hours. Beth rose from the comfortable bed to tug the cable-knit wool over her shoulders.

Most men's clothing would fall about her body like a bag, often reaching her knees, but this cut was snug around her hips and bust. The waist was loose, the hemline just long enough to skirt her upper thighs. Though the sleeves dangled clear over her hands. *He might be wiry, but the lankiness is a challenge.*

After rolling up the cuffs, Beth eased out of the bedroom. The door remained open, allowing their only light source—the fireplace—to leech in. But as the sun faded to night's embrace, it was difficult to see beyond the corona of the hearth.

Beth headed for her phone, more on instinct than with a plan, when the breath caught in her throat. With only the firelight coating his naked body, Tristan sat on the couch. His head was bent over, the once styled hair scattered from their fun, a hand strumming the guitar resting in his lap. One leg was folded inward, cupping around the guitar as if to protect it. He plucked at a stripped-down song while in his stripped state.

An overwhelming urge to preserve the image sent her dashing for her phone. She snapped a single shot, most of his *bass clef* hidden in the shadows of the guitar. There was a faint silhouette to remind her that lean guys weren't lacking, but mostly she focused on the serenity washed over his face. How his once rigid spine bent his body lower to caress his guitar. How he didn't need his striking gaze to look beautiful.

A rotating bar grayed out her screen, sending the tender picture away. It said it was having trouble updating to the cloud it couldn't find, what with Wi-Fi and all electricity being SOL. Beth told it to try again later when it had some damn signal.

"Checking to see if there's word from the outside world?" Tristan spoke, his voice carrying over the tune.

She silenced her phone and left it on the mantel, which was where he'd hung their underwear to dry. *That's one hell of a way to do laundry.* Smiling like a cat in the sunshine, Beth leaned closer to him. "There's an outside world?" she said, catching his silent lips in a kiss. The laugh at her honest joke bounded against her mouth before he calmed to kiss her properly.

Falling to the cushions, Beth faced him. He raised an eyebrow at her thieving his sweater but didn't say a word. She'd never felt so warm in a single piece of clothing in her life. The scent of his body baked into the wool from the past two days only stirred her attentions deeper.

Just the crackle of the logs and the twangy pluck of guitar strings echoed between them. She rubbed her leg against his, their shins touching as Beth tipped back to let the music swirl around her.

"I don't know that song," she confessed, her ears failing to provide an answer to her brain.

"You wouldn't," he said, "I barely do. I've had the music in my head for…feels like years sometimes, but the lyrics keep eluding me." Tipping his head back, he sang to match his harmony, only la's slipping in for where poetic words should be.

"Another good reason to aim for a Christmas album first," Beth threw out, then winced as his sight homed in on her.

She expected a scoff, perhaps a frown, but a knowing smile wound about his lips. "A good point. A very good point. The first original song after nearly a decade since recording one and I fear..." His words faded but the song picked up steam. There seemed to be a rising tempo in the middle of it, or perhaps Tristan wasn't certain what he wanted it to be yet. A forlorn melody for loss or a happy dance tune for gain?

"We're near strangers," he said carefully as if testing to see her reaction.

"Knowing each other for three days, I'd say that makes us acquaintances."

A laugh rolled from the side of his tempting lips. "Associates."

"Social-media friends."

"Oh, I don't know. That seems a bridge too far." Tristan laughed.

"Ships in the night," Beth threw out, her brain too trapped in the pink cloud to drum up more synonyms for the game. To her surprise, the man who'd prided himself on his aloofness glanced down.

The music stilled and he said, "I pray it's more than that."

Pulling in a breath at the raw emotion wafting in his words, she nodded. "Me too."

"You." Tristan picked back up the music but seemed to switch the tune. "Were you ever a Harty-throb?"

Beth snickered, shaking her head. "No."

"No poster on the bedroom wall?"

Shrugging, she stretched her arms out to admit, "What bedroom wall? I didn't have one I could even legally put tape on until after college."

"Fair point." The smile darted around his lips, showing off his sparkling teeth. "I suppose I just…" His words fell away as he kept up the song, his fingers playing like it was burned into his memory for an eternity.

Beth scooted closer, sliding her hand up and down his shin. "Worried I'm only into you for the fame?"

"The expectations built from a poster fifteen years old and…enhanced—they're not easy to shake." He lifted his broken eyes, his face begging for understanding.

He, the svelte, patrician songwriter who'd come onto the scene when all boys were expected to have six-packs was worried that she wouldn't appreciate the reality. Gliding her hand back up his thigh, Beth found that glorious stomach and those abs weighing on him. Pooched in his sit, it bore the signs of adulthood with a touch of sagging, but that meant there were years to it. Experiences. Stories.

"Reality is far better than two-dimensional fantasy," she breathed, rising on her knees. He dropped his hands from the guitar to cup her under his sweater. Kissing him as if she'd never get enough, Beth pressed her chest to his bare one while scooping her palm to his shoulder.

Beth broke away, panting as she breathed in the masculine heat of Tristan's body. At this rate, she was going to wear him down to a puddle, but a satisfied one. Still, as she drew her fingers to the rising standing ovation, Beth wondered how many condoms were left.

"We don't need this." She moved to pluck the guitar off his lap, but Tristan reached for it.

"Wait, wait." While he held it in his arms, he darted a guilty look to her. She couldn't be mad—he'd put in a lot of exhausting work over the day—but she couldn't escape the disappointment either. Time was not on their side.

Tristan extended the guitar above him with one hand and curled the other over her hip. "Here," he said while pulling Beth into his lap. Just as before, when he'd tried to teach her how to play, she fit perfectly between his thighs. Though, this time she savored the stiff cock prodding against her spine.

When the guitar slotted into her lap, Beth looked over her shoulder. "What am I going to play this time?"

"You're not," Tristan said and took up the tune. This one Beth knew in an instant, as did every girl who'd worn scrunchies and watched TRL after school. She rested her fingers on the top of the guitar's body, uncertain where to go as he played with purpose.

"You recognize it?" he asked while seeming to know she did.

"*My Half,* your...song." Beth didn't want to belabor how it was his best-known one, as he seemed to hate that fact.

"It's not a love song as everyone assumes. Well, not a romantic love song, anyway." Tristan waited for that idea to bubble in her brain, Beth trying to remember the lyrics. "It's for my sister. I had a twin sister."

"Had?"

She felt his nose burrow through her hair, Tristan careful to avoid the lump as he pulled Beth tighter into his grip. Rather than dwell on the past tense of his statement, he said, "Tabitha and I were inseparable from day one. The Harty Terrors, our babysitters called us. We'd always try to trick people into thinking we were the other one."

"Had to be hard to pull off." *With the other half being a girl.*

"Not really. She'd keep her hair short, or we'd wear hats. I think people mostly looked at the clothes anyway. God, she loved putting me in the pink tutus our great aunt would send her. And I'd always go along with it because Tabby swore it'd be funny."

Beth laughed along with him at the memory, her brain trying to conjure the image of stern Tristan in something so frilly. But in doing so, it slipped, placing the lean body into a black leotard, his graceful limbs forever at his full command.

"There was an accident," Tristan said, yanking Beth back to reality hard. "A truck t-boned us. Tabby, she…she always took the left side in the back, me the right. But that day, that day we switched. I walked away and she…" His tear-stained voice struggled to form the words. Beth parted her hands over the top of his fingers as if she was directing the music.

Pulling in a breath, Tristan gasped out, "She didn't. For a long time, I thought it was wrong. God got it wrong. Tabby was the real star, everyone knew it. Skilled at the piano, much better voice. Hilarious and charismatic, born for the spotlight. But all that was left was me and blood-stained glass."

Beth spun on his lap, her palm curling to his cheek. The guitar thudded with a twang to the couch as Tristan embraced her. Salty tears dripped to her hand, Beth ignoring them as she tried to focus on the man ripping himself to the core before her.

Pulling in a breath that stung of glass, Beth said, "Survivor's guilt is…" Images flashed through her mind, not of the war-torn refugees fleeing from the missiles, but the families after. When they'd been washed, dressed, fed, covered in a shell of normalcy. But underneath they were screaming, one half begging to move on, the other unable to leave.

"I know, I've heard that quite often. A few discount therapists here, some higher-degreed ones later. Mostly after Sasha."

That must have broken him, to carry so much blame in his heart only to lose another girl he thought it was his job to protect. No wonder he'd fled from not only celebrity and California but music in general.

Beth wrapped her hands around him, tugging Tristan deeper into her embrace. She wanted to comfort him, to soothe away the years of pain, but there was little a near-stranger could do. Even his closest friends and family seemed to struggle with it.

Why is he revealing this?

"I thought that…" he whispered, his forehead nestled against her neck. Each puff of breath curled down the wide neckline of the borrowed sweater. "You probably wanted to know." As he raised his cut hand, the white bandage she'd finally knotted around it visible, a wagon-load of truth struck her.

This had nothing to do with the song. It was a symptom. It was his cracking when the ice did, that fire of panic that feared she might be consumed the same as his sister. Same as Sasha. For someone he'd only known for three days.

Tristan rose from her forced hug, using his wounded hand to try to tame his wild hair. It was almost impossible after it had dried in a haphazard fashion, but Beth leaned closer to help. She wasn't a settler, had forever chased that next spark of interest in her younger days. Trained to hide her emotions when she'd learned how to tie her shoes, she had no true self to show. Other people did the confessing—to her father, to her. *That's what being a good interviewer is, removing yourself from the subject as much as possible.*

But she'd told him things about herself she hadn't whispered to anyone. Only Madeline knew about the book, Beth's father trying to change the subject whenever she broached it. And about her mother. God, she hadn't thought of her mother in years. Certainly not the pain, the fear that Beth was tainted. *Forever tagged as the child then woman that no one could want.*

Why did you tell him?

"So now you know. Sorry." Tristan winced as if he was trying to hide away. Even while naked, his shell struggled to reform, like climbing inside a statue of himself. Marble never cried. "The song, I mean. It, um, puts people off to learn the truth."

Beth smiled. "It's beautiful."

His eyes opened wide in shock, the blue depths glimmering by firelight. "What is?"

"Your song," she explained, fearing he thought she was referring to his pain or loss. "The truth, hearing it and the depth, it makes…it makes it more beautiful, not less."

Beth bent over to pick up the guitar. Tristan brushed his fingers against her back until she scooted into his lap. His warm chest supported her, the arms slotting around her body as she situated the guitar. "How about you teach me how to play it?"

Tristan leaned closer, hot breath tickling down the nape of her neck. His "It'll take a while" admitted to how novice she was. If he'd said as such upon their first meeting, Beth would have ripped into him about his sometimes rudimentary poetry. Now, after just two days of peeling back the protective layers, she snuggled against him.

Tipping her head up so she could stare along the line of his jaw, she said, "We have all night."

* * * *

To his surprise, Beth was deadly serious about learning his song. With only the fire to keep time, he had no idea how much passed with his legs enveloped around hers and her warm body leaning against his chest, but he'd guess at least an hour. While the occasional butchering of a song he knew inside and out would bring a flinch to his face, the adorable cursing from the woman holding the strings made him smile.

"Damn it," she muttered for the hundredth time, restarting the tune once again as if she'd sworn on her own grave that she'd get through it without a dropped note. A foolish endeavor as there was a guitar solo in the middle that he hadn't taught her, but Tristan wrapped his forearm around her waist and nuzzled the back of her neck. The scent of the forest rested in her hair, pine trees and crackling bonfires, of Christmas in the mountains.

"Mmm." The strumming slowed, Beth leaning back into him. He dodged to avoid her bump, which thankfully seemed to be deflating. "Is my teacher not paying attention?"

Tristan trickled his fingers from the warm wool of his sweater piled around her belly down to the naked thighs below. There wasn't much flush skin to find, the rest cut off by his guitar, but the warm pull intoxicated him. "I am enraptured," he whispered against her nape and goosebumps pricked off her thigh against his resting fingers.

"Good, because I'm going to get this," she assured him while beginning once again. Beyond Tristan's natural abhorrence of singing when not at work, the fact that he'd have had to warble the same first verse endlessly kept his lips shut. There was also the delight of pressing said lips to her shoulders, often using his chin to expose the soft flesh below his cruel sweater. His sweater kept her body from him, his guitar her legs. Why were his own possessions in league against him?

Chuckling at the thought, he glanced to the crackling fire. Her lacy bra and panties dangled off the mantel like stockings waiting to be filled by jolly St. Nick. He'd certainly like to fill her panties three hundred and sixty-five days a year.

Fuck's sake, Harty. What is wrong with you?

Chastised by his own conscience, Tristan tried to focus on the music, but his thoughts of her glistening ass cupped in his hands had an unsurprising effect. Rising as if it intended to strike the stars, his dick found itself ensnared between his thighs and said tempting derriere.

There were two options available to him—release his grip upon her body and pull himself free, or try to picture his old music teacher Mrs. Bellheim in a bikini. Tristan chose avenue three and slid Beth forward on the couch.

"What are you…?" she stuttered, clearly mad about losing the song, when he guided her back. As her rounded cheeks cupped against his erection, she said, "Oh." Tristan could hear the blush in her words even if the physical evidence was hidden by that damnable sweater.

While there were few sights sexier than a woman fresh from bed and dressed in only his long sweater, he wished he could remove said obstacle and toss it onto the fire.

Her panties were on the mantel.

A lascivious grin wrapped around his lips as he curled his left hand over the body of the guitar. The right found itself at the apex of her thighs, waiting for an invitation inside. "What are you doing?" Beth asked, annoyance in her tone, but as he began to stroke his fingers back across her pubic hair, her breathing increased to a pant.

Placing his chin on her shoulder, he said, "Helping."

"I can do this," she insisted, even as he felt the gates to heaven cracking open.

"Of that, I have no doubt," Tristan purred, his words forming kisses against her neck. "But I'd really enjoy"—he jerked once with his hips, reminding her of the effect she had on him—"fingering along with you."

"That..." Beth gulped, her beautiful head jerking to a fast nod. "I'd love that."

"Begin with tab three," he said. His left hand was on auto-pilot, trailing along to match Beth's haphazard tempo. His right hand held his full attention, Tristan gliding his fingers back and forth atop the crest of her thighs. Was it his imagination, or were they quivering?

To his surprise, Beth's quick lesson stuck, her notes keeping him on his toes. As she shifted to the chorus, Tristan slipped a finger straight down through her slit. Curling it back in, he dipped the tip inside, soaking it in her rising wetness before circling around the aroused lips pressing against him.

Gasping, Beth dropped a note, her fingers scrabbling to keep up just as Tristan glissaded to her clit. That deserved all the attention in the world. Smoothing over the hood, he took his time savoring the rising pulse of the pleasure entrusted to his care. A moan from deep in her chest did wonders for his self-esteem, but it did throw off the song again.

Slowing his left hand, Tristan whispered, "Best be careful."

"Oh?" Beth gulped, her body trying to rub against his exploring fingers in the tight quarters.

"Dropping a note would lead to punishment by my teacher," he said, pressing kisses back and forth across the nape of her neck, all while keeping both his hands busy.

"God," Beth gasped, struggling to shift down the neck of the guitar in time as he ramped up his trilling. The gentle swirls were increasing in tempo, the panting bouncing her ass against his straining cock. One or both of the sensations caused her to drop her hand fully from the guitar, Beth crying incoherently as he dipped back in for another turn.

"So..." She shivered as the final notes of the guitar rang out through the cabin. Swallowing twice more, she looked upon him. "Do you intend to punish me?"

It was Tristan's turn to gasp, her question freezing him as he churned over the possibility. Hurting her was...he never wished to do such a thing. But if she enjoyed it? "Would you want me to?" he asked, his mouth dry even as he dove to the wettest place on earth.

Beth's unrestrained moans and gasps provided a distraction, Tristan dipping his mouth to suck on her shoulder. The bite was little more than a pinch, but she clamped tight around his finger, her body trembling. "Perhaps another time," she admitted, the words struggling to escape as he danced his fingers up and down her thighs.

Pivoting her head, she stared deep into his wild expression. "When I really deserve it."

Holy hell.

Tristan pulled his hand from the guitar and dove under his own sweater across her warm body. Gliding it up her trembling belly, he curled his hungry palm and kneaded into her breast. As her head dropped back to his shoulder, Beth's exquisite eyes shut in bliss while he strummed her nipple. All the while she tried to grind on his fingers, the index drifting from her clit to inside. She strained to open her legs wider to let him dive deeper, but they were trapped between his.

Raising his leg from the couch, Tristan twisted his calf around Beth's and pulled. Her cry of surprise was quickly overrun by a moan as he extended both legs outward. Now he had more than enough room. While plunging first one, then two fingers inside, he danced his thumb against her clit. All the while, he cupped one breast then the other, darting across her nipples in an unending chase.

Beth squirmed to try to match his pattern, their locked-in legs sinking toward the floor to drag their bodies with them, but he wouldn't hear of it. "God, God," she babbled, raising her hand from the couch to rustle through his hair. She dug her fingers in, pulling him to her whims.

Dipping down with her yank, Tristan placed another kiss to her shoulder, circling a figure eight over her clit with his thumb.

"Please, please. Fuck, I love that callus!" Beth cried while rocking her hips with him.

Just as he plunged his fingers as deep as they could reach, he bit her shoulder. A hiss rocketed through Beth's lungs, her nipples straining from between his pinch as she pleaded for more. Or relief. Or salvation. He couldn't tell as most of it was incoherent.

"Damn, damn, damn," she whispered, her breath whiffling as she tipped back against him. In an instant, her entire body crumpled inward, her cunt pulsing around his fingers. He slipped out, resting his hand on her thigh as Beth succumbed to her orgasm. All the while she babbled like a woman possessed, her abs crunching her in and out as she did sit-ups on his lap.

"Fuckin' hell." Beth finally returned to him, her wild look fading to the warm browns he knew.

Drawing back the hair that had fallen from her convulsions of pleasure, Tristan whispered, "How was that for punishment?"

"I think you're trying to encourage me to fail." She laughed, her face radiant as she abandoned that stalwart guitar and spun to lie on his stomach. God, the feel of her breasts pooling on his naked chest, her belly caressing his groin, reminded him of how hard he'd got strumming her.

Tristan tried to shake it off, focusing on the woman stretched out on him. "I'm afraid my teacher credentials are in question…" He began to laugh it off when she scratched her nails along his thigh. His very naked thigh next to his crotch, all without a stitch of clothing impeding her requests. The firelight danced in her eyes and Beth licked the edge of her lips as she began to slide downward.

He moved to sit up on instinct, as if to follow the draw of her chin down him. All the while, she beamed up at him, daring him to look away, but Tristan couldn't. He was entranced, watching as her lips parted. With the softest whisper of touch, her bottom one lapped around the crown of his cock.

Oh, God! A groan escaped from his lips, the image of her tasting him far more erotic than the light shiver of pleasure from his penis. A puff of hot breath bounded against his cock, Beth finding her undoing of him funny. He wanted to join in, but her tongue lolled out and slicked clear around the tip.

Her heat sent waves crashing up his spine, the wetness driving his hips thrusting out to pursue the promised land. But Beth dipped lower, starting the flat of her tongue at the base. She flitted right above the nest of hair, gliding his tightening skin over the hardening core with just her lips.

Tristan held on for dear life, his toes clenching in anticipation as she climbed ever higher. But, right at the crest, she paused, listening to him suck in breaths as if he'd run ten miles.

Did she want him inside her? That could be a problem.

Why did I only carry two condoms?

Because the chances of being trapped with a gorgeous woman you can't stop fucking for days with no way out seemed rather unlikely. So much for always being prepared. His brain churned through a thousand problems, his tongue falling slack as he tried to work up the nerve to tell Beth it couldn't happen.

Flicking her tongue off her front teeth, she opened wide and plunged him into her mouth.

Fuck! She swirled her tongue around him as she pulled him to the back of her throat. A perfect cacophony of warmth and wetness drove Tristan to bite on his own lip. Every roll of her mouth, Beth twisting her head back and forth to increase the friction, sent him babbling.

A cough caught in her throat, Beth having to break off even as Tristan whimpered at the loss. She slicked her hand around him, using the natural lube to glide down the length of his cock. All the while his leg hung in the air, the thigh straining to keep in the perfect position for the woman bending back down for more.

This time, she moved her hand in sync with her mouth. Both her head and cinched fist rose and fell, her lock tight and perfect. The pleasure built inside as her sucking increased. She switched up her movements, raising her hot mouth as she slipped her hand down, the tension stringing Tristan up like Christmas lights.

He clenched his toes, struggling to think of the least sexy things imaginable. Anything to keep this moment eternal. Then he darted down to the woman bent over his cock, her soft hair brushing his inner thighs, and those freed breasts gliding against his legs.

In an instant, his fight was lost. Tristan, less than gentlemanly, glanced a hand to her cheek to pull her off. Her gaze swung up, almost wounded, until he tipped his pulsing cock back, gave it one last jerk, and transcended into the orgasm.

"Fuck me!" he shouted, shivering as the pleasure arced through his body. Sticky semen propelled clear across his chest, somehow reaching almost to his nipple despite the long and active day.

There wasn't much of a load to catch, his balls giving a warning that they were running on empty. But Tristan didn't care about a little pulse of pain in exchange for the payoff. Beth swiped at her lips, trying to sponge away her saliva, as she stared down at the mess pooling on his chest.

Tipping her head to the side made her beautiful hair cascade off his ransacked sweater. In his pawing, or perhaps her sliding, it'd snagged up, revealing her midriff. "Should I get our lone towel to wipe you off with?"

Tristan flinched, remembering their poor workhorse of a kitchen towel. The last thing it needed was to be sticky with his mess on top of everything else. "We may still need it," was his response.

"Worried I'll be put off by the scent of a little man goo?" Beth cooed. She drew her fingers up and down his thighs, the sensation just on the right side of ticklish. His tongue fell slack, his body wanting to lay down as he gave in to her.

"No." He forced the words out of his exhausted body. "It's me who isn't a fan. Try living your teenage years with a dozen different boys under little adult supervision—or cleaning."

Even Beth shuddered at the thought, Tristan trying to not remember the landmine of stiff socks from his touring days. Though, he'd kill for the stamina of that younger him. This one ached to pass out at her feet, both in worship and exhaustion. But no, she had to stay awake and he had to make certain it was so.

Circling her finger just around the wet spot drying to a flaky mess, Beth shrugged. "There's always the shower."

"The cold shower." He snickered at the thought, but then blushed at remembering the impetus of all of this.

Beth climbed over him, pulling the sweater off her beautiful body. In an instant, Tristan was enchanted by her breasts, the dark tan nipples hardening in the chill. He reached for them as she laid her naked body atop his. Tugging his chin down, she kissed him with the same hot tongue that had pushed him into the stars. With a bat of her eyelashes, she whispered, "I'll keep you warm."

Chapter Sixteen

He should be dragging tail, bemoaning his decaffeinated state, and carrying on as if it were the exhaustion apocalypse. But, despite having remained awake the entire night, Tristan couldn't stop grinning. All right, his smiles were on occasion broken up by scandalous gasps and his lips softened for a taste of hers. God, he could write a song about her lips alone.

Should he?

As the sun crested over the once more new-fallen snow, they both decided it seemed best to dress. This time he watched her delicately slide into her panties, hook her bra on and drape that pale pink silk over her chest. The same one that he'd had pressed against his own for the entire night. Without power, they were reduced to that lost art of conversation, both of them speaking of nothing important but everything vital.

How did three days feel like he'd known her thirty? How did he keep glancing out of the side of his eye, not from fear of her being there, but hoping to find her? How did he become this smitten so fast?

Because you've been alone for too long.

Tristan tried to shake off the cold dose of common sense as he reached out to grab her hand. Finishing the last of her shirt's buttons, Beth slipped to him with her open pants clinging desperately to her hips. He knew the feeling.

"You," she laughed, abandoning her own dressing to run her hands around his body. As she wrapped around his back, pulling herself into his hold, she said, "I thought it was your idea to dress."

"I suppose so," he admitted, regretting whatever fool of logic traipsed about in his brain. Running his lips against her forehead, Tristan kissed her at the beginning of her hair's part. All the while, he tugged on her splayed-open pants. The wily hint of the panties he'd peeled off her sang their siren call, but he pulled the zipper up to silence them.

"Just so you know, I can dress myself," Beth said, even while letting him finish off his work. "But"—her voice dropped into the melting range—"your help is much appreciated."

"Always happy to be of service," he snickered, catching the sweet edge of her lips in a kiss. She puckered them as if they were two kids trading their first real peck behind the swings. It was so wholesome, Tristan was about to lean back when Beth knotted her fingers in his hair. Pulling him deep, it was her tongue that plied apart his lips, her hunger overpowering him.

Don't throw her to the bed. Don't pull her clothes off.

As much as that hunger inside wanted to, he knew it wasn't wise. One, there was a chance of rescue today. Two, he didn't want Barry scolding him in front of Beth and a plethora of plow drivers. And three, he needed to consume a lot more fluids before his testicles desiccated on the metaphorical vine.

Beth seemed to feel the same, her feet falling back to the floor so she landed a head below his chin. Funny, he'd never thought much of short girls, but the way she fit perfectly wrapped between his arms and legs sent his heart racing. Said tiny-but-never-small woman leaned against the bed.

A gulp rattled in Tristan's throat, his mind trying to make the calculations of how badly another ejaculation could cost him. But she reached for the remote left at the side. Pushing some of the buttons, Beth jutted her bottom lip out in a pout. "All this time here and I never get to learn what it does. Cursed power outage."

"It shakes the bed," he said with a shrug as she moved to return the remote. She stared at him, a question hanging inside. "You expected me to not test it out?"

"I'm getting the impression asking you to set a microwave ends in a fire." Beth chuckled. "All push, no manual?"

That wasn't strictly accurate. He could be meticulous if he cared, but curiosity and struggling to not listen to the unknown woman typing on her keyboard had driven him to try. "You know," Tristan whispered, reaching out to hold her hand. Their fingers intertwined, Beth floating over the floor into his arms. As he held her close, he said, "I could make the bed shake for you."

"Mm, don't I know it."

"All you need do—" Tristan drew his fanned-out fingers against her cheek, curling the tips back to rustle through her tamed hair. While he was a bedraggled swamp creature, she'd come out of an all-nighter looking like a fairy princess astride a butterfly. As she tipped her face back, the tiny quirk to her smile increased his rapid heartbeat. Tristan leaned down to finish. "—is ask."

A bright light erupted from the lamp, the bed rumbling off its box springs as the power returned to them. Both glanced up as if a miracle of magic had brought the lights back. "Oh," Beth called, stepping out of his arms. "That's perfect!" She dashed from the bedroom to her once-stilled laptop. The intrepid reporter had to sit cross-legged on the floor, her bare feet tucked under her as she plugged her dying computer into the wall.

With a sigh, Tristan leaned down and silenced the rattling bed. *You didn't want to sleep with her, remember?* That common sense section of his brain tried to argue with the Id that was kicking a proverbial can down the road. *You shouldn't have slept with her at all.*

He flinched at the reminder forever bobbing in the pool of his subconscious. It'd rise every once in a while, trying to rattle him. But then Tristan would glance down at the silky pale skin stretched out across his body and the thought drowned.

As Beth seemed enthralled with whatever needed her, most likely work, as it was technically Monday, Tristan fished for his phone—not for any specific reason. He just wanted to seem busy. Ten missed calls from Barry and a couple of voicemails. He'd even tried texting, no less. No doubt in a panic about something. Tristan dialed up the first voicemail, only for his phone to cry in agony and fall silent.

She glanced up at the sound, a smile highlighting her face as she watched him sigh at technology's failures.

Shaking his head, Tristan lumbered over to plug in his phone.

"All out of juice?" she asked.

"Luckily, that can finally be rectified." He glanced around at the revived lights, a cacophony of them trying to purge the surprisingly blah day outside. When his heart was heavy with regrets, the sky was crystal blue, but when he wanted to fly, it was muck-gray all around them.

So what now, Mr. Harty? That mass of missed calls told him Barry had to be on his way soon. They'd both return to civilization, leaving behind this strangely inviting cabin. *What comes next?*

She had her stories to file, he a half-assed tour and album to put out. That'd keep him on the road, busy. Far too busy to even think of... *Think of what?*

Glancing over his shoulder, he watched Beth rocking on her legs as if music danced through her veins. Her fingers swung wildly above the keys as she closed those heart-stopping eyes to think.

You're thinking of it.

Wondering if...

And what about that article on you? The fact that she is the enemy. Sort of. In league with them, at least. Have you considered that problem?

"Ooh," Beth squealed in delight, interrupting his tortured monologue. "Oh, you have to see this." Spinning around her laptop, she pressed Play on a video of a kitten no bigger than a palm. Its eyes weren't open, but it mewled in impotent anger before a small bottle appeared. Suckling to its heart's content, the kitten flopped down onto its tiny belly and gorged.

"I was worried. Sometimes Mads, she gets ones that are too tiny, that can't make it. Try as hard as you do, even knowing the odds, you can't not care about them." Beth glanced up from the video of the little kitten growing stronger and healthier. "You can't not fall for them."

A flush burst over Tristan's cheeks and he bent his head as if he had to check on his phone at that exact second. In truth, he needed to breathe, to think.

Do you, though?

"My number," he mumbled, raising one hand as if to slap the words away. But he didn't, and glanced to Beth, who must not have heard him fully. "You'd probably need, er, want my number."

"I..." It was her turn to blush and hang her head. She rose from the closed laptop while taking in his request. "I would. Mine, you'd need mine too."

Tristan glanced forlornly down at his phone that was gasping for juice. "Probably best if I give you mine and you call me. I really need a new phone."

A warm smile answered him as Beth pushed a few buttons, then deposited her phone into his hands. The case was an image made up of old newspapers, something he'd scoffed at at first blush but that seemed quintessentially her now. After entering in his private phone number, he returned the phone to her.

She blinked, staring at the screen as if the number was in another language. "What do I...?" Beth gulped slowly, "What should I list you as?"

Client?

Source?

One Night Stand?

Lover?

Or something more?

"Personal," Tristan gulped, butterflies knocking about in his guts. He wanted to wring his neck while also giggling like a kid. "That's my personal number."

Beth raised her phone along with her nod and entered whatever else was required into the index. When those deep brown eyes stared into his, she said all she needed to. "Got it."

Three days, Harty. That's it. Not even seventy-two hours yet and you're acting like a love-addled moron. She gazed out of the front window, where sadly no magical deer chewed through the snow. Tristan stared in rapture at her profile, his heart leaping higher when she pushed a fallen tendril of hair behind her ear.

"You are..." That damn tongue spoke for him, shattering the spell. Beth's focus homed in on him, her open face clouding as he stood there stoically. *Keep going, idiot. You started it, you have to.*

Tristan kicked into the couch, stubbing his big toe. It didn't hurt, but it threw off his balance and sent him scampering toward her. Without a second thought, Beth launched out her arms to catch him. At first, they were steadying. But she slid her hands around his waist, and he wrapped his around her shoulders. "How did...how did you keep your phone charged all this time?"

Coward.

"Oh, that. I always bring a backup battery just in case. You never know when you might lose power while in the field."

That's not what you wanted to say. Fess up. Now. "Ms. Cho..."

She snickered at his using her surname, her head tilting to the side. "Yes, Mr. Harty?"

"I was wrong about you." His lips struggled to voice the words lodged in the back of his throat. "Wrong to—to dismiss you so cavalierly without reason. I never should have—"

"Tristan," she cut him off, struggling to rise on her tiptoes. "I was wrong too. I underestimated you for no reason, assumed you to be a combatant, a...pain."

"Even my closest friends call me pricklier than a porcupine," he confessed, and to his surprise, she laughed at the truth.

"Not a porcupine." Beth drew her hand back through his hair. He breathed in the tender caress awakening his roots. "You're more like a hedgehog. With the right touch, your spines soften. And you're damn cute too."

A snort shot through his nose. Tristan was unable to find himself cute. But it did stroke his ego to hear her say so. "You are..." *Back to this again.* "You're beautiful beyond words," escaped from him. The songwriter, the poet of music was at a loss for his only wares while gazing at her.

At least he knew one way for his lips to explain. Cupping her cheeks, Tristan tugged her higher for a deep kiss. Beth folded against him, fitting perfectly in his embrace as she tipped her face back for his touch.

Honking erupted from outside. Both whipped their heads to stare out of the window as a line of headlights darted through the gray drizzle of the outside world. "They got through," Tristan said. He could feel the excitement trying to catch, to send him rushing to the door and throw it open for their rescuers, but he was frozen. Leaving the cabin meant leaving her too.

Beth crinkled her nose, his heart fluttering as he realized he'd been the one to kiss the wrinkles away. "Well," she said, "good thing I've got your number."

Snickering, Tristan nodded. She moved to slip from his arms, both returning to their requisite squares on the chessboard.

Suddenly, Beth darted to him, her lips tasting his in a kiss. "One more for the road," she said before turning to find her shoes.

Tristan was about to do the same when the door burst open. It wasn't some National Guard member, nor a park ranger, or even a Saint Bernard with opposable thumbs. Barry practically ran head first inside, his arms outstretched to plummet around that wayward charge. Not that Tristan expected anything less.

"Kid, thank God, you're okay!" Barry gasped, his hug less reassurance and more to try to shake some sense into Tristan. "You didn't respond to my calls and I…" The jaded eye of the manager drifted to Beth, only seeing her as a reporter. "I feared the worst."

"Yes, we're fine," Tristan spoke. "The power went down—"

"Shit!"

"Which caused my phone's battery to die. But otherwise, it's been a mostly pleasant long weekend," he said, glancing at the woman gathering up her bag.

"Mostly pleasant," she repeated and her twinkle caught his. Before Tristan could return the look, arms enveloped around his waist, plucking him directly into view of the liver-spotted baldpate of Barry.

"Tris, we gotta get you out of here," he said, frazzled. No doubt the man's ulcers had grown ulcers over the past seventy-two hours. But all was well. *Better than well for the first time in months. Years.* To think, he'd been dreading returning to the music grind, the unending press of being on all the time. He'd never have met her if he'd remained in Bemidji, that was certain. Barry turned a cold glare upon Beth, his hackles raised at her presence.

"In a minute." Tristan tried to pry himself out of the manager's grip. "My belongings are scattered about the cabin, and we should have a few minutes before the snow returns. I hope."

"You just jinxed us," Beth laughed, bringing a chuckle to him as well. Though the idea of having to share the cabin with his manager was an ice block to the groin.

"Kid." Barry snagged an arm around the back of his neck, tugging Tristan lower. "You need to get out of here. Now."

"The schedule, I know." He abandoned his manager to watch Beth gathering up her mass of notebooks. "I think you left some of them in the bedroom," Tristan called to her. She waved in gratitude and slipped inside to find them, which was when Barry whacked him in the back of the head.

"What the...?" Tristan gasped, but his manager wagged a finger in his face.

"I thought you knew better than to get...to get cozy with the enemy."

"She's not an enemy."

"You're the one that called her that, calls all of 'em that. But leave you alone for a couple days and you're all...I can't believe you. We need you away from her." Barry dashed about the living room, cramming what little of Tristan's things remained into the bag. As he couldn't be bothered to fold any of it, sleeves dangled from the jammed-open top.

"Bar, Barry, stop. Stop, okay. It's not whatever you're thinking. Dreading as you do. It's..." *Different. Amazing. Impossible.*

The duffel bag splattered to the ground, Barry rounding on him fast. "Not what I'm thinking there, Romeo?" He hauled up his ancient phone and pressed it awake.

All the blood drained from Tristan's face as he stared at a picture of himself. All of himself. His naked body was illuminated by the firelight with a guitar the only thing keeping the picture from being X-rated.

Tristan's eyes bugged out as he grabbed the phone and squeezed it tighter and tighter. He wished he could strangle the image away. "No," he snarled. "No."

It was her picture. The one she'd taken of him when he… When he'd been vulnerable, when he'd laid out every guarded secret to her in the hope that she'd understand him. Not the music, not the songs, not the poster image. The man hiding below all the focus-group-determined glitz. He'd wanted her to see it all and know him. He'd thought she'd understand and, maybe, feel the same.

It was all a lie!

"Got that this morning from *Thorn*, asking for confirmation it's you in there. Please tell me…" Barry said. A great sigh sputtered through his mighty cheeks. "Look, I don't want to be all nagging Nancy here, but…"

"This will not happen again," Tristan swore, hurling the phone at Barry. Stomping for the bedroom, he froze in his shaking tracks as the traitorous reporter stepped out.

She was all smiles, unaware that he knew. That he was on to her cruel trickery, playing him for the fool and cutting him deep without a second thought. *And what did it matter? You gave her everything she could need to destroy you. Fuck!*

"I think I have..." she said, before staring up into his face. He knew it was red in a boiling rage from the heat bubbling off his cheeks. The look sent her scampering back, her bag swinging between them for protection.

"What is it? What's wrong?"

"I can't believe I was stupid enough to fall for it," he cried, his hands wringing dead air. "To believe a word out of your mouth, out of the mouth of anyone who's only looking to cut a person into bite-sized pieces and sell them for a quarter a click."

"Tris...Tristan?" the liar whispered, darting her gaze around the cabin in an impressive simulacrum of fear.

"I was wrong about you," he cursed. "You're worse than scum—at least that serves a purpose in this world! Barry!" As he turned away from her, his heart hardened against the ghost of tears rising. Tristan focused on his manager. "We're leaving."

"Nice to see you sobered up," Barry declared. Bag in hand, his manager grabbed the coat off the hook. Tristan was boiling on the inside, the rage sustaining him as he marched to the door. He had to get out of there before she spun that same magic that had ensnared him. People like her always had an excuse for everything they did.

"How will I leave?" she asked and he heard the worry in her voice. The same one that had squeaked that she couldn't skate, that she needed his guidance, his help. For a second, his heart tried to bleed for her, but Tristan glanced down at the bandage around his palm. He'd shed enough for her already.

"I don't care," were his parting words, Tristan all but running out into the snow. The cold tried to penetrate, but his skin was obsidian, hardened from the magma levels of rage burning through his body. He focused on the anger, clung to it, because otherwise he might feel his heart fracturing into a thousand icicles. Without a second look back at the cabin, or the lost woman standing in the doorway, Tristan leaped into the snowplow's cab and forgot he'd ever stayed there.

Chapter Seventeen

Congratulations, Beth, you fucked everything up.

She'd managed to get one of the plows to help tow her car to the interstate, which had been annoyingly clear of snow. After that, nothing more than a long, heartbreaking drive back to her editor's desk. Which was when she'd figured out what happened.

Oh, he'd been ecstatic about her 'intimate portrait' of Tristan Harty. *Damn it! Damn it! Damn it!* Why hadn't she remembered he could see everything in that folder? Why hadn't she stopped it from uploading? Why had she even taken the picture in the first place?

In her state of shock, she'd shouted that *Thorn* couldn't use the picture. It was hers, under her copyright, and she wasn't going to allow it. Boy, had that been a big mistake. The happy editor feasting upon the scandalous muck had turned vengeful. So she'd been left with the 'or else' threat.

Write what she knew about Harty, use the image or something just as good, or else that was it. That was her ultimatum, destroy his life or lose her job.

"Gah!" Beth screamed into a pillow made out of an old AC/DC shirt. She sucked in the cloying scent of Febreze while doing so, causing her to hack to breathe in cleansing air.

"What is it?" Madeline called, running from her little en-suite office to check on the worthless pile of scruff that had slunk into her apartment.

"Lamenting every horrific decision in my life. It's taking some time," Beth admitted. Dressed in requisite sweats tattered from mourning, she had her legs tucked under her while merging with Madeline's armchair.

"You're not the first person to mess things up," good, kind, diplomatic Mads said. She playfully tousled through Beth's unwashed hair. It'd been a week since the cabin, seven days of bitter sunshine through the gray city. And all Beth had to show for it was an empty sheet of paper and a broken heart.

"I mean..." Madeline left the useless lump of human dough to check on the cardboard box set up with a heat lamp. "It can't be all that bad. It was just three days."

"Yup. Three days." Only three days. Shit, in this city people didn't even think they were exclusive until it'd been a year and the parents had met them. Three days was nothing. A drop in the bucket. Seventy-two hours she should be able to drink away.

Why did it hurt? Why did it feel like she was breathing in ash and eating glass? Why did she have to beat herself up with every thought of not only him but her entire career on a knife's edge?

Admitting to her sleeping with Tristan in the article might be good for *Thorn* but it'd hamstring her in an instant. Yet, if she didn't mention it, she'd surely be fired. Or there was the truth about him. His ex-fiancée dead of an overdose, her body discovered by him. His twin sister also dead. Two lives he wore like an albatross around his neck even if neither had been his fault. To have the media question it, to bring it up to him endlessly on press stops, to wear him down… It'd crack him, send him back into hiding, or worse.

"What are you going to do?" Madeline voiced Beth's thoughts.

"I don't know." She covered her head with the pillow, crouching deeper into her lap.

On one hand, he was someone she'd met for a long weekend. There were seven billion people on the planet. Stepping on one's toes for her own success was normal. Expected. She owed him nothing. She certainly didn't owe him her job.

"He's so infuriating! Not giving me a damn inch before exploding like that!" Beth cried. No word, no warning, no explanation. Just running out of that door as if she'd transformed into Medusa. As if she couldn't calmly tell him what had happened by accident.

"Sounds like a real peach."

But he had been. Okay, not at first. That had been the most sardonic, acidic man she'd ever suffered. In the middle, when he softened, that had been someone Beth had never known before. Someone she couldn't escape. Maybe it was all in her head. Maybe her punch-drunk heart was making it all up to torture herself.

Beth flipped from the tawdry picture trapped in her phone like the curse it was back to the phone number. His phone number. Private, he'd said. No way would he pick up now. She didn't even try to call, fearing that all she'd get would be a cussing out.

"What are you doing?" Madeline asked, peering closer to the phone so her red curls spilled against Beth's cheek. Her friend was nosy, but Beth was grateful she was here, even more grateful that she'd been allowed to spend the past week with Madeline instead of her three roommates who'd groan at her moping.

Beth sighed. "Thinking."

"No, you're prolonging the pain. Yank that damn thorn out already. Delete him. Forget him."

As if it was that easy. Her thumb hovered over the trashcan symbol, aching to press down. To wipe all memory of Tristan first from her phone, then her mind. His lean body, his nimble fingers, his gentle lips. *Gone in a snap.*

Mad pressed down, making the decision for her. "Oops," she said sarcastically while walking away.

Beth stared numbly at where he had been. Her address book shuffled around, another *H* taking the place of one Harty, Tristan. *Almost as if it never happened.* She'd never interviewed him, they'd never been trapped in that cabin. He hadn't saved her from the ice, pressed his body to hers in the heat of the shower, run his fingers through her hair while teaching her to play guitar. *Erased.*

"You know what you need," Mads said while bustling through the kitchen that always smelled of cat litter. Beth tried to watch her friend, but it was all a blur until Madeline appeared beside her. "A kitten."

Without any warning, Madeline placed the three-week-old kitten on Beth's chest. The weak baby mewled in surprise, Beth cupping her hands around it, but it didn't seem happy. "I don't think it approves of the lack of breasts to cuddle on."

She glanced at her very well-endowed friend, who waved her hand through the air and laughed. "Marshmallow will be fine. All they need is a bit of love and…constant attention, food, warmth, more food. But the love, that's what gives them a fighting chance."

This one had been found in a sewer grate, crying for its life. No doubt some heartless monster had tried to flush the baby away, but Madeline had been there to save Marshmallow. Beth tipped back, keeping the fragile kitten resting on her sternum. From behind, Mads leaned closer to run her pinkie over the kitten's head. It could barely crawl, still struggling to gain weight, but at its new mother's touch, it reached for her.

"They make a mess like you wouldn't believe. And they stink beyond belief sometimes, but…" Madeline trailed off as she stared at the kitten. One of the dozens she'd saved over the years. Pictures of them covered her walls, all adopted to forever homes once they were safe on their own. They might leave her home but never her heart, no matter how little time she had them.

Beth glanced up at her friend and smiled. "But you can't turn 'em away."

"Could you?" were Madeline's parting words as she returned to cleaning up her mess of a kitchen. Having to tend to such a young kitten caused nearly everything else to fall by the wayside.

Wafting her pinkie over Marshmallow's brown-striped head and back, Beth took in the helpless baby. Aching to save them, to protect and shield them from everything, even those beyond someone's reach… "No," she whispered, "No, I couldn't."

"So, what are you going to do?"

For the first time since arriving home, an idea blossomed in Beth's fractured heart.

* * * *

You're carrying on like a moon-eyed prepubescent who had his first crush stomp on his heart. Man up, already.

Tristan plucked at the C string so sharply it bit into the edge of his callus. He barely flinched at the pain. Instead, he took to pouring his wounded soul into the harmonic vibrations. A small part of him knew he was being a right ass, dressed down in hoodies with ripped sleeves and grunting when anyone looked at him askance. That Boston interview would have been a disaster had they not also brought on the newest sugar glider at the zoo, who'd taken a liking to nesting in Tristan's hair. The fear of sugar glider nuggets plopping down the sides of his head was a good excuse for his sour face.

And why? For what reason are you tormenting your friends, your colleagues, the various news crews who have to pretend to like you?

Brown eyes and a wry smile ensnared his imagination. The anger hadn't sustained him, not for long. Maybe a day or two after abandoning the cabin. Now, two weeks since their freedom, since her betrayal, all he felt was despair. And there was no good reason for it.

Three days. Tristan knew it. Barry wouldn't cease prattling on about it, when not trying to gin up a plan to save his ass when the article hit. It was due today, nine a.m. no less. *Wake up. Brew a pot of coffee. Take a shower. And wait for my world to fall apart.*

Tristan prepared by shutting off all his electronics, staring out of the hotel's window at the bleak midwinter landscape and strumming his fingers until they bled. Everyone knew not to bother him. He'd told his mother to hole up for a few days with her stacks of books rather than face the once-friends and neighbors gossiping about her wayward son. What would Beth say about him?

He frowned at her name slipping past the blockade and adjusted in the chair. One leg dangled over the padded armrest, tipping the guitar up into a less than useful angle. Not that it would matter how badly he played. He didn't want to do anything but sulk.

Pretentious? Most certainly. She adored that word.

Callow? On occasion.

Aloof? He couldn't help that image even if he wanted to stop it.

Broken, beaten, alone.

His hand slapped to the guitar, the healed palm barely registering as he tried to screw back in the fear percolating in his brain. He didn't care if she spoke of their unfriendly greetings, of how he'd dismissed her out of hand. It was facing every eye knowing his history, every hand wringing itself over his trauma that sent dread racing through Tristan's body. He couldn't handle it. Even telling her had been…

'What in the seven hells were you thinking?'

That had been Barry's screed on their drive out of Vermont, out of the cabin and away from a lie. But it'd been a comforting lie, a cozy one where for a brief weekend Tristan had pretended that he could trust. *Confess to someone who seemed to understand.*

But no. Soon, the internet would see him stripped, both in the metaphorical and literal sense. Try as hard as Barry did, *Thorn* wouldn't refuse to publish the image they had. Not that Tristan expected much from the old manager faced with this new world order.

Sensationalism won out even in a scratch-my-back deal.

A pigeon landed on the windowsill, its head bobbing as it tried to find relief from the bitter winds. Mid-December wasn't kind to anyone.

The rattle of the door handle and the dangling chain caused Tristan to sit up. He raised his chin but didn't turn to see who entered. There could only be one person. Instead, he picked back up that song without a tale, trying to will his brain to make gold out of dirt.

"Tris," Barry muttered, scrabbling into the hotel room. He paused and flipped on the bathroom light as if checking for ghosts or serial killers before stopping behind Tristan. "It's out."

"I assumed, what with the lack of an apocalypse in the forecast," Tristan said, his voice cold as he continued through the music.

After Barry unwound his scarf, Tristan watching the man's flushed appearance reflected in the window, he sighed. "You're gonna want to read it."

Tristan snorted cruelly. "Isn't that what you're here for? To keep me from facing reality?" At least for a few more hours. He wasn't even at lunchtime yet, though the minibar was down two tiny bottles of vodka.

"Look, it's blowing up. Going all viral and stuff," Barry said, a shiver crawling up Tristan's spine. So it was worse than he'd feared. A part of him had hoped that he was such a small fish, the collective internet would shrug. "And I think you need to see."

The man foisted his tablet on Tristan, but he wasn't having it. "Barry, I am not in the mood to deal with—"

"Read the damn thing already!" Barry ordered as if it was life and death. How much money had Tristan's foolish dick cost him? Was there a calculator app open on Barry's phone that was determining that very number? Canceled tours, aborted deals, maybe even the album itself in jeopardy if this grew gargantuan?

Sighing, Tristan placed his guitar on the hotel table and picked up the tablet. His traitorous gaze found her face tucked up in a little square by the byline. Ms. Beth Cho. Still beautiful, despite everything she'd done. He felt a smile churn in his gut from the preserved one in her headshot. *Grow a pair, Harty, and walk to your own execution.*

Scrolling down, he noticed that at least the first image wasn't of his naked body straddling a guitar. It was one of him taken by the Christmas tree in the on-loan suit. The pocket watch dangled in his palm—he hadn't been able to cease playing with it—but the look on his face was serenity. Most would probably see it as a man gazing out across the horizon, but Tristan recognized his previous self finding something intriguing, or funny.

It was a lovely picture to have chosen. But there was a lot more meat to the article, and they could have hidden the 'money shot' on the next page. Taking a breath as if he were about to plunge into an icy lake, Tristan read.

Hair unwashed, clothes astray, fingernails scratching masterpieces across the rotting walls – this is the fabled tortured artist. Throughout history, we've been sold the romantic idea of the artist struggling against every force in the world thrown against him or her for the sake of art. As if the amount of pain suffered is the only way to truly judge art's worth. While the impoverished who defied the odds to reach the stars holds an allure in this society, it is mental illness and its cruel clutches that infests so many starving artist stories.

"People believe that to make great art, an artist must be tortured. They must know and face in their lives such great turmoil that it plagues them every night. And should that pain be medicated, treated, alleviated from them, so too will the art vanish. This is a lie.

Tristan's heart stopped, his finger hovering over the screen to scroll for more. Where was she going with this? Was it a buildup to revealing his past? Then why mention art in general?

I was tasked with interviewing Tristan Harty, whom most remember for his hit single My Half *from the album bearing his name. While I could describe his attire – meticulous when he was performing, comfortable and wholesome when not – or what he ate during the interview, I see no point.*

There are few facts known about Mr. Harty that truly hold water. While his fans know his break came courtesy of a local New York daytime talk show, the average person might be aware of his rise to join the heights of other late '90s bands. But in the matter of his fall, there is naught but conjecture and hearsay. It was not avarice by his own demons or untrustworthy friends from his inner circle that brought him low. Nor was it an inability to innovate, a fandom aging out of his style, nor simply exhaustion.

No, what chased Mr. Harty from the world of music was us. The world demands a blood sacrifice for what it gives. In exchange for fame, for a modest fortune, it wants a story to salivate. What it craves most is tragedy, one that the artist must mention endlessly, forever reliving for us while standing upon the world stage of entertainment. They must wrap their pain around themselves and wear it as a coat they can never remove. Otherwise, we would cease caring.

I was gifted a unique experience with Mr. Harty – a man often described as cold, distant, as unreadable as a frozen pond. I too believed the first impression, finding him bafflingly callow and aloof…

A smile knotted around Tristan's lips to find he'd guessed somewhat right.

…but in the snowy mountains of Vermont, I discovered a man I'd never have known otherwise. He suffers pains, same as many other people in this world, pain no amount of fame can cure. Laughter in the form of surprising self-deprecation. Warmth radiates from him that every other interviewer before missed, because they wanted that pain and not the joy. They wanted the loss and not the gain. They wanted a story and not a truth.

I, for one, am glad that Mr. Harty has given us a second chance. After the world was robbed of his songs for nearly ten years, we will once again be gifted the opportunity to hear both his classics and enthralling new ones. We must look differently at our artists, to stop demanding that they suffer for our amusement, to alleviate the pang to the ego because we are incapable of doing what they can. The task of creating, of brightening this world with a reflection of itself, is a continuous struggle when someone's boot is on your neck. When hands help pull an artist up and give them the room to breathe, imagine the amazing splendors that can be gifted to the world.

It's up to you to decide which world you want to see, but I know the perfect soundtrack to grace its new dawn.

This is Beth Cho for Thorn. *If you liked my articles you can find me…*

The bottom of the article smudged as drizzle built in Tristan's eyes. He moved to swipe it away but nearly sent the tablet tumbling from his tentative fingers. She hadn't sold him out. Hadn't ripped open his old wounds and twisted them to her advantage. She…she'd spun gold from straw and he'd once called her a glorified blogger.

"Uh huh, yeah, Tuesday works great." Barry's on-the-phone voice punctuated through Tristan's enlightenment. Planting a hand to his knee, he glanced over his shoulder to watch the manager nod vehemently and raise a thumb in the air. After ending the call, he kissed his phone and shouted, "That was the *Morning Show*!"

"Which one?"

"No, the *Morning Show* with the trademark and everything. Nationally syndicated. They read the article and want you on to talk about it, along with a musical segment."

The studio had shaken its head on any national news segments for his tour, no one caring about a washed-up songwriter putting out a Christmas album. *And now…!* Tristan's leap of glee was postponed as he glanced down at the illuminated words that had made it possible. How he'd stomped on her heart without a second thought, hadn't even waited for an explanation. Just once again assumed the worst and run to brood in his cave.

"Kid!" Barry threw his arms around Tristan and tried to haul him into the air in a great bear hug. Where it would have lifted him off his feet as a kid, Tristan remained stubbornly on the ground. "This is fantastic! Oh shit, we gotta get you cleaned up." A professional look took in the mountain of stubble clumping off his chin and jaw. No doubt his eyes were red from first the drink and drama, now the swallowed tears.

Tristan nodded along as Barry laid out the plan to freshen him up before the big time. While his manager hunted for a reputable spa to slot in a prickly customer on short notice, Tristan scrolled back to her picture. Was she doing well? The article had to be a good boost, but how was her book coming along? Or her friend's kitten? The need to hear her voice, to listen to her thoughts, to touch her sweet lips, clanged down his nerves like a bass hit.

"When is it?" Tristan asked, throwing a wrench into Barry's surge in scheduling. "The TV appearance?"

"Tuesday morning, nine-thirty a.m. Which means us waking at five and me having to listen to you make those godawful gargling noises." Barry groaned about the tuning-up exercises, but it was all in jest. He was clearly over the moon at this unexpected score. From death and scurrying under a rock to shining in the national spotlight. It was all thanks to her.

Hauling up the guitar, for the first time in an age, inspiration struck Tristan. He hooked the strap over his neck and began to play. As the vibrating cords transferred to a hum on his tongue, he bent down and wrote in his notebook the first words to enter his head.

"Barry." He glanced at the flustered manager. "Any chance you can work your magic to polish me to a gleam in this room?"

"I guess. Why?"

Tristan smiled while scribbling out the next line in his chicken scratch. "I found the tale. Oh, and I need you to do one more thing for me..."

Chapter Eighteen

There was no descent of balloons, no eruption of fireworks, no standing ovation, but people at least smiled at her as Beth walked into *Thorn*'s offices the day after the article's publication. 'Congrats,' they cried, some patting her on the back as if she'd won them a world series. It felt good to watch the numbers climb, the link-backs increasing as more and more outlets began to dissect and add their own articles on her short peek into Mr. Harty.

Passing the bank of monitors set up for video editing, she caught George working on splicing an old music video of Tristan's into the next broadcast. It was peak late '90s, with the backlit musician in an open shirt, baggy pants and the rain. *So much rain.* The two editors watching snickered. "Shitty dancer."

A shame they couldn't see him on the ice, controlled, collected, directing every inch of his body at his command. *Or in the bedroom.*

Beth flushed at the thought, her embarrassment quickly burning to shame and regret as she scuttled past without saying a word. Upon reaching her desk, she pulled in a breath and signed in to officially start work. New day, new celebrity to pick at. Or maybe her boss would finally let her dig into some real meat. *He did just get a two-million-click article.*

Boy, had he been mad at what she'd turned in, grumbling at the lack of sordid details or her once again refusing to use that picture. He'd said whatever happened was on her head, leaving Beth to pick at the drooping succulent at her desk while waiting for the order to pack up her things. Then a miracle from the sky had happened. It had connected, it had spoken to people and it had grown legs fast. By the end of the first day, her colleagues popped corks and toasted to the major increase in ad revenue.

Beth glanced at the side of her desk to find a brown box sitting where her notebooks would go. Ice squeezed her lungs. Had her editor changed his mind and decided she wasn't worth the hassle? Heart throbbing in her chest, Beth reached for the box, when Emma strolled into the mostly open, one-walled cubicle.

"Excellent work, Cho," her fellow entertainment reporter said. Beth smiled at the greeting, well aware of the barbs inside. While they were happy to support each other on the outside, everyone here was circling like sharks, wondering what strike they needed to make to hit it big next.

"Thanks. Got lucky. You know how it is." Beth tried to shrug it off while glancing down at the box. It was taped up with a mailing label on the top, so probably not a sign she was being fired. *A bonus?* God, knowing her editor it'd be a sign that said, *Get back to work.*

Emma glanced from Beth's confusing unboxing to the editor's office. His door was shut, but everyone in the entire complex could see his silhouette ranting into the phone. "Word is, all the big networks picked up your article."

"Oh?"

"Sounds like the *Morning Show* snagged Harty first to discuss it."

Her hands froze, Beth pulling in a ragged breath. She'd tried to end it with him in that last period of her piece. As if publishing her article would erase the ache from her heart. How many here could tell that her smile was as phony as a three-dollar bill?

"He's pissed that they didn't tap him instead," Emma continued, talking about their boss.

"I'm guessing he doesn't care that I'm not wanted," Beth surmised, watching the tight-lipped nod from Emma. Their editor was a known camera chaser, often starting feuds on social media just for the attention. But he was the owner's something-or-other so he was allowed to fester like mold crawling across the printing press.

After yanking the packing tape off, Beth cracked open the box. A single white square envelope rested inside. Turning it over, she read her name, not printed in a fancy calligraphy font, nor done up in gold for a party. The hand was not illegible, but not particularly neat either. It pressed the ink deep into the paper.

Cracking open the envelope, Beth fished out a plain card. It was the simplest Thank You note one could find, with the declaration printed in black in the center and two gold lines outlining the edge. Not very creative or exciting, and it didn't give her any clues as to who'd sent it.

With a haphazard toss of her fingers, she opened the card, glanced back to find her boss had finished his ranting and almost fell to the ground.

I read the article, the card said.

Oh, God! This can only be from him. He…he had to have read it. His people had known it was coming, but… *Stop panicking, Cho, and finish this.*

There was only one more line under that.

Call me, followed by the initials *TH*.

Little hard for her to do, what with her deleting his number. Not that she was exactly lining up to be berated for doing her job. That had to be it. His reason for sending her a cheap-ass card to remind her once again how worthless her work was. He probably found the 'Thank You' aspect ironic. What other purpose would this serve since he couldn't even muster an apology in the card?

Emma broke away from their boss, curiosity leaning her closer to the box. "What is that?"

Closing the cryptic card and sliding it into the envelope, Beth finally dug into the package proper. Hidden below a scrap of brown butcher paper was…

A giddy laugh escaped from her lips as she pulled free a silver pouch. The label on the packet bore an image of a plate stacked with delicious pancakes. Pancake mix? He wasn't mad. He wanted to apologize? To talk it out? To see if they could start again? *He wants to see you, to… Shit, you deleted his number!*

One of the most reclusive men in music, who had no social media presence, who went out of his way to avoid people, wanted her to find him...and she'd deleted his goddamn number.

Fuck, fuck, fuck!

How in the hell could she get his attention? No way would he deal with his 'fan services.' No chance of them letting her through, not until it was too late. Not until...

"Tristan." Beth spun to grab Emma's arm. "Harty, when was he going to be on TV?"

"Uh, nine-thirty, I think. Why?"

Shaking her head made tears of joy fly off as she tried to calculate the chances of her getting all the way to Times Square before it was too late. Even if she made it in time, there was no chance they'd let her in. Not without help. Grabbing her purse, Beth left her coat on her chair as she dashed for the elevator.

"Where are you going?" Emma tried to stop her, but Beth was set in her course. Just before she rounded the line of monitors, she grabbed up one of the press badges for *Thorn*. Winding the lanyard around the badge and stuffing it into her pocket, she picked up speed running for the lobby. Half an hour until showtime, half an hour to catch him before he could be gone for good.

* * * *

"...and we'll be back with an exclusive performance by Tristan Harty after the break."

Karen, as she'd insisted she be called, turned away from the number two camera, though her smile didn't dim until the producer waved a finger at her.

Massaging her jaw, she said, "Interesting discussion, Mr. Harty."

"I suppose," he responded, glancing down to find he'd been digging his fingers into his knees the whole time. Beth's voice flitted through his head, pointing out his own nervous tic to keep his thoughts in check. As her voice faded from his memory, an ache rose in his heart, one that Barry must have noticed as the man came rushing from the stage side.

Normally, the manager was left in the greenroom, if they bothered to let him into the studio at all. Tristan was hardly a minor who needed escorting from gig A to interview B any longer. He didn't need Barry henpecking above him. But it was nice to have that familiarity as well. Almost as if the years hadn't passed without him in the spotlight, despite the abundance of technology he wasn't used to.

Frowning at the pancake makeup necessary for every person who walked onto the HD cameras, Tristan moved to run a fingernail under the slop when a producer stopped him. "Mr. Harty, we have you set up over here."

The woman with the clipboard—at least that hadn't changed—jerked her head to the side set. It was the typical Christmas village scene. Piles of flat white batting gave the illusion of snow stretched atop raised boxes. A single tree decorated in twinkling yellow lights rested beside it, and there was a snowman. There was always a snowman that looked nothing like the ones real children made.

"Kid, you're doing great," Barry cheered, then frowned at Tristan undoing the last button on his jacket and shrugging it off. "Uh…maybe you want to keep that on. For lighting, or whatever."

Tristan knew it was really because, to quote the dresser, he was 'skinnier than a birch tree' and the jacket helped disguise the fact. But he was far more concerned about his second debut performance on live TV than his presentation. Passing the jacket to Barry, Tristan undid the cuffs on his crimson shirt and rolled both sleeves to his elbows. The ebony vest pinched to his midsection as he sat on the stool, but that could be ignored. It was also impossible to sell 'professional adult' with a vest partially or fully open.

After adjusting the guitar he'd tuned for the two-hour greenroom wait as the show worked through its other guests, Tristan glanced up. He stared through his manager to the captive audience whispering and checking their phones until they had to be silent once more. There were millions more beyond, all about to listen to his song. No doubt they'd wonder if he still had his voice or his skill.

And he was going to break the cardinal rule for performing live.

"One minute until we're back," the main producer called from his little booth.

"You better get off the set before they make you play a tambourine," Tristan said with a smile to Barry.

A shudder at the thought rolled up his manager's back before he paused and placed a hand on Tristan's shoulder. "Break a leg."

"I hope to break...something," was his cryptic response. It was clear Barry wanted to ask more, but the line producer was shoving him away. With Tristan's suit coat strung over his shoulder, Barry wandered outside the camera's view with the rest of the non-talent.

The lights around him dimmed, leaving Tristan in the shadows of the studio. Only the yellows from the Christmas tree gave him comfort, reminding him of a lone fire in a snuggly cabin. It was time. He tugged the microphone closer as Karen stepped away from sucking down her smoothie, the makeup artist quick to retouch her lipstick.

Hands jerked beside the main camera, counting down to zero. "Welcome back," Karen said, pausing for the polite applause of an audience growing bored after three hours of sitting. "Here with a song off his holiday-themed album is Tristan Harty."

Spotlights clicked awake, burning Tristan's vision to a crisp. Funny, he'd forgotten about that pupil-searing pain. But while blinking to focus, he tugged the microphone closer and excised a single scrap of paper from the back of his pants. "If you don't mind, Karen, I'd like to play something else. This song is…exceptionally new."

"Um…" In an instant, the studio was thrown into chaos. There was a backing track for the original *Silent Night* choice, which the sound guy was killing dead. The producer was whisper-shouting at everyone around him, no doubt wondering if they could yank Tristan from the set and go to more commercials. As for Barry, Tristan couldn't handle the glare off his manager.

"Sure," Karen cooed, as if anyone in the studio had the time or ability to stop him.

That was the one plus to doing this live. Pulling in a breath, Tristan started himself down a path he couldn't escape. The music he knew by heart, each note simple on the acoustic guitar, but also earnest. Here he didn't obfuscate, here he didn't dodge. In his music, he was all of himself, even if most couldn't see below the surface. Those, he didn't care about. This song was for the ones who knew the heart below his ice shell.

Leaning into the microphone, he loosened his lips and let fly the words not even twenty-four hours old.

Snow falls from the skies
Forgetful and pure
O'er mountains they rise
Erasing the cure

I reach out to feel
Glass cold as a grave
Mirrors never heal
Reflect but ne'er save

Reach for me, reach for me
Give me a chance
Sing me a hope
Gift me a dance
Words from your lips, pure and wise
Colors to wash the white from my eyes…

* * * *

Damn it!

Traffic crawled through the tourist traps, hordes of sticky families darting from one mega-corporation store to another while every car and cab refused to move. Beth glanced down at her phone and flinched. It was fifteen minutes to ten. They'd be wrapping up soon. Then what?

Close the stage, kick out the audience. Doubtful Tristan's the type to hang out and sign autographs. It wasn't as if

Beth could work her way through the crowd to reach him anyway. *Why did you delete his number?*

She wanted to knock herself in the head for that mistake, but there wasn't time for self-pity. There wasn't even time to wonder what he really wanted to talk about. On one hand, the pancake mix seemed a good sign, though the card about the article was stark and cold. But that was Tristan Harty to a T, and…

"Damn it all!" Beth cursed as her Uber slammed to a halt. She could see the hint of the studio's mass of windows two blocks down, but reaching it would easily take another twenty minutes at this pace. She'd miss him. He'd walk away never knowing she was there, and he might never speak to her again. What if this was a passing mood? What if he took her silence as anger? What if…?

Cracking open the door even in the midst of in-theory moving traffic, Beth said to the man who smelled of anise, "I'm getting out."

"Uh, Miss…" Whatever he was going to say was lost as she rocketed from the front seat and ran around the back of the car. Horns blared at the insane woman walking into the middle of a busy New York street, but she gave them the standard salute and dashed for the sidewalk. It too was surging with people, Beth having to twist and leap to avoid every collision as she ran for the studio building.

The seconds ticked away like sand in a glass. That reminder wasn't helping, and neither were the throngs of both visitors and locals packed outside the Times Square building trying to get a look inside. They were cordoned off by a series of winding aluminum barriers which Beth did not have time for.

Grateful she'd worn pants that day instead of her skirt, she hopped over each one like a kid jumping the turnstile. The bitter December cold seized her bare hands, trying to chill Beth to the bone, but she wasn't stopping now.

"Sorry. Excuse me. Please move," she babbled whether her foot came close to beaning someone or not. Reaching the front of the line, Beth adjusted her messed-up clothing when she felt a cold eye stare her up and down. Two hundred pounds of muscle was poured into a navy-blue suit, his arms crossed, but they were starting to move to toss her back to the masses.

Barely thinking, she whipped out the press badge and shouted, "I'm with *Thorn*! Your show is covering my article and asked me to be here!"

"Shouldn't you use the performer's entrance?" the man of muscle asked, raising a look over the tinted glasses turned black by the glint of sunlight off the windows.

Beth's thundering heart threw out the most beautiful lie. "Just got the call. Seems there was an unexpected cancellation. Came over as fast as I could. Guess they forgot to mention this other entrance."

To her gasping relief, the guard snorted. "What else is new?" he said and stepped aside while pushing open the door. "Reception's through there."

Nodding in relief, Beth slowed her steps but elongated her gait, trying to move as if she belonged there. Once the door closed, the muscle gazing back at the throng, she turned from the friendly desk with the logo of a rising sun plastered behind. *Five minutes left to find him.*

* * * *

Tristan shook off the angry glares of the producers he'd hurled a curveball at. It seemed unlikely he'd be invited back anytime soon. He didn't glance around at the audience, who were at least politely listening in. No, all his focus was turned inward. His heart had written the lyrics, his veins piping them to his lips that breathed them into life.

Snow falls from the skies
Cleansing my face
Heart breaks from the lies
Swirling through this place

I reach out to feel
Glass cold as a grave
Mirrors never heal
Reflect but ne'er save

Reach for me, reach for me
Give me a chance
Sing me a hope
Gift me a dance
Words from your lips, pure and wise
Colors to wash the white from my eyes

All the while, he had a vision of flint eyes, a wholesome face and pink silk drifting through his mind.

* * * *

"Excuse me, ma'am..."

Fuck! Beth knew better than to say such a thing aloud, but she sped up her hunting. Why hadn't she looked up a map of this place in the car? *Because no one in their right mind would put that on the internet. Probably.*

Her heels clicking on the polished floor, Beth swerved when she spotted a studio number beside the wide door. She reached for the handle, only to catch that the *On Air* sign was off. *Damn it!* That gave her pursuer ample time to draw closer. She'd picked him up when she'd stupidly crammed her head into a break room, then made up whatever excuse she could to get out of there fast.

Clock's ticking, Cho. And having to explain yourself to a bevy of security guards while waiting for the cops will not help you find him.

A glowing sign in red caught her and she lit up. *On Air.* Two minutes left. It had to be that one! Abandoning her pretense of belonging, Beth broke into a run. Her pursuer joined in, but she didn't care. She was almost at the end of this song.

* * * *

While bridging out of the solo, Tristan's fingers trembled, repeating the refrain as his mind churned. This was some foolish, throw-of-the-dice gesture that could backfire horribly. What if she didn't see it? What if she didn't care? Would she even understand his meaning?

A warm smile bloomed inside. Yes, if anyone would understand him, it was Ms. Cho.

He'd been obsessively checking his phone ever since receiving notice of his package's delivery. It had gotten so bad, Barry had swiped the outside link before Tristan headed on stage. But there was no call. No sign that she…she wanted to speak to him ever again.

Hope. When all is darkness, when you're stranded on a lake of your failures, the only oar at your side is hope.

With a smile on his lips, Tristan leaned into the microphone and belted out the last lines of his song.

Sun breaks through the snow
Its rays so strong
Fool at last knows
You were there all along

I reach out to hold
A hand fit for mine
Hearts become bold
And our stars align
Words from your lips, pure and wise
Colors to wash the white from my eyes

He strummed through the final bars while the lyrics he'd scratched into his old notebook carried through the studio. He'd never even sung them aloud until that moment, stupid as that was. That'd sink damn near anyone. Who dragged a barely mixed or written song before the world to devour? But he didn't care. He had to try and, as he raised his hand from the strings, he smiled serenely at the attempt.

Applause erupted around him, shaking Tristan. As he blinked in the spotlight, tears blurred the people who'd been forced to sit through his heart's praying. And they were all rising to their feet, hands slapping into one another in surprising abandon.

A goofy smile twisting his lips, Tristan gave a small wave to the audience before slapping his hand back to the safety of his guitar. As he stared at Karen, she seemed to realize that the ball was back in her court.

"Wow, that was," she whispered into her hot mic, before flinching. "Tristan Harty, everyone. You can find his latest album *Christmas Time* on Amazon, iTunes and at Target."

The cameras panned off him, the light of the snowy diorama fading to black. Once again, all he had to keep him company was the twinkling lights on the tree as Karen moved into the show's final wrap-up.

His heart thundered, all the nervous energy of this dangerous decision zapping down his legs. Shaking on the stool, he glanced up to find Barry giving a slow thumbs-up. While it was nice to know Tristan wasn't going to be tossed out on his ass for this move, that wasn't the person he was hoping to hear from.

I pray you saw it, Beth.

Chapter Nineteen

Beth darted around the mass of wires covered by duct tape. Above her loomed the backside of the bleachers packed with an audience mumbling in anticipation of leaving. *No. Damn it!* The studio lights were focused on the blonde woman seated behind her desk, leaving the rest of the set in shadows. She darted into the aisle between bleachers, hopefully losing her tail, who was no doubt calling security.

Looking at charges of trespassing and potential jail time all to catch the eye of a man? What the hell is wrong with you?

She didn't have time to weigh the consequences. Beth slipped closer to the circle of cameras and technicians trying to wrap up the show. Stopping just before the blinding wattage of light touched her, she glanced around the sides of the set. Guarded faces waited, the look reminding her of children when the dismissal bell was about to ring, but none were recognizable.

There was no thinning hair swept to the side, no lanky body unfolding into a wide stretch, no sapphire eyes peering into the darkness.

"That's our show, everybody!" the host called, pumping her hand through the air to wave the at-home audience away. "Thanks once again to Zookeeper Marco for…"

She was too late. The studio lot was clearing. All the talent the woman had thanked had already been shoved off to avoid the audience's exit. She'd missed him.

The small flame of hope that had kindled upon finding the pancake mix snuffed to smoke. As it curdled through her veins, the lights switched out. Beth fell off her stretched tip-toes, abandoning her foolish miracle. The cameras rolled back, feeds cut and the audience rose to their feet.

She'd failed.

People moved toward her en masse, their faces rendered formless as her heart crumpled. It had been one last Hail Mary risk-everything chance, and for what? What chance was there really? Three days. Seventy-two hours that should mean nothing. How could so little time mean anything? *Mean everything.*

She prepared to face the cold December morning alone.

"Beth?"

It was her imagination, no doubt her stupid heart trying to relight that spark of hope. Or there was another Beth in the audience. That made the most sense. Shuffling with the hapless crowd, she hoped to meld into the pack so the security would miss one small woman in the throng.

"Min-Ji!"

Her body froze, blocking up the herd, who cursed immediately at the woman getting in their way. She was so shocked, Beth's boilerplate apologies stuck in her throat as she stared back into the friendly facade of the studio. Dashing from the darkness came a wiry body with a chest of scarlet. "Tristan?" she asked, holding a hand to her forehead to try to see through the glare.

The shadow stepped into the light and a lanky silhouette stared directly at her. He was here! Beth gulped, goosebumps rising up her body at the determination in his face. For him, the crowd moved aside, parting like the sea as Tristan walked to the woman shaking in confusion. *So he's here. Now what?*

What if he's still mad? What if he…?

"I'm sorry," she said first, but Tristan was quick to overlap her.

"I read the article."

Beth shook her head, trying to knock away the tears of frustration at her stupid actions. "It never should have happened, that picture. I forgot about the damn cloud on my phone. I wanted to…hope to…"

Dashing through the crowd, Tristan scooped one hand around the small of her back. Without a second's pause, he plucked her onto the tips of her toes. Their lips met, Beth's endless apology fading to a kiss. In an instant, the ice shield enveloping her soul shattered, warmth flooding her heart as she fell into his embrace. He cupped her cheek, those beautiful lips puckering for two more gentle kisses against hers before he leaned back.

"I wrote you a song," he said, sounding surprised he'd done such a thing. "Sang it for you on live television."

Beth frowned. "Damn it. I missed the whole thing. I was too busy trying to reach you. To explain…"

A heartwarming laugh rumbled through his chest. Tristan pushed back the hair that escaped her ponytail. Tipping his forehead against hers, he said, "I can sing it again."

She snickered at the joy in his voice, wrapping both her arms under his and up around his shoulders to pull herself tighter to him. Tristan held her, his body fitting perfectly around hers. Parting his gentle lips, he breathed in a shudder. "I've missed you."

"Probably not when you thought I was going to torch your life and dance on the ashes." She cursed at herself, then winced at the reminder of how badly it had all exploded in her face.

But Tristan, that private man who diverted anyone from plumbing his heart, whispered, "Even then. Can you forgive me for being so foolish? For not trusting you?"

"Well," she said, a grin rising on her lips, "I dare say you owe me for such a slight upon my character."

"Oh?"

"I can only be recompensed with pancakes…" Beth dropped her voice, whispering in his ear. "In bed."

At that moment, the flock of gawkers launched into hoots and hollers. Both glanced at the studio to find that the producers, not about to miss a story like this, had turned the cameras around to capture them. A blush burning up her cheeks, Beth tried to hide her face in Tristan's chest.

"Sorry. I didn't mean to make such a spectacle…"

He didn't glare at the audience, didn't cast more than a cursory glance at the camera. No, he lifted her embarrassed face to his, and said, "If this is what it takes to have you in my life, then I happily accept it."

Beth leaped up, kissing him with all the joy and serenity in her heart. Three days, that was all it had taken to never want to live without this man she had hated with all her heart. As Tristan held her close, Beth raised both middle fingers to the camera, ensuring they couldn't use this shot of him—of them—for their story.

Chapter Twenty

One year later…

Mud splattered off the tires as the car came to a halt on the dying grassy patch. As he glanced away from his phone, a pang of nostalgia flitted in Tristan's gut. Nothing had changed. Well, there was no snow on the ground, this December proving to be bereft of winter's magic touch. But the porch was there, the sturdy chessboard, the rocking chair, the wood-cutting stump.

The memories of that alone had sustained him on the road. Though he'd certainly enjoyed other perks along the way as well.

"Is this right?" the driver asked, glancing behind his shoulder at Tristan.

"Yes, thank you," Tristan responded, already rising to his legs to exit. As he walked to the trunk to remove his things, the driver rolled down the window.

"What are you going to do in a cabin all by your lonesome?" he asked, showing the first real interest in his fare since the ride had begun.

Tristan pulled out the guitar case, the last of the anxiety washing from him once that reassuring weight was in his hand. "Hopefully, write another hit song. If all goes well. Thank you for the ride." He tipped his head and squelched through the mud to the stepping stones he'd had no idea were even there. Shaped like cross sections of a tree, they led in a quaint, haphazard pattern to the front door. Snow had a way of hiding the most surprising of secrets.

He expected the car to reverse course and drive down the mountain, but the driver seemed to be studying him intently. Perhaps he was trying to place him or attempting to work up the courage to ask for an autograph. Either way, Tristan watched the man, waiting for his words.

"Just...you got a plan to get out of here in case you get stranded by the weather?"

Tristan gleamed. "More than you can know."

"Well, all right." With those assurances, the driver finally rolled up his windows and left the old honeymoon cabin. Tristan waited until the car was back on the gravel road proper before walking up the stairs.

With each step, the grime of the road, the long nights, the empty days and the unending push to repeat his unexpected success faded away. He felt a new man reaching the top, about to push on the doorknob, when it kindly opened for him.

"My God," he gasped, staring in rapture at the woman dressed in a pale pink blouse and tight black trousers.

"Mr. Harty," she said, tipping her head to him. The tone was all business, but her look was not.

Rolling his tongue in his mouth, he responded, "Ms. Cho."

"I dare say we have the mountain to ourselves." Beth smiled brighter, her body curling against the doorway as if she intended to block him. Or she wanted him to scoop her up in his arms and carry her straight to the bed.

Dropping his luggage on the threshold, Tristan wrapped his hands around her waist. She laughed, the lightness filling him as he said, "A small part of it, at least."

"I think we can make do," Beth whispered, batting those soulful brown eyes up at him. He braced himself for her to surge forward and take command, but she seemed to wait patiently. He had been the first to kiss her, after all.

"You know what?" Tristan breathed against her ear, watching as the words left a trail of goosebumps rising along the delicate skin of her neck.

"What?"

A smile twisted up his lips and he whispered, "I love you." Before Beth could return the sentiment, Tristan kissed her. Burying her hands in his hair, plying his lips with her wanton hunger, pressing her chest to his, it was more than heat that swirled through his veins. His heart had found the succor it'd been seeking for these past two lonely months in the only place he'd ever thought to look.

"I missed you," she said, wafting her fingers over his fashionable stubble. Beth pulled her bottom lip into her mouth, biting down until a smear of peach-pink lipstick stained her teeth. She was adorable and finally live in front of him.

One year was nothing in the scheme of the universe, or even a life, but those twelve months had changed everything for him. Even when he'd been plagued by doubts and regrets, she'd been there. And when she'd cursed the very idea of setting out to write a book, he'd propped her up as best he could. It hadn't been easy, the studio insisting they make hay from his unexpected solo on live TV, but when the lights had been dimmed and the makeup wiped off, they'd had each other.

Twelve months back, he'd walked into that snowy cabin thinking his life would change. It was to be done via studio deals, charts, touring and recording. He never imagined it'd be his heart that'd change most of all.

"Shame about the mud," Beth mused, gazing at the supposed winter wonderland that bore a decidedly brown hue.

"Well, I…" He was about to say he had no intentions of leaving the cabin when a wet dot land on the back of his neck. After wiping at it, he strained his head up to the clouds and watched as a dozen white flurries tumbled from the sky.

"Is that…?" Beth asked, but Tristan barreled to her. Gripping her waist, he hauled her over his shoulder. Her infectious laugh shook his entire frame as he carried her to the bedroom, where they could finally try out the shaking bed as snow buried the cabin for a perfect winter. Tristan knew he never need worry as long he had Beth in his arms, her love in his heart…and a box of pancake batter in the pantry.

Want to see more like this?
Here's a taster for you to enjoy!

667 Ways to F*ck Up My Life
Lucy Woodhull

Excerpt

If there's anything more calamitous than being fired by a scumbag, it's having to be polite about it. I bit back all manner of choice words, lest a barrage of 'screw yous' and 'blow it out your asses' smack the venerated editor Carmichael Burns in his florid face. He was the king of choice words, after all. What could I say to him that he hadn't already spewed across the *New York Times* bestseller list?

Besides, sweet Dagmar Kostopoulos never, ever used words like that.

"But... But..." I did manage to get out, my mouth as dry as his pretend ennui. "You're promoting Jazmine into my role? How can that be? I have a Masters in English from Columbia." And she had a certificate from the Brooklyn Irony Emporium.

Carmichael laughed at my earnestness, as he always did. He pitied me because I actually did my job studiously and worked hard, even as he told me I kept him honest. And why shouldn't he chuckle? Jazmine had banged this ponytailed ball of pretension the moment she had gotten the job as his secretary, and now she'd 'earned' mine as editorial assistant. She wouldn't know a good nonfiction book platform if it bit her on the butt. She'd let him bite her butt, though. I cracked a mirthless smile at my stupid inner monologue, then sucked in a breath because...horrors—I had just lost my job.

The whole room went hazy. My head spun like water down a toilet bowl.

"You're too expensive for me, Dag," declared the man who'd given me a raise not a month ago. "Jazmine has a certain...flair for this work. You don't need a degree to develop *je ne sais quoi.*"

I didn't know *je ne sais quoi* was French for 'showed her thong like it was 1998'.

No—I would not be angry at Jazmine. Or her thong, which had been hella cute. We'd both known how to get promoted in Carmichael's office. Hell, the entire publishing industry understood that you gave head to get ahead with him. She'd been willing to go there, and I hadn't, for I'd thought my stellar performance would bypass his editing-couch antics.

The blame lay entirely with him.

He who smirked at me anew and said, "I know you'll land on your feet, Dag. I'm really doing you a favor. You can do so much better than me." His modesty rang hollow and dull. His last four books had debuted at number one everywhere—tell-alls from globetrotting manly adventurers, over-sexed Instagram stars, and jailed politicians.

"No!" I chirped. I smiled my summa cum laude, brilliant-girl smile. "No. You need me, Carmichael. Promote Jazmine, of course"—that last bit came out a little teeth-grindingly—"but I am an essential part of this team. Now, if you don't mind, I'm going to get back to the business of selling books."

I stood and buttoned my navy blazer. Yup, in a year and a half on the job, I'd found a future bestseller myself from a long-lost Kardashian cousin with a combo sex/Mason jar recipe blog. She made great salads, although I hadn't ever tried one naked in a hot tub as Khandye had recommended.

He said, "I do."

I blinked sweetly down at him. "What?"

"I do mind. You're fired, Dag."

A thousand rational arguments crowded my brain and I had to squeeze my eyes shut to form them into dynamic sentences that showed, not told, him how absolutely necessary I was.

I—

He—

No. Nope.

This was not happening. *Not* happening!

"Carmichael—" I blinked and realized he no longer sat in front of me at the rugged desk that used to belong to Ernest Hemingway. He was now perched outside the office on the arm of Jazmine's chair. Her cackle blew into my ears on a frigid breeze.

Carmichael had called me frigid. He'd grabbed my boob at the Christmas party and called me a frigid slut when I wouldn't advance my career by screwing him. I'd asked him how one could be both frigid and a slut. Probably a bad move, since he was now firing me four days later.

Rage bubbled through my gut, into my throat, a wave of heat that nearly knocked me over. I clenched my teeth and willed myself to call him what he was. An aging hipster douche sniffing the pretention of his own backside while selling bullshit to the lowest common denominator for only fourteen ninety-five.

Not that it hadn't been super fun while it lasted.

I couldn't find the words to defend myself, to talk him out of it. I performed excellently at my job. I'd found talented writers and changed their lives for the better. I'd worked endless hours, putting aside my own personal life in the process.

All for nothing.

I squeezed my eyelids shut as I shuffled past them. Jazmine sing-songed, "Bye, Dag-marred."

The eyes of the entire floor bored holes into my back while I gathered my purse and coffee mug. Nobody said a word—the Swiss cheese would stand alone.

What the heck did I do now? I'd never gotten a B, much less a pink slip. And my colleagues needed the largesse of Carmichael—they couldn't afford to anger him or Jazmine now. But Dagmar, well, Dag-*marred* was literary roadkill, so *Don't let the door smack your backside, darling*. I had many friends and amazing colleagues in this building, and I knew we would stay in touch, no matter the manner of my departure. I waved to them all without being able to meet anyone's eye.

Moments later, I shivered in a gently falling snow, not even remembering the trip down in the elevator from the lofty sixty-third floor. I pulled out my phone and dialed the first number, the tears already bubbling from my face. "I got fired, Blade."

"I'm in a meeting, babe, I'll have to call you back. Wear something sexy when I get home—I've got great news." The line went dead.

Snotcicles formed in my nose and I wondered what he'd heard me say. At least one of us had good news. We'd just moved into our first apartment together, and yesterday I'd thought that my life was going perfectly.

Maybe Khandye Kardashian would give me a job stuffing Mason jars with dildos.

I hailed a cab, reconsidered the expense since I'd lost my income, but decided that I would economize another day. Right now I was blubbering on Fifth Avenue while clutching my 'You Have as Many Hours in a Day as Beyoncé' mug.

Time to slink home.

* * * *

Four hours later, nose raw and eyes aching from the world's longest scream-cry-punch-a-pillow fest, I greeted Blade in my only Spandex dress. I'd never actually worn it—my friend Mel had forced me to buy it—because it was just so tight, you know? I could see a rib through it, and I wasn't really a 'revealing ribs' kind of girl. But getting dressed up for no reason had offered a little comfort. It'd been preferable to rage-stroking over Carmichael the @#&%.

Blade picked me up the moment he swept into the apartment and I clung to his wide shoulders and soft blond hair. He was a doctor, just as my dad always wanted, so I had that going for me, which was nice.

He set me down and said, "Break out the champagne, baby. I've got a new job at the hottest plastic surgery practice in Beverly Hills!"

Surprise melted my knees and I nearly collapsed onto the hardwood floor. "What?" When had he applied for this? "*What?*"

He trotted into the kitchen and I followed behind. With a satisfied smirk, he said, "Got the word this morning. I'm going to be a partner." *Pop* went the champagne we'd bought to christen our new place. He drank straight from the bottle. "Sun and fun—no more of this snow shit for me."

Blade hated the snow so much that I always had to shovel out his car for him.

I leaned against the kitchen counter for support, my stomach regretfully empty from not eating all day. "How stupendous! This is perfect timing." I laughed and took my swirling head (and the rest of me) to the cabinet to fetch our two champagne glasses. I held them out for him to pour. "Carmichael fired me today. Can you believe that? Fired me to promote *Jazmine*." Blade knew how I felt about Jazmine. Even though she wore the best shoes—always tall and vibrant, like she was a *Sex and the City* character. If I were an *SATC* character, I'd probably be Miranda's work ethic.

Blade pulled a face at my news and didn't pour the champagne. "Guess you shoulda slept with him, huh?"

"Ha ha." My arms shook as they still held the empty glasses. Man, did I feel queasy. I'd skipped lunch in favor of crying. He took another pull of the booze and still didn't pour it. I put on my best happy face. "But now it doesn't matter—we're moving to L.A.!"

"I'm moving to L.A."

That queasiness seeped from my stomach to my arms, legs, throat. I opened my mouth to speak but, for the second time today, nothing came out.

He took the champagne bottle past me and into the living room. I took a deep breath. Another. He was just being oblivious, he hadn't really meant what it sounded like. He could be that way—selfish. But it was because he worked hard to save sick people. From their lumpy noses.

With a forced laugh, I followed him. "Blade, do you know how that almost sounded? It sounded like you were moving to L.A. without me."

"Oh." He turned around and tilted his head, a sheepish smile on his magazine-model features. "Yeah."

I waited for more.

I waited for more.

My heart started to race and I waited for *better*.

He nodded his head and said, "Yeah."

"Yeah, what?" It came out so shrill, and I tried never to be shrill with Blade. Guys don't marry shrill—that was one of my dad's words of wisdom.

Blade plopped onto the couch and shrugged. "I'm sorry about this, babe. But there's literally nothing I can do."

My shrill increased by twenty percent. "That's not how one uses 'literally'. Blade, I lost my dream job today. My job that I've been working years to get, and thousands of hours to keep. I've yearned to work with books since I was a little girl."

"Look at it like…it's a whole day of new beginnings for you. And for me. You're not really an L.A. kind of girl. I mean, you're a brunette." He chortled at his 'joke', and I lost my grip on reality. The world clicked into fast forward and I slipped to my knees. I fought the hot vomit simmering in my throat.

"Oh, geez, Dagmar. Why can't you be happy for me? This thing with us hasn't really been working out anyway."

What what *what what what*? "This is some kind of mad joke. We just paid first and last on a new apartment!" I screamed.

"Ugh, I hate it when you get emotional." He thunked the champagne on the coffee table. "So you'll find a roommate. Maybe then you'll stop bitching about me doing the dishes." He held up his hands. "I told you, I can't do chores because I must save my hands for surgery." Then he disappeared into the bedroom.

Clarity. My entire existence became a camera lens shifting into focus:

My hard-nosed, perfectionist boss hadn't been pushing me to make me a better editor, he'd just been an abusive asshole, embittered that I wouldn't bang him.

My focused, intense doctor boyfriend wasn't absent because he was working hard, he'd been avoiding me and seeking a job three thousand miles away.

I cleaned up after these two men not as a supportive, brilliant helpmate, but as an overachiever desperate for the approval that was abundant in the beginning, in order to snare me, but that had stopped flowing long ago.

How could I have been so impossibly deluded?

I threw up, all over the hardwood floor that I would, apparently, be paying for solo with funds from my non-existent job.

So I heaved even more, accompanied by the plaintive cry of "Ew, gross" from the douchebag who'd had sex with me just this morning.

No telling how long I lay there next to the puke, throat on fire, while wearing my sexy dress. Blade passed me on the way to the kitchen several times, once craning his neck to look up my short skirt.

My cell phone rang. Could it be that somebody loved me? That someone cared enough to call and check on me? I got on my knees and crawled to the coffee table to answer. "Hi, Dad," I said, tears slipping out with the words.

Blade yelled, "You gonna clean this up? It's nasty! You see—this is why you'll never get a man to stay, Dag." He breezed by with another bottle of booze.

My dad sighed on the other end of the phone. "What's wrong, Dagmar?"

"I got fired and Blade is moving to L.A. without me." I sank next to the coffee table and set my forehead on it. "I can't wait to see you in a few days." Christmas was next week, and the plan was for us to take the train to Connecticut to visit. "Hey, maybe I should just come right away. I've got nothing here, anyhow."

"Well..." It was the way he said it. It was the way everyone had said things to me today—hesitant syllables with a side of two-by-four. "I'm going to Hawaii with your sister and her family. They bought me the ticket, isn't that generous?"

Without my go-ahead, my cheek slid off the table and I descended slow-mo style to the floor. This is where I would reside now—me and the floor that would never move to Southern California without me. My butt stopped fighting gravity and sank all the way down. "Dad... Can't I come?"

"They can't really afford you too, Dagmar. Not with two kids and his parents. You'd know that if you had a family."

"I do have a family. You and Vanessa are my family."

More sighing. "Dagmar, you never get it. She has children. A husband. She's doing something with her life. I just don't know why you twins turned out so different."

We weren't twins so much as actors in the sad melodrama *The Golden Child and the Scapegoat.*

I wanted to cry and hurl again, but, apparently, I'd been drained dry. The hollow ache that used to be my eyes twitched, but emitted nothing.

My loving father kept talking. "All those degrees of yours, and for what? You don't have a job anymore? Selling those vile books?" He didn't wait for a reply.

"And Blade is a man, Dagmar. He wants a wife who's supportive, who will give him children. Children are the most important thing you can do in this life, not gallivant around New York doing...whatever. Reading other people's writing? What is that? Get with the program, and then you won't be alone on Christmas."

As talks went, this one ranked up there with, "At least the play was funny, Mrs. Lincoln."

"Thanks, Dad," I whispered.

"You should spend the holidays thinking long and hard about what's important in life and make the right choice for once."

He hung up. He hadn't even invited me on my own dime. Neither had Van.

I turned onto my back and stared at the ceiling. It had those little sparkles in its craggy white peaks. Laughter erupted from my dry, cracked lips. It kept coming, and coming—the cackle of the damned. I'd been fired. I'd been dumped. And I was worthless because I didn't have a husband and babies. Twenty-eight years old, and every single dude in my life had given up on me.

All my life, I'd worked endlessly in schools and jobs to achieve, just as Beyoncé (of my coffee mug fame) had told me to do. The more Dad lauded Vanessa for being prettier, the higher my GPA. The more cars he bought her, the more I volunteered at the soup kitchen. I'd been praised by guidance counselors and bosses as a paragon of hard work. Valedictorian of everywhere. I was going places!

What was the frigging point? No, to heck with being so namby-pamby. What was the cock-sucking point?

Or *non*-cock-sucking, as it were.

It was like...I'd gotten so used to the unhappiness and the withholding of affection that I thought it was normal. That I deserved it. My stomach twisted with self-hatred. Self-hatred, even now! Even when I knew I should hate them instead.

I managed to get myself to my knees. Blade called out from the bedroom, "Clean up that gross shit, Dagmar. I'm not gonna tell you again."

My eyelids closed and a peace soothed itself into my angry shoulders. My inner 'give a crap' bucket stood depleted and empty. For perhaps the first time in my life, I didn't care anymore. About anything.

And a plan formed in my vacant heart.

I walked, calmly, into the bedroom. Blade lay on the bed, texting. He didn't even glance at me. I proceeded into the closet and took stock. The back corner of his side was filled with expensive suits and cashmere. Blade had always been a snappy dresser—I'd noticed right away the night we'd met two years ago at a New Year's Eve party.

I hugged my arms around his soft, expensive sweaters and snatched them off the rack.

I returned to the bedroom.

Once again, I wasn't worthy of a turn from his noble, blond head.

I dropped the cashmere onto the floor and opened the window. We were three floors up. I leaned down and grabbed every single stitch of Ralph Lauren and Hugo Boss.

With a grin, I tossed them all out of the window. They sailed downward, colorful arms flailing in the breeze.

No sound of protest, so I returned to his expensive closet corner and started in on the suits. They seemed to plummet to the street much faster. I didn't know how much faster, because I wasn't a science person. I was a language person who'd read instead of getting married.

"Hey!"

A wide grin bloomed once again on my face, but I didn't look at him. I bolted back into the closet and went for the shoes this time. Blade had his shoes flown in from Italy.

I let his shoes fly into the setting New York City sun.

He lost his mind, screaming and yelling. Men—so emotional. He told me no one would ever want me because I was such a bitch. Dagmar the boring, the plain. Living with me was like screwing an accountant's ledger. Then he ran downstairs to reclaim his stuff.

After he left, I hollered down to the faces upturned toward me on the sidewalk. "It's the wardrobe of a douchebag! He talked me into an expensive apartment rental and now, three weeks later, is abandoning me to move to L.A.!" I spread my arms wide. "Take it aaaaaaaaaaall!"

I got applause from a group of women strolling by in suits and sneakers. They ran to grab the sweaters just as Blade made it down there.

I closed the window and sprinted into the living room. Splendid—he'd left his keys in the decorative bowl next to the front door. This was the first good thing that had happened to me all day. I slipped in vomit on the way to the deadbolt, but I deliberately chose not to care. I slammed the door—*blam!*—and shoved a wooden chair from our dining set underneath the handle for good measure.

Next, I cleaned the ick off my foot and flew to my laptop. Two months ago, he'd finally convinced me to obtain a joint bank account. We'd done it, but I hadn't closed my old, single-girl one. They were with the same bank. In three minutes, I'd transferred the bulk of the joint account into mine, then I severed the connection.

At least this money would buy me a little time. Two months' worth, perhaps, but it was better than nothing. A smile of surprise graced me—shocking that he hadn't done the same thing to me before he'd cut me loose. He rather had, though—I'd wanted to save more money before we moved into a pricier zip code.

Bastard.

Bang bang bang! He beat on the apartment door and hurled curses upon my head, but hell would freeze into Ice Capades before I did one more thing for that jackass.

His words sniveled through the door. "Dag, what the hell is wrong with you? You'll be alone forever, you bitch! I tried so hard to love you, but you're just—just a boring fucking nothing! Let me in!"

Well, that wasn't very nice.

Drink. I needed a drink. Why not? I was unemployed and alone. I'd always had a rule about drinking on weeknights, but to heck with that.

I ignored the throw-up again as I splashed his expensive, twelve-year-old Scotch into a glass. My pool of sick seemed a fitting representation of the day. Just this morning, I would have freaked over such a mess, but now? Now my insides had snapped loose and flailed about my ribcage.

I took a huge pull of the strong stuff and nearly breathed fire from it. The taste soured my whole mouth, but it warmed my gullet all the way down to slosh in my empty stomach. Why did I have a rule against this? Monday drinking was excellent, damn fine stuff. I drank another swallow, another, and finished the glass.

I poured again.

Leaning against the counter, I drank and considered the stupid rules I'd followed all my life. Be the best, the most efficient, no wasting time, no slacking off. I did my taxes on January first. I went to bed at ten p.m. I drank eight glasses of water a day. I hadn't consumed a donut in ten years. I was a serial monogamist who'd slept with only two men. Two men in twenty-eight years—what a wild woman.

I poured another drink and came to a realization—I *was* boring. Just as Blade was currently screamed in the hallway.

I'd never traveled to Vegas. I had no idea what happened there, because it stayed there. I wore khakis and sensible blazers in professional colors. My bras were all beige and black. My hair remained its natural hue. I followed every single rule from *The Basic Bitch's Guide* (a tome Carmichael had edited).

And for what?

I sank down the cabinet face, bounced off a drawer pull, and fell onto my butt. I was twenty-eight years old living like a sixty-year-old woman. Not even! Mrs. Delgado, my downstairs neighbor, was sixty-three and had two boyfriends. They played strip poker and all spent the night once a week, after *Wheel of Fortune*.

Oh, wow. My head really started to swish now. I grabbed a bottle of cleaner, a roll of paper towels and my Scotch, and crawled out to the vomit puddle. I drank and cleaned and listened to Blade rant outside. He was now threatening to call the police.

Let him. Let him call the police. Following the plan of my life had failed spectacularly—maybe if he called the police, they'd arrest him and give me a medal for Locking Out a Plastic Surgeon Who *Literally* Deserved It.

Once I'd finished with the vomit-soaked paper towels, I gathered them into a plastic bag and took them into Blade's office, namely the second bedroom.

Into his gorgeous, hand-tooled leather briefcase they landed with a disgusting, wet *splat.*

My phone dinged with a text message. Hopefully, my sister calling to remind me that I was the short one with the bigger butt and the empty uterus. 'I've birthed two miracles, and I'm smaller than I was in high school, lol.' Yes. I had actually received that text. On our birthday.

Nope—thank God, it was Melanie.

Holy fuck, that piece of shit fired you?

I called her. "I'm on my way," she blurted by way of greeting. "We're gonna get you so drunk."

"Done and done," I replied. "Oh, and Blade dumped me. He's moving to L.A. to give Jennifer Aniston bigger tits. And my dad is flying to Hawaii for Christmas instead of seeing me."

She uttered a sound of total comfort and commiseration, something along the lines of "Uuuuggggghhhhrrrrrrrrr-oooooooohhhhhhhh-aaaccccckkkkkk."

My heart swelled. "Thank you."

"I'm one block away. We're going to order every kind of greasy food known to man, cut the crotches out of Blade's pants, and leave one-star reviews on Amazon for that asshole's books until you're too blotto to stand."

"I love you."

"I love you too. You're going to get through this."

"Be careful of Blade. I locked him out, and he's screaming and yelling in the hall."

"He needs to be afraid of me."

We hung up then, and I just sat there, drinking, unfeeling. Un-feeling, as in trying to 'un' my feelings.

Mel worked for another publishing house. We'd met in Columbia undergrad, and she was truly the bright spot in my existence now. I'd grown up being told that women were catty and hateful, that we were in competition with each other for only one thing—men. But I'd fallen for Mel's friendship the moment we'd been tossed together as roommates. She'd taught me that women were here to support one another. I mean, if I was smart, and she was smart, then it stood to reason that ladies were wonderful, right?

A knock sounded at the door and I scrambled to my feet to answer. When I swept it open, I spied Mel standing over Blade, rolling on the hallway carpet and clutching his balls. "He attacked me, officer," said my best friend in her most drawling Southern accent.

I cackled. I waved her in and snatched Blade's wallet from the side table. *Whap!* My tipsy aim was true, for it flopped open over his mouth. "You're staying elsewhere tonight. See, you already have clothes." Only about half of what I'd thrown downstairs lay in a pile beside him. He started to curse me more, but we slammed the door in his face.

"I've never kicked a man in the jewels," I said to Mel.

"You should totally try it! It puts the 'ball-busting' in 'feminist.'"

She threw her arms around me and I started crying anew as I sank into her embrace. Soon, her equally non-L.A. brown hair was wet with my blubbering. My every muscle screamed in tired agony and I sobbed until I'd expressed every emotion known to woman, and probably a few heretofore only available to bears.

Later, who the hell knows how long later, I lay on the couch shoving egg rolls into my mouth. Mel told me that the news of my axing had run through every editorial staff in the city. They all felt sorry for me, for I'd earned a reputation as a great editor.

"What's the point of being great?" I asked her drunkenly, and also rhetorically. "I'm tired of being

Polly Perfect while horrible men use women like Kleenex and then sneeze their snot into them."

"Ew," offered Mel.

I shoved a wad of chow mein noodles into my ravenous maw. "Carmichael will go to his cushy job tomorrow. Blade will soar to L.A., straight into a model's bed, no doubt. But not Little Miss Dagmar Boring. She'll send out tasteful résumés and meet a Wall Street wanker who'll cheat on her with an artist from Williamsburg."

"It's not fair," Mel agreed, with a pat to my leg.

I sat up and leaned against the arm of the couch. I really had no choice, for my bones no longer functioned in their proper, rigid manner. "I'm done with it. Done. Every *good* and *sensible* decision I've ever made has flopped. I'm in debt up to my eyeballs from school, and my own father thinks it's a waste."

"Yeah, well your dad lives in 1952, and his treating you like shit is nothing new. Sorry to say, hon."

Mel was the only person in the universe who could call you 'hon' or 'sugah' and you wouldn't mind. She couldn't sound more Georgia if she sang about midnight trains.

I waved an egg roll. "I'm not following the rules anymore. I'm gonna get some shitty job I don't care about. Because caring only hurts you. And then—I'm gonna bang the boss."

She cocked an eyebrow. "Well…at least choose a hot boss."

"Duh." I switched to a sushi roll and pondered aloud while I chewed. "Den, I'mf gonna bang shome other guy. Wish tattoos! Mayshe *I'll* get a tattoo."

She nodded. "Careful—you're spitting tuna on the couch."

I swallowed. "It's Blade's couch. He can take it with him. No—maybe I'll keep the couch and have lots of nasty sex on it. I've never had nasty sex. I've had very polite, sensible sex because that's what I learned from the book I was given about sex when I was thirteen."

She gasped as if I'd just admitted to wearing double-knit polyester.

I leaped to my feet, fell down, and got up again (more slower-ly) to find my notebook, the one I usually used for grocery lists and reminders to collect dry cleaning.

Notebook and pen in hand, I plopped next to her on the floor. I ripped out a page with a list of chores on it, and another with a packing list for Christmas.

At the top of the fresh, new page, I scrawled *Ways to Screw Up My Life.*

A giggle escaped Mel. "I like where this is going."

"Wait—girls who don't care don't say 'screw.' They say 'fuck' in a most unladylike fashion." I scratched out the 'screw' and printed in all caps *FUCK.*

"How many ways?" Mel asked. "You should aim high so you don't quit."

"But aiming is for achievers, and I'm not doing that anymore. I'm giving up, Mel. I'm giving up." I waved my notebook around. "I'm fucking giving up! No more shoes with sensible two-inch heels. No more washing my bras after only wearing them once!"

"You actually do that?"

I sniffed mournfully. "By *hand.*"

"That's madness!"

She whooped, and I whooped, and we whooped. Then it came to me. "Six-hundred-sixty-six. I'm going to do six-hundred-sixty-six numbers of fuck-ups."

"Damn." She placed her hand over her heart. "That's a fuck ton of fuck-ups."

"It's the devil's number. If assholes always prosper, which they do—they always, *damn it,* do!—then I shall become one."

"Don't sell your soul, though. Gotta leave room for a deathbed recant. Just in case."

"It's what an asshole would do."

And we clinked Scotch glasses.

I added my numerical goal to the top of the sheet so it read *666 Ways to Fuck Up My Life*. Under this non-lofty title, I put the first item on my bad-girl list:

1. Get shitty job I don't care about

I left the period off the sentence, because who cares about grammar and shit? Nobody else in the world did. They abused punctuation as if it were a hard-working underling.

"Bang boss," Mel reminded me.

I added:

2. Bang the boss

3. Use him to get ahead

"What's the point of the sex if you're not also taking advantage?" I said of number three.

"That's just good sense." She grabbed the pad and scribbled a few words after number two. I turned the page and blinked until my drunky eyes focused. *She'd put and have nasty orgasms in inappropriate places* after *bang the boss*.

I crooked my arm around her head. "That's an excellent point."

"I have another one." Her green eyes danced as she offered me the last of the spicy tuna rolls. "Let's do what a dirty attention whore would do...what Carmichael Burns would do. I think you should start a blog."

4. Start attention-whore overshare blog

What could go wrong?

About the Author

Ellen Mint adores the adorkable heroes who charm with their shy smiles and heroines that pack a punch. She recently won the Top Ten Handmaid's Challenge on Wattpad where hers was chosen by Margaret Atwood. Her books, Undercover Siren and Fever are available at Amazon as well as a short story in the Lucky Between The Sheets anthology. Married, she lives in Nebraska with her dog named after Granny Weatherwax. Her hobbies include gaming, painting, and halloween prop making. The basement is full of skeletons because they ran out of room in the closets.

Ellen loves to hear from readers. You can find her contact information, website details and author profile page at https://www.totallybound.com

www.ingramcontent.com/pod-product-compliance
Lightning Source LLC
Chambersburg PA
CBHW021522240626
47154CB00002B/742

* 9 7 8 1 8 3 9 4 3 8 1 9 6 *